LAND

CW00825671

CATE BAUM

Land of Hope is a speculative novel about survival and obsession set in a near-future Brontë-esque England. Written in an invented poetic vernacular, expect dark themes of abuse and terror of the unknown.

'Has the land come to mimic us vile deeds, or have we only mimicked the land?'

Daughter. Mother. Glory. Wife of The Devil O' Th' Moor. Hope Gleason has many names. The child of a shepherd raised in the remote moors of Northern England, Hope has always understood the satanic brutality of the land.

But when an ear-splitting, unknowable sound destroys the nearby village, Hope must embark on a dangerous journey to survive through the ravaged land with a lad, newly orphaned and alone, under her wing. As they trek the wilds together to find her husband, her violent past chases her at every turn and long-buried memories begin to resurface.

A pitch-black, magnetic, and unforgettable meditation on the nature of love, evil, and the power of redemption, *Land of Hope* mixes history and the myths of the English moors to tell a compelling modern English fable of serial killers at the end of the world, by way of the apocalyptic hinterland of *The Road*, in the style of *Everything Under* or *Elmet*.

© Frederick Henle

CATE BAUM was born in Cambridge to a magician and a big band singer. She grew up in the East Anglian countryside, spending summers roaming the wilds of the UK. She studied screenwriting at UCLA and gained a Masters with distinction in Creative Writing from City University, London. She now lives in Spain. *Land of Hope* is her first novel.

LAND OF HOPE

CATE BAUM

THE
INDIGO
PRESS

THE INDIGO PRESS
50 Albemarle Street
London W1S 4BD
www.theindigopress.com

The Indigo Press Publishing Limited Reg. No. 10995574
Registered Office: Wellesley House, Duke of Wellington Avenue
Royal Arsenal, London SE18 6SS

First published in Great Britain in 2025 by The Indigo Press

Cate Baum asserts the moral right to be identified as the author of this work
in accordance with the Copyright, Designs and Patents Act 1988

A CIP catalogue record for this book is available from the British Library

This is a work of fiction. Names, characters, places and incidents are
products of the author's imagination or are used fictionally and are
not to be construed as real. Any resemblance to actual events, locales,
organizations or persons, living or dead, is entirely coincidental.

ISBN: 978-1-911648-91-8
eBook ISBN: 978-1-911648-92-5

Cover design © Luke Bird
Front cover images © Helen Hotson/AdobeStock (house)
Moixó Studio/AdobeStock (frame)
Mike Enerio and Caleb Woods on Unsplash.com (sky)
Jonny Gios on Unsplash.com (bird)
Art direction by House of Thought
Typeset by Tetragon, London
Printed and bound in Great Britain by TJ Books, Padstow, Cornwall

1 3 5 7 9 8 6 4 2

EU GPSR authorised representative
Logos Europe, 9 rue Nicolas Poussin, 17000, La Rochelle, France
e-mail: contact@logoseurope.eu

For H.

CONTENTS

LAND OF HOPE

'A Retrospective of The End of The World'

This notebook contains my handwritten transcript of the last, and only, known testimony of Hope Gleason, from audio recorded at my photographic exhibition *Land of Hope* in the just gone hours before we fled for the ship.

I enclose the remaining small-format photos of the land from that exhibition, each captioned accordingly. If possible, the photographs should align with the places Hope leads us to, both physical and unearthly.

ERSKINE ELGAR,
KNOWN HERE AS 'THE AMERICAN ARTIST'

Somewhere in the North Sea, England
– Night –

By day the sky is blue and grey
Ont moor
by night tis dark
Aye, tis when I fly
away come by come bye
like a dream of a lark
when village sleeps I fly past
o'er the fell the flocks sleeping tight
come by come bye
but be you ware, wary there, tis when the wolf,
the dog will bite
I'll come by come bye
come bye
come
by

'BLACK DOG PYRE'

Gelatin silver print, mounted on board

320 cm × 250 cm

Far west from here and north with the ghosts, the stories of this land wait to be heard. We ken them in the light of cloud, the salt wind crack, the stars. Folk ont moor would pass them round fires, the dark at us backs. And to see us flocks safe, we kept custom with the old gods: the unturned furrow left to wild, the plague stone washed with honey; the bairn in May, a song in the night, the blood of brids in crop. Small pagan acts were the ballast here, and the world went on. For a time.

Seems everyone's heard my story, but I've yet to tell it myseln. So, aye. Gather round. You and me at the end of the world, the dark at us backs. The sky on fire.

In these parts, we'll begin a yarn with the weather. And so let me tell you, the cold come in harsh early the year I run, and for that, I reckon most had me for dead. The low gilt dawn for miles was muted by snow that first morn us two black shapes slid trees to village, hungry as ghosts all white breath. In Bill's winter boots I must of seemed like a survival

nut strayed; young and frait, a woman alone in all that nature.
But folk gave an easy wink, sold me their bread. They ken
straight up I was hefted, see, working Jip round my ankles like
a gripper lent me substance. Some asked, you sheep stock?
I am, I said. Glaiswold, mine lot.

I'm not, course. I'm Houlsdale.

Round there, I don't suppose none had much to hide, with
their big ald pans for faces all open and meek as sheep. The
little what they did was for reasons I wouldn't care to pry in.

That's the thing. To my advantage or nor, I never was the
nebby sort, so I reckon they paid me the same mind for it.
Never used to leave, sheep folk. Hefted as the beasts. The
land is in us blood like dip; seasons bind you to a place. Soon,
the years spread on thin, and I was Glory to them, one of
their flock inherently accepted. I played my part well enough.
The kiddies come up knew no different than me being in my
shed. These kiddies, who'd supposed to work this land for life.
I mean, I'd see off a few skitting on me, but a flash of my knife
in an amiable fashion and they'd scatter. Glory the weir witch
and her dog, who lurk in yon trees with rare ideals for nature.
Nowt like a good tale to keep folk settled.

In truth, all they cared for honest was the weather and the
price of feed. Sure, they'd mutter to each other over ale, at
auction, church: 'Hear about them kiddie murders ont news?'
Rocking on their heels, 'Yar, shame, all them nippers; gotta
feel for the mams.' Then that would of been that, cause there's
always ten jobs to be done for every one you can imagine,
and that stops you thinking too much of outside, and what
outsiders do.

I come upon my shed a nithered night we'd wandered too long in them trees seeking shelter, about to give ghost up to the snow, when there it was, Jip sniffing the door. An abandoned observational base for the forestry division during the war, unlocked. Christ, I could of died. Dug under copse, trees over in wood hid. Inside, just about room-sized, old wires and plugs up wall long gone, corrugated tin with a lavvy of sorts, a garden hose shower. It was just reet, me being on my own. And a few old books had been stuffed in the weep holes where the wind comes in; these military handbooks on survival that saw me through that first mean season.

For sleeping, I'd a mattress, thin and striped and piss-beaten, by all accounts abandoned by a vagrant they called Huw in village, gan off some year nobody ken where. Such is the migratory sense of this country deep in. A couple wood pallets from round back of shops dragged with my own bare hands far brant up the gully one hellish evening. By then, course, my hands were no longer soft and weak and polished pink, and I'd my farming skin back on, hardened with weather and will.

The roof's wood slats I nailed over tight, bright green with moss that oranged thick with slugs. And them big ancient trees shielded us from prying eyes, thinner boughs whispering my secrets to the metal. Aye, me and Jip were warm at night enough, a camp stove and wood for burning. We's well used to bitter winters ont fell.

Jip's a scruffy ald merle, int he? Stormed fur, long in the snout. A bit warty these days. Mismatched eyes: one hawk brown, one gannet blue. All fish breath and cracked claws like a manky gull. But a faithful, clever breed is a merle. Bill brung him for my twenty-third birthday, a wriggling shirt ont table. Miserable with Bill that day I was, but them mad doggy eyes come out all bright and knowing, and I fell in love.

Me and Jip, we saw too much around Bill before, and that's us bond. He keeps me in a strict routine. Wouldn't of made it this last week without him. There's nowt like having a dog around to make you get out of bed and stop moping about the things you cannot change. If a bag of puppies is thrown int river, Bill used to say, they don't help each other like folk might. They swim for the side and keep going, happy to have their own life. That's what I do naw, keep swimming for the side, just like dear Jip, who resets hisseln each morning no matter what went on before, chirping for his breakfast. When you go and think on what he's seen, it's a bloody holy miracle he's alive, let alone happy enough to keep on.

The wood runs a good few mile down the ridge of them giant wet ferns afore you break into the clear. There, the land rushes in to meet the eye, dressed in its grand patchwork coat of fields. The colours, both gaudy and somewhat dark, are all rusts and rich greens with them yellows and purples in the stone and scrub, the wind doing its best to shunt the grubby fat clouds to sea east of it. A red kite or two might sail cross, wings with markings like eyes, drawing you to ponder the horizon, where them great watery hills north yon seem painted in, vague and shadowed in blues and greys, a charcoaled marsh eternal soaked in ancient loth.

This place has such godly intentions. And naw, well. I reckon we always ken, deep down, folk don't belong in them plans. To understand you need only pick up a pebble or feather, a leaf landed in your path, and you'll sure feel the flutter of energy come off it in the palm of your hand, like some wee beast softly breathing there.

Felt it yourseln when you come up, no doubt.

It was the June you arrived, was it? I recall the weather was good, almost too good for us up here, and all was hot and green and buzzing with bees. By the day you and me crossed paths, time had rendered a version of me so different to that photo they kept using, what with my weight up, hair long and its rightful colour, I was sure I'd shook free of it all in that wild. A dark copper red, would you say, my hair naw? Like the rusted earth dug fresh in May. Thick and waved as electric, no grey yet. Warrior hair. Like Boudica, I used to say to myseln. The hair of survival.

But *you* knew straight off, did you? When you put eyes on me, ken who I was? Then again, *you* were with the intention of looking me out.

The American Artist, they were calling you in village. A craic going about you were famous, and well might you be, but what did folk ont moor know of art? Most round these parts don't as much rightly ken Leonardo da Vinci, so. The young'uns come round saying you were some 'feminist rebel' they knew from 'the socials', but I wouldn't know about that.

And so. Erskine Elgar, your name. The American Artist. What a grand ald name she has, we were all saying between usseln. Funny name for a woman. We rolled your name in us mouths, laughing snobby at the elegance of it.

Erskine. Elgar.

Come to the barrens with your cameras, they let on. Tasked by the council with taking back the land from what happened there, to make it beautiful again. Rebranding the place for tourism, they said. Beauty spots. On account of it being the tenth anniversary of when The Devil O' Th' Moor confessed; since the kiddies' graves were found. Yet still there was no peace thar round. About time, they were all saying in village. Sommat needed to be done.

See, folk'd had a belly of it all summer. Rotten goings-on abroad. All that death, and war. Strange weather. Mass shootings. Yarns of weir sights in us skies. To have it wiped on their doorstop an' all? Nay. They longed to move away from the world, as if it was a different place to moor altogether. When they got the funding for your 'beautification' project, it was all anyone could natter about.

On the wireless, they'd this woman from council. Apparently, we were 'lucky' to have Erskine Elgar staying in the vicinity, stopped at RAF Morton taking pictures of female fighter pilots. This councilwoman had clocked how you'd brung the Americans into us community with your photos. Reckoned your portraits of them lasses captured a strength in their eyes; a hope that was lacking in most of the world by then. 'These brave young women want to save the world,' she said. Christ knows we all needed to believe there was a world worth saving. But that sentiment felt worthy, too late, not nearly enough. Even then.

Bridget seen it in a magazine: The American Artist had a 'residency', whatever the gods that was, in this new farcy art gallery in coast town some mile off village. The council's letting her live scot-free in little cellar flat under, to do her pictures and whatnot on a 'rural development' grant. Reet for some, int it? Free accommodation at the expense of the working man!

But womenfolk in village, they'd eyes on their eyes. All spied you previous when you come give a talk at village school, chelping with the mams by the gate, kiddies round your elbows like flies. Specially that little lad, Bridget let on, nodding at me as we sipped us paper cups of bitter coffee.

Aye. The lad.

Spuggy ald mare you were, Sarah reckoned, lighting a fag. All long and snevverlike, she says, holy black clothes like a priest. We laughed then, us mean shoulders flapping like wings, all close and ruffled. I was pleased none of them was chatting on me.

But the thought of you dwelled. This so-called artist come delving fer The Devil O' Th' Moor. I swiped up a copy of that magazine from Sare's shop, all pie-crust promises to bring it back. And I read your interview, over and over, till I had it off by heart. What was it naw? *Elgar's images hold a mirror to the broken soul of a place, a thing, a person; reflections are caught in her lens, dancing with memories of light.*

They'd printed some of your 'award-winning' photos: a bombed-out building filled with sun, a flooded dump where a tree still grows. One of them American lasses, hair greased back, grinning by her great looming jet up RAF Morton. Face all shining, like a kiddie to me. Was she one of them roiled the sky, attering us flocks? There was sommat about them planes, all screaming low over moor in the weeks before it happened.

We'd murmur deaf blasphemies and holy words and technical explanations, worrying for the lambs.

Then, a picture of you.

I mean, I should of expected it one day, that someone would get too close. You said in that interview you'd researched the murders thorough, intending to record *oral histories* of the land. Bridget said that sounds reet mucky, and oh, we did laugh.

But Ms Elgar, you said sommat in that magazine, that you'd found yourseln *poring over the court transcripts, studying the faces of these two monsters*. Figured the husband as *strange, not quite handsome, though sharp*. The wife *had something you recognised*.

There'd been true-crime fans gauving hill and dale for selfies at the known graves year out, and it'd not mithered me. The land is too fierce for most to get far. But when you said, *Why, in all that wild beauty, would two people in love do such things?* Nobody asks a question like that without already skirting the answer. I wondered what it was so awful sent you running to the wilds.

Aye, I said to myseln, this lass has got herseln a bone.

Even though this coast town, this gallery, is far off village, that interview pricked me for days, waiting for sommat I couldn't define. I did consider flitting farther north, but my dear pal Copper Mark would of sent up the cry in a flash. Vulnerable woman missing ont moor? After what'd gan on there? Imagine the gossip in village, endless speculation. I'd of burned my bridges straight. And I thought on them dogs they'd bring out for me, just like before. The heat-seeking air search, the dragging of rivers. I didn't have the strength no more. Nay. I'd my flight zone, I reckoned. The space I felt safest. So I just sharpened my knife. Anyone gets in it, I'd step up, show my horns.

But that's not how it went, is it?

The first time I spied your glinting lens in the shadow of evening trees, I didn't quite know what to make of it. I was fair shook, you being that close to my shed, and I made the hissing noise and lifted my hand. Jip took to growling, and you faded back in the dark. More clout than dinner, I said to Jip, heart beating like a brid. And hoped to the gods that was that.

But next evening, or maybe one next? I was chopping wood in low sun, blind near, and I hear a shutter going from bushes, like one of them cameras a reporter might of used. I'd imagined that same clickclickclick when Bill was in the papers, when they'd snapped at him relentless rushing from the prison van with someone else's jacket on his head, sped into court for sentencing, the shape of him haloed in flashes. So the clickclickclick put a horrible cold feeling over my edges when I heard it in my own wood, and I stepped into the sound aggressive to look it out, and clickclickclick you'd gone again, and that's when I caught your gold stare in the black.

Course, naw I almost understand what you wanted; but fancy, lass, would you for a song, what was going through my brain then! I raised up my axe, yelled like a warrior, did I? And you ran like the wind got the shits.

So, well. I'm sorry. I only wanted you gan. I roused Copper Mark to threaten The American Artist with the trespassing charges. And five, ten minutes later, I see his faithful blue light swinging red up the path with the squelch of his walkie, and well, I dunno what he said to you, but the Yank bitch never did come by after that, did she? He reckoned you'd left village sharpish, gone back to your damned 'residency' in town. Surmised I'd never see a harr of you more.

But then one morning early, couple weeks later, was it? I'd been out first light for rabbits. I was resting my legs ont cairn at Black Dog Pyre, that ruin of stone and wood from the time of bloody queens. Far enough from the ramblers' trail, on a clear day, you'll catch the glitter of sea on skyline. But that dawn, 'twas thick as soup. I could just make out the dots of violent summer stars through the brume fading hot in pale scrub, a muted chorus of brids, Jip panting in the mud. Always like to sit in the fog, me. There's a stillness to a place in fog, a slack in the tide of the land, like a catching of breath.

Sudden, a great shape struck out towards me from the mire, taking way to them dun ruins. Beyond, a church bell echoed ghostly in mist: the dead being announced. Cameras slapping heavy like guns on that broad shoulder of yours, them tiny weir lights flickering in heather we all used to think nowt of. Some trick of the morning, we'd tell usseln then, peg o' lanterns, will-o'-the-wisp. Before.

Your big gold eyes come at me first, peering. 'Good morning!' All cheery and loud, you were. And I was like, fock this for a game of soldiers.

Well, I'd nowhere to run, had I, in that flat land? ''Ow do,' I muttered bitter, did I. 'You again.' Tight hands on my trap wire, Jip round my feet with a low growl, coat lined with dew, tail going.

You smiled all open, best ends first. I couldn't read you. Reet bloody friendly, in fact, putting down your gear all precise. Glad of the living, I reckon. 'So, they burned witches here?' you said.

I nodded serious to the charred rock. 'In wet skirts.'

'Pretty gnarly, right?' Huffed in the chill. Forcing an answer, were you, making everything out your mouth a question. Fiddling with zips and latches. One eye on Jip, who was nosing the bags you'd set from your back. You took off a glove. Tiny symbols and lines on dark fingers, tattoos of all your codes. Black jeans, like the young'uns wear in village, knees all shod. More like a fella with your shaven head and set jaw, that great black coat hanging like a broken wing to your boots. How very tall, I thought, one of them lanky Yanks they grow in compost.

Round here, coming by a stranger we'll pass a solemn word. Places, not names. I stood by that custom. 'You stopped up coast then?' I sniffed.

'Yes!' You sniffed an' all. Mirroring me, like a slape with an errant sheep. 'I've never been this far inland before.' Your eyes, like a dying brid, wandering my face, taking it all in like a map you ken so well. As if affirming the paths you'd previously studied, and the fact you could see them all there as you half expected was a bloody revelation to you. 'Glory, right?'

My heart jumped.

You smiled. Knew you got one in. 'Lady in the store told me.' Sharp as a stick in your weir velvet voice, like an actress in a film. Pulled out that little wood fox you must of bought at Bridget's place in village.

I carved them little animals from fallen branches; you know, all eco-friendly like. Sweet little beasts whittled from soft fell trewe. What tourists want these days, Bridget had said, displaying them on a glass shelf in her shop. BY LOCAL ARTIST GLORY on a little paper, a red inky stamp of a leaf, and it made me a bit proud to see them. Till you come up had one.

When I first settled, see, I was so exhausted by all the guilt and terror soaked in my bones that I hadn't felt the poison of it doing its work. And it made me enough to live on, and better sure than labouring in the killing sheds or beet fields where I'd of had to leave Jip behind the best part of the day alone, as well as having to take a bloody bus out to the middle of some industrial estate with all the slappers and the drunks, and them that'd been in prison, and the rest. And course, I worried I'd know someone, if I ever went. Whittling with my knife in trees, it did heal me, strengthening my mind, my fingers. This one artistic endeavour was a small way of holding onto myseln, telling stories of the land with little knots of wood.

A bit like you, with your pictures.

It's affected me in funny ways, what's been done, but then who can say how sommat such as that affects a young lass? I'd hid in the land some four months without a soul but Jip for company, and by the time I come to that abandoned shed, I reckon I was suffering with what I'd call the morality of my own solitude. What I mean by that, in a somewhat self-effacing light, is that most folk who go out on them dales alone enjoy it well enough, but by the time the sun is setting and there's a nip in the air, they'll be chuffed to get back for a brew or an ale and chew the cud with any ald soul around the place, just as the howls of wild animals start up with the dusk wind.

Trust when I say that when you're out there nights on end with the stars peering down on you, rotten and judging, there's all infinity come glaring to scrape over the ashes of horrors and watch as you swallow them down scalding in your sleep. What with the headaches, and arms that weaken some days, and pains in my chest like I'll keel over rigged as a ewe, I had moments them first months akin to Jane Eyre ont road to Whitcross.

But nowt of it killed me.

You held up that little wood fox to me as evidence, eyes wide like a pair of suns, looking on Jip. Were you reminded of them self-styled murder experts who reckoned I'm the fox in that so-called poem of Bill's? They could of said about the pup being with me, I was thinking, heart in my head. And naw there'd been questions in village. 'Erskine Elgar,' you offered, lifting the fox to your breast. The American Artist, going on and on with the asking, '*Is* it Glory, your name?'

I turned away quick, cause it frait me proper, and I took to rifling in a panic with these silly souvenir pole badges I'd stitched on my jacket for decoration, rubbing a rough thumb over and over the tiny engravings of cloud and hill to catch myseln back again. Nebby caw, was Bridget. Telling this one my business. 'Glad you like my fox.'

And you gave a smirk, did you, and put it away without saying further round it. But I could tell by the gaze on you that *you knew*, and were using a code with me.

I careful looked deep into the Pyre as if I was looking for my soul. Christ, I might well of been! Pinching up them badges in my fingers tight and spiteful, they rattled like bones being cast for a fortune. Part of your interview flooded my mind: *In the blurring of zoomed pixels, I find alchemy in her eye. A light in the gaze of the frail young wife that holds an untold story.*

You'd sniffed it in the ink of her shapes, I thought, this frail young wife who'd run away and buried herseln in the vast cold moor. *There were sightings, you know, after she ran… We're about the same age.* That present tense mithered me most. You'd rolled her name in your mouth same as I'd done yours and tasted it like augury. *Hope.*

How far do you have to be from death to see it as a story, do you reckon? It can't be all that far.

I sudden saw us two transparent outlines in the fog, imposing on each other the lines of us experiences, till the lines merged, becoming one shape neither of us ken. I shook it off, a weir sort of notion I sometimes get. Whistled to Jip through my front teeth, come bye.

'I wonder if you might help me before you go,' you ventured quick, rummaging in your bag. 'On the airbase, you know, it's a mini USA. Taco Tuesdays, *Oh say can you see, by the dawn's early light.* And boy, do they love concrete.'

I didn't get one bloody word you said. I grunted.

You read my face. 'Oh. All I mean is, it's not, like, *here.*'

'I should think not,' I said, making ready to go. But them lines were drawing me in, and you waggled your little grey stick with the blue flashing light.

'Would you do a recording with me?' Waving it at me, some sort of device. 'Locals have been telling me their stories.'

I threw up my hand, shook my head. No focking way was I falling for that! 'I'll see ya, lass,' I said, pushing up my collar ready for the off.

'Wait!' you said, urgent like.

Blessed liberty, I says to myseln. But I peered over curious anyhow. See, to be a woman in all that nature, tis brutal and strange. I did admire how you followed that growl. That deadening in the belly, a shift behind your shoulder. You must of thought many times of this wife out there. Just like you, all alone. Lonely. And just like her, you kept on.

I watched as you pulled out one of them maps they sell in village with a great paper clack like startled wings. Spread its folds on that damp cairn like a cloth for a sacrifice, smoothing it with a gloved hand. Then, from a pocket at your chest, first some kind of cap for a lens, then a pen. You held it out to me, taking off the top. 'Would you write on this for me? Given you're local?'

Local. The word grated. 'Wha' d'ya want me to mark off?' I said, feeling rough and stupid.

You hesitated, city eyes flashing. Bright and wide, like a lens. Like a fox. You snatched off the other glove with your teeth, threw it down. 'Give me the beautiful places.'

Forced down to paper territory, my unsure eyes sank to the offerings of inked terrain: concentric curves, watercourses, sea levels, ramblers' signs. 'What like?' I muttered, uncertain pen bleeding where I'd rested its felt edge.

'Memories,' you said, voice floating like a poem through the mist: timeless, immediate, clean. You had a way about you caught me in a lull.

'Would I draw on it?' My voice thickened; damp dawn stuck in my gums.

'Be my guest.' And you went back to your farcy machines, setting up cameras, one ear to my scratchings. If I'm honest, it struck me as downright arrogant, this project. Somehow callow. Over-egged, how you did anything at all. I smiled to myseln, feeling wicked. Aye. There was a way to do it that pleased me. I slid the pen to the location of the Pyre. Drew a star of lines like the inside of an eye.

I must of lost myseln a time, scrawling here-there. Explaining my world to this stranger with her 'mini USA'. Arrows and crosses, scraping out boughs and dips; watch your footing here, better two mile north if sun's out, brook shallow for crossing, mind nettles, brambles, shooting, toads, old hills shape of a woman's hip, resting. The kilns, the howes, the wood, the narrow, the hollow, the prison, the outlier with the stars.

Jip come by, rubbing legs with his woolly pelt, impatient. I'd been letting down my guard, had I? It'd been so very long since I'd talked about the land to any soul who didn't ken the place back up and front down. Suppose that's what you relied upon. Vanity. 'Pardon,' I muttered, putting down the pen sudden. 'Don't much know what'll make a good photograph, but.'

'Fragile creatures, photographs,' you said all toity, an eye to some whirring device in your hand. 'The meaning often births inside the lens.' You looked up from your machines so very friendly like, and so very kind. It was meant as a comfort. Met with my judging face. Flapping hands, the intelligence coming off you. 'Like, something else can appear in the work, after.' Blinking. 'Something akin to magic.'

I swallowed any bitter retort I would of normally had for such casuistry and found myseln giving a nod. Truth is, I was intrigued by you more than frait, with your strange city turn of phrase, this idea of magic. Cause I always thought that of this land an' all. It's got a life of its own, and things hidden inside. And sometimes, just for a moment, you see them things.

Maybe I understood you, woman. Maybe that's why I'm here naw.

You put a gold eye to your camera, took in the rot stink and wet, looking for light. I imagined them gan bitches of the Pyre, graves never dug. Dancing. A shift in the air. Clickclickclick. You breathed out, fog scattering like hot ash, the burned bones of weir women, tiny husks to scald watching eyes. 'What times we live in,' you sighed, and the years seemed to vanish between us and them hags, just how they cram an empire into one printed dash between dates on these gallery walls. How many women suffered in this land, do you reckon, in that one black line? As time passes, a billion years will be nowt but a thin drawn dot on the paper of forever, and we'll never know their names.

You ran your hand cross the memorial plaque that's bolted to the cairn. An old shepherd's song, that, words cast in iron, warning. Not of the women set alight with superstition, but an ancient story of a beast that lurks in these parts, killing. *When village sleeps I fly past / O'er the fell the flocks sleeping tight…*

I felt watched in that moment; by the ghosts that dance at the Pyre, the magic in your lens. You shrugged, as if you heard my fears. Said, 'I'm hunting monsters, I guess.'

'Careful lass.' I turned tight for the ridge, Jip's tail still wagging in the Pyre with the creep. 'Hunt monsters long enough,' I growled, 'they'll start hunting you back.'

But the land, when it calls, it's a savage beast with wonderful fur, and you lifted your face to the pale sun anyway.

'VILLAGE'

Gelatin silver print, mounted on board

320 cm × 250 cm

I woke with a start the night it come, dog barking. A violence in my shed, a sudden thud like an empty chair. The sky sank heavy through the roof, a weir panic in my skin, crawling. 'Here, Jip,' I said quiet, and he lowped shivering paws to my bed. And we both closed us eyes again. It was only when I come to Sarah that last day I thought of Morton Hill.

It must of been the week previous them jets swooped so low over village that we all of us gasped baskets to cobbles, sure it would crash straight down. Old man Dutton nudged me, said, 'Scower that, Glory lass. Yank base up Morton Hill. Lord only knows why.'

'Training exercise, suppose,' I said.

'Training for what like,' he said after a bit, old Dutton, more an answer than a question.

'Aye,' I muttered by way of a reply, and fearful we were, but nay shape t' it. And we stood there together, ears buzzing, watching the kiddies run the green rise in the great shadow of the craft, a flash of roaring metal on ink clouds.

Me and the pup made a habit of going through trees to village weekly. I'd buy the same stuff from each shop, and they'd mostly ready it for me, ken I was the sort that don't hang about. Seasons, we'd ramblers and offcomers buying my little wood carvings for a few quid. Just like you. Course, I was well wary of thrang townsfolk peering too close. I never could know, could I, what they'd heard of Hope Gleason.

Every Wednesday like clockwork, Jip would fetch his collar off the hook in his gammy ald teeth and bring it to my pillow, so as when I woke I'd see it, all wet and stinky from his bad gums; his way of telling me to look sharp.

But Wednesday last, he did not fetch it.

We'd not ventured out much for the rain being so heavy, and I wanted to catch up with my carving. And, course, I was still nervy about you. But when I woke that morning, I could feel what Jip felt: sommat was off. I reckon it was the silence. Brids don't much sing in the rain, but a pale bright sun was flooding shed in dry air, and there was nowt to be heard but the swish of branches on the roof. I lay there for a moment under my blanket, listening, watching. Sommat off, I said to myseln.

I studied the window, where a thick white pollen fell silent cross the glass, forming heaps on the sill. I couldn't place it, what seeds were coming down. I worried it was ash from a nearby fire spreading, cause my eyes aren't all they used to be.

I tried Mark on my walkie to check all was well in village, and honestly, just to snap myseln out of it with his cheery voice, but all I got for my trouble was static and swooping.

'Nowt to be done fer it, pup,' I said, my voice sounding a little tighter in my ears. 'We'll hafta be off.'

Heaving myseln from the bed with misgiving in my chest, I threw on the clothes to hand. I slipped my knife to the inside breast pocket of my jacket where it always was, and collared Jip.

There was no smell of burning outside the shed, and despite the queer white seed that kept settling, the air was clear and warm, so I was calm enough to leave the wood untarried.

Soon, we were halfway down gully for village with the sacks for shopping and my new carvings all packed, hopes of fresh-baked cobs and the notion of bitter hot brewed coffee already fizzing on the tip of my tongue.

That wretched white stuff was in everything. Did you see? Like when woolgathering cards in heather, all sparkling and dew-sticky. As the sun took swift hold of the morning, it melted away with a funny smell of sulphur behind it. 'More like catkins, that stuff,' I said to Jip, studying the strangeness of it on my fingers. Delicate it was, perhaps a slight sting to it, like a nettle. I wiped it on my jacket. 'Or what d'ya m'call it, spring snow? Willows.' But I didn't ken of any willows about near, nor catkins, but then nature's strange enough, and I'd seen rare things ont moor.

Reckoning it as pollen brung in on a strong breeze, despite it being the wrong time of year, I careless shrugged it off, my thoughts drifting back to folk in village, them that I might exchange a few pleasant thees and thous with, and which of my figurines I might get off to Bridget. 'Come naw, woman,' I said to myseln. 'Don't be a soft 'ap'orth.'

I took long strides through the mud. Bill's thick leather boots hold a tread still. Jip was gripping my heel as we went, naw and then giving out a tiny whimper, as if frait of the stuff getting on him. 'Tis queer, pup, I'll give ya tha',' I said, roundly whistling through the gap in my front teeth to keep him coming, shaking that stuff off my hair.

My da bred them heavier than Jip. He'd hisseln a black and white slape with a wiry temper called Flo – well, they were all called Flo. Phwip, phwip, he'd say, come bye, gentle like, wisht, and Flo, she'd drive them right in gates, square. Da taught me to whistle proper when I was a kid, a piece of long wet grass in my thumbs like a brid's neck for a reed, till I could do it without. 'You've the teeth of a shepherd, lass,' he'd say, proud.

Course, naw everyone in the sodding world knows what I really am. 'You're just like me, Glory,' I remember Bill whispering to me in bed at the heaviest of times, the heat of his breath in mine, possessing. 'You don't ken sorrow or regret.' And he'd push his wide dirty fingers to my neck, squeezing. I kissed him, as if I agreed with this sentiment, but that wasn't it at all. I just felt so much for Bill that all other feeling was like water in water; but see, if you keep pouring in what you refuse to feel, it spills over and drowns you anyhow.

Over time in them trees, in my little shed, as I went on in the same patterns, the past somehow took to changing itseln, as if I'd worn it away with repetition. It become less and less real to me, what had been done, and Bill, some old wives' tale I only half remembered from long ago, fading all the while into dim snatches of memory. I'd plain expected it to come smashing the edges of me when I was clear of it, the way the wind booms on the crag cross an empty dale. I'd braced for some time at the beginning, hardly daring to feel in them first years on my own, case it broke me when it did come in. But it never did.

They say, don't they, that the cells in a human body change completely and replenish every seven year. Well then, I venture that who I am naw wasn't there at all them year with Bill, when it happened. Cell by cell, I shed that evil bitch as dust, one and a half times over.

Sometimes, when I got with the knife to my wrist glooming, I'd remind myseln in the dry of mortality that I was alive in them trees that guarded me, naw part of a kindly community, folk who found me magical and different – or at least a distraction. Glory the artist, who lives in yon wood, they'd say. I'd the shimmering of a life. And Jip.

But cause the changes I'd had to make were so extreme and complete and sudden, I could never forget Bill Gleason, for he was the sole reason I existed at all in this new form, with this name, in that sunless place.

We all live two lives, I suppose. The wild form we are born with, that we break and wear out; then the one we learn to accept after, made in the ruins of us. My soul may be dark-cracked and raw, but it's who I am. The fragments can still breathe in and out.

Anyroad. That morning, me and Jip, we went through the loke with the trees over, a mud-lined track that horse folk used for hacking of a Sunday. But he kept dropping behind, barking at the sky. 'What is it, pup?' I moved myseln aside the hedge,

expecting local lads to race round on pedal bikes as they sometimes did: thanks miss, thanks miss, they'd each say on passing, as if I was their teacher. But no bikes come rushing, nowt
on the breeze, only a strange deadness I half recognised.

Da's voice come saying in my ear then: *The dog barks to
warn the pack of danger.* Only I paid his voice no mind, cause
I didn't have the head on that morning. I was instead fretting
on hot coffee and fresh bread in front of us, not what Jip was
trying to tell me. 'Too much eye, pup. C'mon, Sarah's waiting
wi' yer snack.' He tilted his head, love him, trying to understand. 'Snack?' I said, and he raced to heel, tongue hanging
out like a wet sheet.

Once we reached the end of the loke we come out flat,
then it was a few hundred yards afore we'd break into what we
round there called the field: a bronzed blanket of stubble with
a high narrow copse that tickled low cloud. We'd often meet
a few dog walkers, and Jip would perk up and rub noses with
a few he liked whilst I was forced to make awkward with their
humans. He'd ignore any pups racing round his tail trying
to entice him to a quick game of chicken. He didn't care for
young'uns these days, and I'd have to explain it to folk, deter-
mine it wasn't sommat wrong.

Funny how dog walkers judge each other based on their
dog's behaviour. But then I suppose that's right, cause my da,
like a lot of men round here, would of done an' all.

Well aye, there was not a soul in field, just a strange magnetic pull that seemed to swipe tones cross my ears, like a
radio wave pointed on us. I got a creep on then, like I'd many
times previous when walking alone out, crossing some oddly

haunted marsh or frosty bit of sward I wouldn't much like the look of but had no choice in traversing. So I pushed my mind to one side, come bye, and rambled on.

But as we two picked us way to the end, I'd the strongest notion we were being watched, and Jip's ears kept on swivelling like a cat's, receiving the weir sound I could feel as a dullness in my head. I peered into the sky, wondering about them jets from Morton Hill.

At first, it seemed a perfect cream-coloured morning, sun spiked and low as a moor sun often is. But there was a foreign movement to it too, far above, like a rush of oil on water. It made not a bit of sense. I put it down to the floaters in my eyes from staring into the cloud so long. 'I'm gettin' on, Jip biy,' I said, and stopped myseln looking. We sidled half dizzy through the stile and hedges, coming out to the thin path cross the maze of allotments that backed vanna on village hall, some stale caution bitter in my mouth.

Jip ran ahead, and I let him, as was us custom from there, expecting the lad to be waiting on the wall for him. A pewr little scrap he always was, never at school, a feckless bastard of a mam, snot up his face and a piece of biscuit for Jip in his dusty pockets.

But when I caught up to the corner, Jip was standing there alone and not with the lad at all, tail straight up, watching like a hunter. Too much eye.

I pulled my jacket tight, looked about.

Leaves scuttled up the path, as loud as clogs on cobbles in the quiet.

My body keeled inside itseln.

The place was still.

It sounds funny to say that was the moment I knew sure that everyone was dead, but that I did. There's sommat to it, the way a place breathes with its people: a rise and fall, like a tide we only ken exists when it's gone. And after, there's only what it is when life leaves. When death steps in. I've held it to my cheek and felt its grasp. So, aye, I knew it then, I did so.

And I ken the land like my own skin. Swathes of night and change, and the wind coming up from nowhere, off the very soil. It screams and sighs and bellows, and sometimes you can make out murmurs that almost sound like language; poems of its existence in the grass, the pull of its history in the iron-cored rock, how it eats and shits and vanishes all things that don't leave.

This moor, it presents as a great English desert when you first walk into its vast flat skies. It can feel like you'll sure die there for lack of nourishment; that you will dry out and crumble and blow away. Course, many souls have. But if you let it in, the colours will swirl into your eye and you get so as you can taste them; out here, a new palate forms in you of moss and fern and clay moving slow in great ancient curves inking with light – and sudden, sommat so derelict and rotten and parched is beautiful and richly patterned, with all the life you could ever want.

Home. I dug in my heels, and my roots reached up to meet me. I repeated it to myseln like a spell: Look, the narrow brick houses, their red tile roofs and faded wood gables, so tight-built they seem to sit atop of each other. The bright grass square with the flint of St Ann's and her spiked slate steeple. Copper

Mark's police station; dear Mark. And Sarah's place, for the walkers, with the bitter dark coffee in them shiny paper cups. Bridget's souvenirs, with her patriotic polka-dot red, white and blue bunting hung up outside long torn to shreds in gales.

The red telephone box the Parish turned into a farcy free library, with its dog-eared paperbacks not a soul ever reads. The run of guest houses and alehouses that slop up the path I've never been in, their sunken bottle-end windows amber and lead shining far vanna in the night when I see them like sparks on the black glen from my window. And there, the white wire racks of postcards, the massive paper maps of the land stacked in baskets on cobbles: great documents as hallowed as Bibles out here, those maps – or used to be, anyroad – folding out into mystical blankets, revealing escape east to the sea. Them, you know well.

Farther up, the ugly little terraces with their pebble-dash walls, where steadless lasses keep all sorts of hours with no men to keep them neither. Single mams all, as soon as they can get it done for the sake of the child benefit, seems to me. Necking chickens up Hill Farm cash in hand, or cleaning arcades on the coast nights, cause nights pay 50p more an hour. Like the warm'un who cleaned your gallery. Aye. His slag of a mam.

I looked to the noticeboard on the green, its dub wood legs sunk under the scrog; notices done on cheap lined cards that I stopped and read all empty in my eyes: coffee mornings, union meetings, choir practice, harvest festival committees; cash jobs for bolters, shearers, wallers, balers; stud sheep, pups, cast ewes, machinery, video games, knitting wool for sale.

I sighed long. How the world went on without me.

Then, the graveyard; its grey slabs looming over two hundred and three – or was it four since old Jerwood in the spring? – rotting underground. The mossed drystone that runs round it all, jagged jewelled sea glass stuck in gaps by children and witches for keeping out the wild, that slight sniff of ocean in the stone. And the dead.

I could hear this thumping, real close. Then I realised it was the terror coming up slow in my own veins. Standing on them cobbles, I thought on that jet coming over from Morton Hill; to my gut there was some connection. Village had shifted by nare, like these clouds through this window naw, shadowing me like a curse. I thought to myseln then: We're no longer safe here.

I slid a few steps up the high street's narrow, and the sweetness of the first body washed in, a greeting to thou that knows. Mrs G's cottage. Bakers, her lot. Would start making patties three, four in the morning rambling season. Bovine, my nan would of said of the woman. In her faded cooking pinny, flour still on her bloodied hands, she'd fallen sudden, halfway in her front door, dried blood in her ears with the flies.

I thought on old man Dutton, that jet. *Scower*. Aye, he was not stupid.

I stepped over the woman into her house. But I did not call out. See, just like naw, the whole place felt like it was watching. As if at any moment, I'd be caught.

You feel it too?

The husband, a plump and balding fella, was in the obligatory wing armchair in front room, one of them beige ald ships with doilies on the arms, flies in his nose and the jelly of eyes, box blaring a black-and-white film as if nowt had gan on.

Till later, when the lad told me how it works, that film playing in that house gave me cause to believe that whatever'd happened, it was only local, and help would soon arrive. 'It's Glore?' I said up the stairs, my voice a grey whisper. The silence answered.

Slipping in a line of black blood on the tile with a curse, I found the mother in the kitchen, tiny maggots dropping into a bowl of onions she'd been cutting with a little green knife resting on her chest, as if someone'd laid her out for ritual. I laughed out loud at the sight of her. Well, that ald caw. She'd been a reet nebby one.

Her ugly brown skirt was up her middle, bloomers on show – you know, knee-length cottons with the thick brown stockings hooked with garters, veiny legs all covered in dried orange piss where she'd let go. Unrushed chewing come from her belly. I stood over her a moment, my bloodied boot on her thigh. Made a camera with my fingers. 'Clickclickclick!'

Before you say owt, course, my behaviour troubled me greatly. I'd stepped back into past habits, and truth be known, felt a rush with the stink of the place. So I pushed myseln quick out to where Jip was standing guard over Mrs G, bless him, lapping at her ears. 'Come bye, fella,' I said. Remarkably cool and sensible I sounded, thick in shock. 'There's sure sommat better than that ald bitch to be lickin'.'

I was high and light, my words faraway. My brain had took its cue to act up, pulling old shapes. All this death and I'd soon taken to drifting.

I'm sorry if this sounds awful cold to you, but you see, I left the world long before it left us here. Jip was rushing for his snack to Sarah's shop, and whatever gods were watching had become blind to my behaviours long time ago, and naw only devils spied, waiting.

Bridget's place was shuttered, but Sarah's I found unlocked, so we went right in with a ding of the bell. She was sat propped at the till, lights on where she'd been doing a stock check, the ledger on the counter sprayed dark with blood from her eyes, sealed shut with the red. And I clouded in the terror.

See, it's funny, but I'd never seen anyone I knew as well as Sarah dead like that. I said her name a few times for a prayer, dizzy from the stench of her. It was a rare shame. She'd been a real good pal to me over the years, one of a few who'd truly stuck their neck out when I first got to village. I found out later they'd all made up their minds I'd a violent husband somewhere far out and I'd run away. Sarah was the one they put up to asking me if that was the case. 'Sommat like that,' I'd replied all wry like.

I resisted the urge to turn off the lights at the wall naw it was morning. Nowt could be evident of my presence after this. Out the corner of my eye, I made out Sarah's skin moving where she'd bloated, a new pulse growing under-neath. How long ago had this happened? I poked her arm with a farcy long fluffy souvenir pen to figure out any part of it, and she was soft as butter. It was curious to me, that softness. What I ken was the first hours, when they're stiff and heavy, as if on death us bodies are instantly exchanged for a weighted doll.

I allowed my eyes to run over Sare's face proper then, and though it was a flaysome thing, silent said my goodbyes.

Jip was too busy for superstitious ramblings, well used to me gabbing on to myseln. He was nosing about counter for his snack as if nowt queer had happened, ignoring Sarah after an initial sniff. He found his jar open; a milky selection of dog treats spilled out, and he stuck his long face deep inside. I let him eat his fill, pondering how we'd retrieve supplies before the clean-up arrived. The pup would need his energy.

Jip's always with me. I would never leave him in shed for one second alone in any case. There are too many dark things that can happen on this land.

You ken that much, Ms Elgar.

And that's when it come to me. They'd all bled from the ears. It had to be sommat to do with that sound few days previous. That jolt, a weir thud in the night. I thought about how Jip had been so scared; how he'd come quick to bed. I had to wonder if whatever happened in village – a terrorist attack, a natural thing, an industrial accident – we'd been just out of range of it, me and Jip. It'd missed us shed by some miracle.

And you an' all, Ms Elgar. Think we're the lucky ones?

I took to pondering on what Copper Mark had been telling me some month back, about these curious lights they'd been seeing late at night swooping over airbase far off in sky, speeding low over moors in greens and pinks, racing around for miles like peg o' lanterns, then streaming up more like kites caught in a jet. Paddling and zooming till they were tiny bright dots no more'n a speck of dust, and then they'd blend into each other in front of your eyes and disappear, whoosh, just like that.

And sometimes after, there'd follow the dun slow shapes of helicopters from Morton Hill, hunting.

'Allays been the unexplained ont moors,' Mark told me one night as we sat in his truck, gazing into the black. He said 'moors' like farm folk used to say it, like my elder family, with the 'ooh' sound soft and lilted, two syllables, full mouth parted in red lips you see deep north of this country on men that change little from generation to generation. Ruddy, suitable Scandinavian faces that useful hold blood in the head in a ripping chill.

Copper Mark was different to Bill in every way, thank Christ. To look at, Bill was thin and dark and sharp, a mouth that snarled even when he kissed me. Mark's face was, in contrast, bright and blunt, breath all cloves and stale milk. Blue eyes in a mud face. A pleasant face, Mark had.

I never was sure what it was between Mark and me, but he wasn't married. Maybe not the marrying kind. Nowt ever happened with it. I suppose I felt too left off from myseln to involve anyone else. But when we talked, it was us custom that we'd come away from the others around, like we were us own flock.

Well aye. Mark was someone I cared quite a bit about, and it very much mithered me why he'd not been on the walkie. It made me fret, the fact I'd not been able to rouse him that last morning, but I put it down to the rain interfering with the connection. You don't want to think anything's wrong till it is, derthee?

I was pondering whether I shouldn't go straight to his station, see if his truck was on the corner where he'd park it, or if that was too risky for me. Could the military be there, the authorities? Seemed they'd go to the cop shop. I hoped with all my heart Mark'd been out of range like us, searching for his blessed poachers or unhooking deer from barbed wire.

What had gan on? Were we at war? There was that conflict overseas last I looked, the strangeness at sea with the brids. But like most folk local, see, I never trusted the Americans. It's a tic in the English for sure, country over, though perhaps only them up north's brave enough to admit it out loud for fear of being heard.

No offence to thee, mind, Ms Elgar. You're the first one I ever met.

Anyroad. I wiped my eyes and grabbed some Kendal mint cake off Sarah's counter. Many a stranded offcomer's saved with a bit of mint cake they'd forgot in their pocket.

And there, she'd been having a glance at the local paper, folded nice by her brew. The headline was sommat about flocks dying unexplained out by Cresswell. I took it up and read the date. Saturday. So that sound, it come Saturday, early Sunday.

Less than a week ago. Can you believe it? Seems like forever ago I was having a natter with Sare and Bridget in that very doorway.

We left shop cautious like, Jip trotting up front, round corner, flat to the wall, into village proper. I come cross three or four more – one, a smaller size curled up in her mam's arms in pyjamas, as if she'd run out to meet her from her night shift. I stared a moment at the scene till the dread come in with my blood.

Aye, the sky certain watches us as we go, low and cold as an owl quartering.

There was a pram in the middle of the road, a big old-fashioned navy blue thing like a ship on springs, likely passed mam to mam for generations. A flood of fat green flies was buzzing about the hood. Jip ran up to sniff at the great white wheels, spying a cheap sliced loaf sitting in the rack under. The lass had likely took a walk sleepless with a teething bairn down petrol station 24 hour. Jip tugged at her bread's cellophane with his gentlest teeth, causing the pram to glide off silent on its big old wheels down the dip. He was reet forlorn, eyes deep in his little head, paws ticking on the tarmac, clamming with a whine escaping in little breaths.

'I'm not goin' fer it, pup,' I said quiet to his disappointed mug. 'Wouldn't catch me looking inside that for owt.'

Don't get me wrong. For all my bluster, I was scared as a rabbit in a trap. Fighting the instinct to bloody gnaw off my own proverbial leg, that being the idea of hanging about for the authorities. But I also had this nice image of being wrapped in a foil blanket, perched on the edge of an ambulance, being asked what happened here. I'd recover in a clean white hospital room with a telly, Jip all washed in a basket at my feet, the news reporting it was some natural disaster far off, like when you hear about a forest fire or a flood somewhere you've never been, and it's nowt to do with you, but you feel a passing worry for the folk involved.

But them thoughts were only fleeting. I was doing my usual rounds, not letting in the truth of the situation. And when it come into focus, all bright and close, I doubled into my knees and heaved a while at the ground, head sick full trying to muddle it out. Deep breaths, spit, stilled. 'Come on, woman, daft caw,' I hissed. Shook it off like a cat out o' mud.

Whatever this was, if I stayed in village, there was no way of getting my basics. The shops' supplies would quick all go off rotting. Even if I gathered enough scran and water and that, at some point soon, even if the authorities never showed, other folk who'd survived – cause they sure existed if I did – would arrive within days, searching for those who never turned up as expected to their shift; or a lass that'd never come to meet them, or a brother never shown to a mam's birthday do, or whatever it was. And then I truly would be focked, excuse my French.

I looked up at that weir pale sky and I thought out these others coming, wanting my ID and answers. They'd ask my name, and I couldn't very well just say 'Glory', could I? They'd demand to know exactly how I alone – a strange-looking woman in her thirties with nowt but a dog and a mouldy ald ranger's shed for a roof over her head – had survived, when all others had not. They'd push at my shoulder. Get close. Why didn't I live in village like a normal person, in one of them little cottages with the other abandoned women? It seemed inevitable they'd find out who I was quite quick, Jip snatched away, put down, and that scared me sommat rotten, how terrified that sweet little chap would be. I just couldn't stand the size o' it.

And if they failed to put me to my photo from the papers, if they didn't have another better answer, they'd say I must of done this thing somehow, being the only one left.

Most folk might of broken down seeing the world in this way. Given my situation, I should of been laughing, laughing, the only one left in all the world, free as a brid in the land I loved! But survival kicks in hard with me, some high form of hysteria, and instead, I was reeling with panicked visions of hiding up in wood and waiting it out. Or maybe I'd be caught, attacked. Maybe I'd starve to death! All the angles. So I figured if Mark had the truck still, I could filch a few gennies from farms nearby, take the fuel from cars, go hide, filled with supplies.

Sounds mad naw. I don't know where my head was when I look back. Everyone dead, the world to spelken, and all I had was a vague, scrambled plan that meant lugging a freezer up to wood on my tod and jamming as much scran as possible to wait out this clean-up I was convinced would soon come. Course, anyone would of heard the gennies faint in the distance, if only they stood in the quiet of village for any moment at all. Stupid.

But the reason I'd some faith in this muddled idea was that when I first run into moor, I'd survived four months on a plan just like it. A plan full of see-what-happens, not really a plan at all. But course, there'd been no time to think on it, lest I got taken down like my husband.

'HOWES'

Gelatin silver print, mounted on board

160 cm × 250 cm

See, by the end Bill was a broken god to me, floating about on a tawdry planet he was far too grand for, what with all we'd seen. My heart bled and bled when they first took him, till I reckon it was dry.

You mayn't know this, but I was only allowed to see Bill the once after they arrested him. At the time, I believed they'd not enough on us, so I played the innocent wife just as Bill's solicitor advised me, with a pretty hankie at my eyes. The truth was they'd figured that if they let me go free, gadding about worrying, yapping to my mam and Bill on the telephone, they could tape the conversations and build a stronger case against the pair of us. I'd been slipped at the bull a'ight.

I didn't know that though, did I? I was only young.

That last time, Bill and me, we'd sat in this narrow concrete room in the local nick for less than ten minutes, me playing the devoted wife to the monster as the coppers listened in. He'd a black eye that day, broken ribs, wheezing sommat rotten. They'd beaten the shit out of him, see. For being a nonce, he told me.

Nonce. That was the first time I ever heard that word, but Bill seemed to ken it well.

And so, as we sat in that damp coffin of a place where the walls had ears, he whispered instructions between puffs of his cigarette, swift and quiet, using us code. So sure he could talk his way out of it all, he was, thinking he was such a silver-tongued genius that all he'd to do was turn on the charm, throw a few bits of poetry about between his own orations, and they would all be hypnotised.

Bill mumbled to me that the solicitors reckoned the coppers had no real evidence, a claim I was flummoxed by, as the cops had already been right through us house and his truck with swabs and tapes. When dog walkers found the first grave, they'd quick found that other one nearby. It hadn't taken them long to match Bill's DNA, already on file on account of what he did before we met; nowt I'd known about till right then.

And them newspaper bastards stood at the end of us street every day, neighbours chattering in their doorways to any bugger with a camera and mic, as if the ald bitches ken a harr of me. I'd catch the flash of lights through the window of a morning, but I kept indoors, curtains half closed, willing it to all go way. Even then, there was talk of some connection between what Bill had done and the world dying. It seemed tenuous, that link, but naw I have to wonder.

One day, near the end, I gathered myseln and come out to go shop for teabags, and this crying woman run up and slapped me hard cross the face, called me an evil bitch. I never looked, kept on walking, cheek flaming, lip shut. When I got back, they'd smashed my windows with old bricks, little pup Jip on the sofa whining at the bits of glass. Thank the gods he wasn't hurt.

Then there was the smiling school pictures held up by the mams on the telly every teatime. Had been for a while, by then. I was not bothered at first. I didn't recognise the faces. I longed to ask Bill in that horrible concrete room why was it I didn't know the ones they'd found, and why they were talking about that missing Wrigley boy again, and some lass up Glaiswold who'd gone off two year back: prossie on internet, they said. She looked just like me before I had the bairn. But there was sommat in me warning I didn't want to know the answer he'd of come up with if I did.

Bill floored me in that last meeting. He stated quite cold that they all saw me as his weakness. The solicitors, that is. The cops. It cut me deep, course. I felt betrayed, but also, when his words come to settle, I felt I'd let him down. They were completely right. I'd never of been able to stand up to the sort of interrogations they were pushing Bill through, especially after the way they'd taken him off and beat him to shreds. I was feeble with it all by then, specially with finding out about his previous record, and he was rightly worried there was a part of me wanted done with it all.

Course, Mam was on the phone to me day and night, terribly worried, asking what had gan on, was any of it true, and I told her it was all a great big misunderstanding; that some rotter had borrowed the truck off Bill, and he was the one the cops were after really, only he'd run off.

And Da would be there in the background, shouting about from his chair, commentating. 'Bullcrap!' he'd be yelling. 'He did it! He bloody did it!' And Mam, how she trembled! I could hear it in her voice. 'Pet, why don't ya come up 'ere, be wi' us at farm?'

But she didn't know, did she, till later. 'I shan't Mam, I've to stop 'ere, wait fer Bill,' I kept saying to her, tears coming fast every rotten lying word I uttered to the woman. I knew even then I'd never see her again.

In that coffin of a room, Bill reminded me to think on all them conversations we'd had in the dark previous, at night in bed, ont moor, close to each other. 'Remember, Glore,' he whispered, 'how we said you'd hafta run, if owt happens. No harm will come to you if ya make off into land. These townie pigs,' he muttered, 'they can't find no place at all without a fockin' map. And Glore,' he whispered low, 'the best places, they're not marked.'

And I set to thinking then. It was true I ken the land, I knew its give. I'd been walked out miles and miles as a kiddie in the worst of weather, come home in thickest fog, the sort where you can see nowt but your toes and all is muffled and stinks like iron in blood. It was as easy to me to find my way as a brid soaring high in the jets. I could hold out my arms and taste the wind and know my place in it all.

On the Saturday after my visit, the solicitor rung the house to say the cops had been talking in interrogations with Bill about how comes I knew certain things about it all, testing Bill on the details, and it hadn't gone as well as Bill had made out to me. The solicitor said Monday morning was the next shift of the detective who'd spoken with me some days previous.

Monday, he said firm. *Monday.*

I left the greasy pots I'd been doing in the sink, and I folded my little yellow apron on the chair. I went round Bill's ugly little house where we'd never been happy, touching the things I thought I loved, to see what to take along. Little ornaments, my high-heeled shoes. A photo of Cheryl Ann. But nowt seemed to matter to me at all more than leaving.

I grabbed the thickest coat I could, Bill's best winter leather boots from the hall, three pair of wool socks, his best gutting knife the coppers hadn't carried off. A wire for trapping, a flint for sparking. Tins of beans in a sack, an opener. Soap and a toothbrush, toothpaste. Bog roll. A cup. A box of long matches. A candle. Tins of sardines. Flask for water. Sleeping bag and blanket. Plastic carrier bags, for all sorts. I could use my bag as a pillow. The last of an old bottle of antibiotics, that later, I reckon, saved my life. A bit of cailo tucked in my bra – oh, cailo? Cash. Pulled a hat down past my ears, then another. Waterproofs. I considered my old paperbacks, broken at the spines. Pages like old leaves, brown and thinned and cracked. Turned them in my hands. Threw them at the wall.

I tried to think proper on all what Bill had told me. What I ken already in my bones. Where I could go, all the nooks and rests. Abandoned cars, dry dips. The howes and old kilns for hiding.

I was too thin then, like a stick, but I could bend. I was fast, too. Could walk miles in the cold. And my slender form, turned out, gave me an advantage when hiding at the start, slipping down narrows to sleep.

Jip was waiting at the back door when I was ready, his collar in his mouth making feet on the lino ready for action, bless him. Only a little guy back then, as I said. But so very brave. A tear had come with a lump in my throat, cause till that moment I'd thought I'd best leave him behind, that my da would sure take him. But then I thought on how Da didn't favour merles for workers, and Jip already had too much eye. Looking on Jip in that moment I saw he was my dog and nobody else's. He was coming along, no matter what. I fetched his little blanket from his basket and stuffed it in my bag.

I put the key under the thin brown mat outside where my mam would find it when she'd certain come looking for me, and as I was walking off, I sudden remembered that she would likely find the box of ugly embroidered tea towels she'd got me for the last Christmas, still in their wrapping in my drawer, all rejected, and in it all, that was the sadness that hit me.

I walked normal with my head down, Jip close at heel, convincing myseln I was any other dog walker forced out into the cold, strolling late through the emptying town that Saturday night. About one in the morning it was, going past the last of the drunks shouting about, and the prossies all sullen and dirty by the phone box, waiting in the rain. The cop cars that sat on the town square by the nightclub with their windows rolled down and their lights on, flashing whenever some git started playing up. Young plods, flirting with the pished lasses. The poncey cocktail bar all in pink neon reflecting in the wet, and the few dark taxis that still waited. I hated that grubby sad town and was glad to be leaving it for the open air.

I went up the outskirts of the place, up, up, where Bill and me had walked often, past the rotten country-style pubs Bill loved so much, and the office. Past the rows of stingy brick houses with their squat blackened chimneys against the grey night sky; up past that wretched church where we'd buried Cheryl Ann, by the long broken weeds and the shadow of the hill.

I kept walking.

Like a fox finished hunting, I skulked the fell road till the street lamps finally give out to the bluff, and on to the dark rise where estate lads work souping cars. Past the reccy and allotments where the land turns to scrub, and under the Roman brick bridge through the creepy underpass cross the A-road in orange light, feet echoing the curve. Straight down what they call the gypsy track, and the dim again where the caravans park, and a dog barked once, a rustle in the air, but Jip kept quiet, and we passed.

When we reached the empty grazing near the end that seems always to belong to no one, we trudged the muddied lane, hard on my heels, a scuffle in the earth as we went. Disturbing sommat, we were. Plover, or rabbits. A memory of Bill.

There was no moon that night, and the rain was sharp as teeth on my cheeks. We'd walk all the cold night, was my plan, then all day Sunday, far as we could manage. Make some distance before Monday started dawning with that copper back to work. It helped being young: I was cocky, and not scared to die.

I shoved little pup Jip in the front of my jacket and legged it over the drystone, and evil Hope Gleason disappeared forever into moor.

Where was I? Sometimes, I go round in circles. You're right when you say it's sommat us moor folk do in conversing, though I'd never noticed it previous.

I was telling you about that last day in village, was it, and the lad.

Well. I needed to find Copper Mark as my priority. I reckoned he'd know what to do, and as I've let on to you, I cared about him quite a bit. I don't suppose I'd know real love if it bashed me in the gob, but I'd the sour rind of worry for him in my gut. I started up riffing on how I could tell him who I really was. He'd help me, I was after convincing myseln. He'd known me eleven year, after all.

What I was thinking, I've no idea, given what a good man Mark was, but you don't think straight when it's all happening to you like. I mean, who'd help Hope Gleason with owt, let alone a copper? Joker, I am sometimes. Nay, I thought, I'll stick to being Glory. Whatever's occurred, I'll always be Glory to Mark.

But as we crept up the concrete path to the door of the low-blocked police station, Jip started to growl, very slightly, like he didn't want anyone to hear except me. 'Wisht,' I said, and he gladly went in the bushes under the windows to hide with us bags.

I always had Bill's gutting knife. I touched it then, the newly sharpened blade familiar cool in my breast pocket. I pushed the door; it gave with no buzzing in, so I stepped into the reception, light on my toes. No bodies visible, not a soul stirred. But that stink.

I tried the double doors to the overnight cells, where Mark was likely to be if he were here at all, but I didn't call out. The doors were unlocked, no security on them. A red light flashed above, like someone had set off a silent alarm.

Then a lass's voice come up, not too far, yelling, struggling, men laughing, muttering. A pair of cheap red heels lay abandoned in the way, scuffed and kicked off for running.

I turned low on the wall, into the pale green corridor I knew would lead me to the heavy wooden desks with the filing cabinets under, where Mark would take the fingerprints and book rowdy folk for the cells. I crouched down far as I could and peered through the crack between the desks. I got out the knife from my jacket and pressed its edge to my thumb, and my heart swooped at the thought of it.

I could see the lass clear from there. She was on the floor in the next passage where it widened to the cells, skinny legs kicking wild. The mam of the lad that liked Jip. The warm'un who cleaned your gallery of a night.

Aye. Horrific.

Two bloated ruffians in police jackets and hats that didn't fit them right, as if they were in party costumes, had her pressed down like butchering a pig. One of the rotters had off her jeans in a great dirty fist, waggling them about as his prize. A lot of dark blood from somewhere deep coming off her, pooling on the tiles, these sods slipping in their socks as they went, the feckless bastards, all red-faced and loony. She'd be dead soon enough.

I wondered first if they was them the villagers called 'thar pikey brothers' settled some mile off caused a load of grief for Mark a good few times poaching and fly-tipping, but I'd not seen the louts myseln, so. They were sure too big for me to save the lass, and too gan in the head: their eyes were blank, like animals when they take prey in their jaw. I'd come to harm just like this one if I tried, so instead I had to watch careful, searching for an end to it. But it was clear as it went on and on so long without respite there was none that wouldn't leave Jip alone in this world, or with his neck wrung in the bushes, so I could only watch quiet, and wait.

One maniac pulled his fat hand cross her mouth, and like magnets, her pale eyes glinted direct on mine. She'd sensed me there somehow. Often, I've seen it that when a person knows they will sure die soon, they become for a time almost magically in tune with the world.

I felt a warm breath just then on my cheek, quiet and small to the side of me, from inside the desk shelf. I turned slow. The lad was curled tiny in the shadows of files and folders. He put one snotty finger to his mouth, shh.

I gave a half nod back, *aye, be fockin' quiet as a mouse*, and then the big bastard was raping his mother, and the lad's eyes were crawling like lizards in his head, and he smothered his ears with his little hands when they slit her throat, and I gazed curious at her wan face staring back at mine with all sorts of songs and words in it whilst she made a sound in her throat like witches casting curses.

I watched careful through the desk with plain fear as the man slammed intoherintoherintoher. She was like a white brid when she soared, cheeks wax and snow. The blood pulsed black and pure as it fell from her jaw, like cherries through red lipstick. That colour took me to the lake at low tide, a rusted diamond dust that washes into your toes. I was far off floating in the empty with her for a time.

Then one of them lunatics sat heavy on the floor near; the thump of him brung me back from my reverie. See, he'd leaned on the desk, pushing it towards me an inch with his girth, the crack widened just enough so as I could of got my knife into his fat neck like into cooked fish, and slid it in the artery and ran it quick, and gutted his system so smooth that he'd just cease to be. But my hands fell to dumb lumps of clay in my lap; the knife might well of been as blunt as a rod. For the man was dead already sudden, a stripe of hot black blood from his ear.

The other, he was pounding her frail junkie body and never noticed his brother wasn't shouting out no more, not till he shot, and then he looked over for his congratulations, victorious in his sick mind; he said sommat as he did it that sounded like nonsense, and only then did he see the other one dead, and he caught the flash of my eye in the crack I suppose, and he went for me over the desk, sharp animal and fierce.

And I hisses to the lad, *Run!*

The ald fella's tough little cock flopped about, trews at his ankles, and he's tugging me spiteful by the roots of my hair, and him in Mark's police jacket an' all – the very cheek of it dashed me, it did – and somehow, the fury come on quite calm for me once he was squeezing at my neck with them big wet rough thumbs, wolf breath in my eyes, the scrape of nails dirtied with death and earth and the poison of his soul.

The thought of ending up like the lad's mammy was enough to take my knife and return the favour, intohimintohimintohim, and he was so very surprised, flailing in his own mess on that desk, smiling like I'd told him a joke he didn't understand.

That's when I saw his wrist. Not the brothers then. The unmistakeable neon green band round here we're trained to look fer, studded on tight. Once the brute fell, I crouched over him, heart pounding hot and wet, and I checked the printed letters. BELLEMERE. Shaking sommat rotten from the rush of what I'd done, I checked the other fella's wrist. Jesus Christ help us, I thought.

The lad hadn't run at all, and was standing on the desk quite still, surveying it all like a captain with a right glazed expression. 'She's dead naw, me mam,' he said, in that strident little voice children often find when death is close, as if their whole unlived lives come to them in a thick second of knowing.

My hand was cramped from the stabbing, that iron taste in my mouth. I'd caught the blade on my thumb. I wiped the blood on my knee and put the knife away fast so as not to scare the little fella further. 'Where's Copper Mark at?' I said, straight as I could. The lad pointed to the corridor, where the cells were. 'Stay here,' I said, but he sort of followed from a distance, like a lost cat smelled grub.

I went quiet as I could into the cells, finding Mark on the floor, blood drying thick down the walls. I might of said his name. I lost the sight of it when my sorrow gave. I allowed myseln the count of five. And then I wiped my face. Mark was gone from this world, and I'd no intention of following.

'Jip's outside waiting,' I said, striding back, grief so sharp in the throat I was dizzy with it. The lad jumped down playful, as if everything was normal, but when I touched the top of his head it was extremely hot.

He reached into his pocket as we left the place and pulled out the biscuit for Jip. 'I allays have it fer 'im,' he said quiet, and I suppose then I knew he was coming with us.

'DARK SKIES'

Gelatin silver print, mounted on board

160 cm × 250 cm

I determined to get to Bellemere straight. There'd be lunatics the spread of the land if village was owt to judge by. A woman and child alone would not fare long. I only had to look at the lad's mam to see how that would go. If we were to survive, I needed Bill. He might naw be free, I reckoned, if those two crazy bastards were. At first, this was a mote of an intention dancing sparse about my head like spoondrift on twigs, a fancy that comes over after a terrible event when your brain's all used up on menial tasks from shock. But every moment the fear grew in my belly, it come to reason that only Bill would be dangerous enough to protect us.

A dreadful decision, perhaps, Ms Elgar. But this was a dreadful world.

I slumped on the wall outside the cop shop to catch myseln after seeing Mark. After what I'd done. There's sommat bio-logical that goes on with your body after killing, where you feel distant yet focused for a time. I looked on the blood pooled in my hand as the usual flashes of what had just passed rolled through me like a train in a forest, catching the branches and kicking up rocks. Tiny details. The shape of blood on the floor, like a map to some place dark and far. Mark's hair soaked with it. The flesh of the neck, open, smooth, pale as a lamb. The slim cut on my hand where I'd slipped with the knife. The feeling of metal on bone. Her eyes.

Then, as always, it went by.

The lad was perched next to me, alert as a brid disturbed, took to looking at his funny square knees against the moss, gasping with shock. Always thought he was a pleasant-looking lad. That sandy sort of hair, cut round his flat head in thick waves like the footballers wear it naw. A big jaw, chocolate moles splashed at the mouth. Teeth like sucking mints, my da would of said about the lad. But a pretty sort, and polite enough. Nine or ten years of age; a dangerous age if he was coming with us. If he was going to run into Bill.

But I couldn't think on that too much, for fear of bringing old ways up in myseln.

'What went on wi' that sound?' I said in the still.

The lad caught my hand in his, and he was shaking, hot and sticky. Little lads have done this before with me, taking my hand, hoping to have my trust. I went cold and loose. And he must of bided that alien warning riding against his fingers, cause he let drop then. 'Were long time off, seems.' He rubbed his eyes and yawned, exhausted with it all. 'Me and me mam was kipping in thar, in cell. Got bladdered Saturday, she did, threw hammer at cops. Copper Mark called Social Services. But weren't nobody thar.' The lad sighed, chatty with the upset. 'Same night, well…' He sniffled, remembering what hell he'd seen.

'Where'd Mark been off when it happened?'

'Lights up moor, near abbey like. He went look. Couple folk reported it. Just fore.'

'Ruins on Morton Road?' The abbey was farther than shed, t'other way. So, Mark had been there when it happened, looking for them lights. Survived. Only to be murdered by them animals! It was a hateful shame, and I despised the very thought of it. He must of suffered terribly. If not for them bastards ruining everything, Mark would be with us naw! My belly turned dull and empty. Mark!

'Mam said they was fairishes.' The lad drooped his head, holding his own hand naw for comfort was all he had left, squeezing his little hot fingers white to the sinew. 'Them lights.'

'Aye, maybe so,' I said, shaking myseln as bright as I could, for the tarradiddle of fairies in the heath was certain less to fret on for the lad. 'How comes yous stopped at cop shop?'

The lad sniffled again, looking at his hands. He shrugged. 'Mark said it were bad out. Let me read his motor magazines while he tried to fix the walkie, tryin' to rouse ya.'

Oh, I did feel sorry when he said them words, Ms Elgar, let me tell you. But I kept it to myseln, said, 'Oh, aye?'

'Aye.' The lad rubbed his head, thinking. 'I seen 'im whispering to me mam couple times, mithering on sommat, but he didn't lock her up no more. Give us a Pot Noodle and that, so.' He put a hand on Jip and stilled. '*Bad out*, he says to us, Mark.' The lad set his intelligent eyes clear on mine. 'I thought he meant th' weather.'

I sucked in the flat air and watched the lad feed Jip the biscuit from his pocket. It was a comfort of sorts that all was well at least in that small scene. But then I got a creep. 'We'll head off,' I said firm. 'Get thee to civilisation. Find someone to help ya, lad.'

'Who, though?' He looked up at me with them level slits of deep blue. His school jacket was too short in the arms, as if he were much older inside his little lad's clothes.

Somewhere in my head I dredged up a scrap of village gossip that he'd a nan wanted to take him on, but the mam was fighting it. 'Where's yer nan live?'

'Never can say the name.' He sighed, rubbed his forehead, gearing up his brain. 'Petting-sommat.'

'She on a farm?' He was thinking of Pettingrew, some fifteen mile north, nearer the water.

'Think so.' He wiped his nose. 'Horses an' that.'

'Hm.' She might of made it, I thought. She was far enough off. Farther than Bellemere.

The lad studied me, trying to read my thoughts. 'Me da hates us, so no good thinkin' of 'im.'

'Where's he at?'

'Abroad. Tay-lund, is it? Does kick-boxing or sommat.'

I smiled, trying to comfort the lad. 'Sure he don't hate ya. Likely just busy.'

'Me mam always says that an' all,' said the lad, rubbing his eyes like he was tired of hearing things like that.

We went back to the shed first off to collect us thoughts, the pup shivering, trudging back up the ferns through the weir glubbing sound that still echoed in the field and hurt my head, vanna the line of wood to hide from the silenced world. 'No brids,' said the lad, and he was right. This time of year, we should of heard the peep of plover and the c'mere, c'mere of grouse barking in the scrub, throstles in the trees, a rustle in the hedge with the wheatear.

'Early, is all,' I said to him, but we both knew that wasn't the thing, and I ran cold with it. Them kiddies used to hunt brids must of all been dead an' all, along with Copper Mark, and Sarah, Bridget, Mrs G, old Dutton. Oh, how I wanted Bill in that moment! And we hurried through the silence of trees and the gully, the sky turning on us its bloodshot eye.

The lad was quite taken with my shed when he saw it. I suppose to a little lad it had the shine of a tree house, or a den for playing in. 'I like yer house,' he said, quite canty like, eyes roaming the tin walls I'd covered with sacking and blankets for warmth.

'Nowt much, but it's home,' I said, shuffling off my coat.

I got the fire on quick, and we gobbled almost the entire rabbit stew I'd saved for the week, him sat on the bed with Jip at his elbow. The death had somehow made us ravenous, as if we needed to prove we were still alive by eating all we could, some ritual to keep us safe from harm. The sorrow was hanging deep and hungry in us, and we fed it till we couldn't breathe, till we smothered it; till the blood was needed in us bellies instead of for turning the thoughts in us heads over and over of all the horrors we'd just seen, and eventually we were feeding chunks of gristle and the crusts of bread to Jip, and it was a nice little normal thing to do, like the biscuit in village, and that's why it healed us some to laugh at Jip jumping for the bits.

By the time dusk fell, the lad was quiet on the bed with gravy on his cheek. Quite sudden, as the last of the light fell into dark, he burst out crying, tears shattering his cheeks with great hot splashes of grief. I patted his little head, Jip circling smaller and closer tapping his claws, whining along, licking the lad's knees. 'Christ,' I muttered. Rather terse, I can be. It was shocking though. He'd been so accepting till then it took me out of myseln.

'Me mam!' he groaned, dramatic teeth all full of bubbles and spit and tears, frightful images playing behind his eyes, shining in the dim. 'I want me mam!' he whickered, shaking his jaw all loose like a puppet. I'd seen sommat of it previous, but this lad had the force of an ox in him, heaving his breath in a great tide of woe on the pillow.

'There,' I said again, with a little stiff rub to his shoulder. Jip jumped up on the bed and the lad grabbed him rough by the neck as if drowning, and Jip, bless, let him. The lad buried his face in his fur and sobbed mournful like.

I fetched a strip of flannel from the side and doused it in water. I meant to wipe the lad's face a bit, make him calmer, but Jip looked round at me all solemn, almost guarding the lad, and I thought better of it. I stood at a distance till the pewr little sod ran out of steam, his eyes closed and snivelling. Clinging to Jip, he lay still on the bed. Jip settled in his arms, all claws and knees, and put his head down wolf-like on the lad's belly with a resigned growl, raising his eyebrows to me only once before turning away.

Christ, I thought, this is going to be a battle. A child in tow.

I left them to rest and tried the walkie for a bit with no luck. All white noise. A rush kept rearing in my blood, some fury of impatience. I couldn't catch my breath.

I ken this condition. I'd had it early on, after. A pattern of yearning in the skin, a tiny pressure on the soul. Here was I, and there, Bill, yon. And naw what remained between us shone cross moor beacon-like, a calling, on that first strange night.

I turned the bloodied knife in the bowl and washed it clean. Looked over the lad sleeping, his pale thin neck, wondered if I should end it for him quick. Tis easy to mistake a slow death as comfort, and darkness as dreams. But I didn't mind the company that night. 'You'll be wi' yer nan soon enough, lad,' I whispered like a prayer, and put the knife aside to dry.

I went and sat on porch to catch my head straight, taking up any stray runners that grew on the strings at front with my fingers for us leaving, and to look at the sky. See, I don't always sleep of a night. Been alone too long. Could be hormones, a woman my age, turning in her hole. Could be the mad of us don't ken we're gan soft.

The stars that night sprawled wrong in the darkness, cut down at the feint of the sea, waiting for sommat to arrive. We might be living through the end of the world, I thought then, and there's nowt to be done round it.

Sommat about village you may know already, it has these famous dark skies, and often I'd make out folk with telescopes in tiny silhouette gazing at constellations atop the sandstone outlier by airbase. But that night, course, not a soul, and I wasn't gazing, but searching, for patterns in the sky that didn't belong. There, Cygnus, Delphinus, Equuleus to my left. There, the blur of the Milky Way, coming in faded to shimmering Altair, shooting up to the bright pin Vega, Lyra dimmed to its side.

And then I saw it, a bounce of purple, a glint of white, pulsing at first. It shouldn't of been there. Was it a plane come to rescue, some helicopter, a military vehicle, a mirage caused by headlights on thick cloud? The sky was as clear and dark as ink on glass, and the high moon flooded bright at my back, whole and dappled. It's a known phenomenon that on occasion, a ship far out can be caught in its shadow, even from way out here, by a house light left on late at night ont moor. And it comes off eerie, sliding cross the fell like a great spirit lost.

But this was none of that. Speeding down, these lights were, and just like Mark had said, they could of been as small as my fist or as big as a planet. I couldn't make it out. And bombed, they did, from so far up in the sky it took my breath away the pair of them, like seabrids do for prey, and then the lights faded into heather miles off, returning as gassy glows in the black, perfectly round, gliding on the windless fields east straight, as if they'd their own path marked out for some sinister purpose.

I watched them for a time, and the more I looked the more solid they seemed, animal-like, embryo-like, a dark mass inside, veins at the edges, and it made me run cold. I was seeing things, I told myseln. The shock of village playing games with your head, woman. But my heart was thumping about like a pig in a box, a weir sensation in me, a warning from the land.

And as I watched them lights dancing low in the fields, just like Mark had said, they zoomed literally miles up, faster back into the sky than was even possible to my mind, where I swear they split into nine, ten orbs of tiny pinprick light, circling each other in a frenzied revolution, then just as fast faded as if they'd never been there at all.

Did you see it?

Well. I gasped sharp at the sight. Sommat walked on my grave, and the wood around, sudden evil and cursed, took up whispering, hemming in with its black. A strange voice calling, silent. I knew that voice from before, did I?

The sky went straight dark. And there was nowt left but the eldritch wash of the earth come in.

Slipping in the sod, I scampered indoors with the door double-bolted fast behind me, and wishing for dawn, I readied us with trembling hands to trek the eighteen or so long miles to Bellemere Crag. Only, after them lights come sinister in and all the death, more than anything, despite all what had gan on before, I wanted to be with my husband. Is that so strange?

You'll know from your research the experts concluded Bill was 'criminally insane'. They'd given him a 'barrage of tests', it said in the papers. It's what folk prefer to reason, that Bill is mad. But that reasoning to me was no more than when a priest might wrap a cursed relic in cloth to keep it tame, truly believing they've trapped the evil in a vast hellish empty where men keep their wantings.

Bill never showed no remorse, the papers said, least the ones I read in village. The eyes of a killer, they said, the face of the Devil. His police photo under the headlines stared out at me in legion from the front pages of Bridget's newspaper rack in black and white: defiant, sure, as if his eyes were following me like one of them portraits in a grand ald house. He hadn't looked like hisseln in that picture at all.

Oh, Bill. I'd at one time thought he had a beautiful face. His face saved him to me. I never wanted to lose that face, and so I'd say to myseln, let this be the last one, and then I'll get us away from here. But have you ever heard that saying, wherever I go, there I am? I reckon I ken the truth of it even then. Cause I would also sit put in that horrible little house in town, imagining how good it would feel to yell at him like he yelled at me, to stop with all this 'new wave ideology' and 'deep social reckoning' he'd got onto, messing with his head. By the time I knew what was happening, Bill was out too far from what was real. It was the very fabric of his being.

Bellemere was the best option, his farcy solicitor said on the wireless during sentencing. By then, they'd all had enough, the whole focking country. Best outcome for everyone, they said. It gave him a chance of rehabilitation. In my naivety, I first thought that was proper Christian of them. That they'd let him free after he was cured, that he'd be let go from prison.

But it didn't mean that, did it? He'd what they call a Whole Life Sentence. Once he was deemed 'better', he'd be chucked in what they call the GP, 'General Population', down south, with all the thugs and hooligans. There were threats being made on his life as early as his arrest that I only found out about recently on one of them true-crime radio shows. They said he'd do better to feign mental distress to keep in the hospital, if he knew what was good for him. They said, just look at what they did to that Willy Fregg inside, once he was deemed 'fit and well' and put in the GP. Glassed him, almost cut his damned throat ear to ear. Raped him with objects. Pissed in his food. Not even the worst of devils gave a shit for that feckless bugger no more.

What folk don't seem to have figured is that Bill Gleason is the most honest man you could expect to meet. He can't tell a lie for toffee. He must of told the truth to the authorities, about how it made him feel, and they kept him there all them years based on what they called his 'psychopathy'. 'He's a disturbed individual,' one reporter said on the wireless when he was taken down at the end. 'He thinks he's God.'

But that was sensational talk. Bill hated God for what happened to us little girl, and for a long while, that's what I thought had set him off proper and why he was dabbling with other forces, calling out to devils to give him purpose once more.

Grief's a strange beast, in my experience. A fever of entitlement in which you float delirious for a time, convinced you're the only person who ever knew loss.

You ken what I'm saying, don't you, Ms Elgar? I see the sad tale in the gold of your eye.

Like I says to Jip when they come took my husband from the house in cuffs, I said, Bill's the sort couldn't just bloody cry about it. He had to act. Int that true of most folk when death comes in? Like when my da chopped wood enough lamb to mutton in the nithered snow, no coat nor cap, the morning his mam passed on. And you, what's that about, wandering the moor with devices, peering in strangers' stories for sommat or other, muttering to yourseln?

Don't fret, woman. I used to do that an' all. The muttering. I'd even Bill's voice in my head the first years he was locked away; all what he'd said. *Glory love, we're reborn. You and me, we've stared death in the face, and we'll live on, victorious.*

I should explain that Bill first left off calling me Hope when us bairn died, which was what I was baptised. 'Hope?' he'd hissed at me at her funeral, as they sank her little pink casket in the frosted hard ground. 'What's Hope to me?' I can remember how the sky looked when he said it, the churchyard's black bare trees like slashes in the white, as if we could see reet through to the void of elsewhere. The weeds that choked the gravestones, the chill, the stink of foxes in the nettles by the gate. I'd not eaten days but for the half-stale sleeping tablet of my mam's slipped between my lips in the car. So I'd nowt of substance to say on my name. Bill took to calling me Glory after that, just like this song they'd chant at his football. It was his magickal name for me, he announced, magickal with a k so as not to be confused with conjuring tricks. As if what he started to dabble in was any more preternatural.

Though Glory was a secret between us, for a long while I fretted chronic he'd written about it in them so-called diaries they found in the house, that the whole world might know that name. You said it, did you, at the Pyre: *Is it Glory?* But looking back, you were just confused, Ms Elgar, with your watching gold eyes. Cause you knew me as Hope.

But by the time I found my shed, the cold hard land had changed me. I'd lived off the land some four month, barn to abandoned car to ruins, campsite to bothy to shepherd's rest. Like a hedge hag, see, wandering with the stars as my navigators, burrowing myseln well again with mutterings and herbs, chewing on mushrooms and moss, trapping rabbits, scraping sides of deer off the road still twitching where they'd been battered by trucks in the night. I'd creep in milk a caw straight into my hands just to warm them; steal a couple eggs from steads I'd ken as a child.

No doubt it was the wildest I'd eaten all my life, and for that I become different-looking, ruddy in the face like a butcher's lass, calmer in the eyes from not starving myseln to look pretty for Bill. My bleached hair grew out like weeds, thick and curly; I reckon half out of the need to keep its head warm. I hacked off Hope Gleason's damned townie blonde with my knife and burned it on the ground like witchery, till all was left were these raw fire copper rings I'd been born with.

Sure, I was bloody freezing sometimes, and it was damp as all hell in the bothies that winter, but at least somewhat clement compared. I was often sad and lonely, even with Jip at heel. It was as if Bill had died, see, with Jip my only saviour them nights in the open.

And a couple of times, excuse me for saying it, but when I'd get, y'know, women's problems, I'd risk a rambler's bunkhouse far off as I could, one that allowed dogs, pay with a bit of cailo. I sometimes bled so much from the stress I had to get a wash and a lie-down in the warm, or I'd of keeled over. I shouldn't think you ken them sorts of places, but how it goes is you help yourseln to a bunk and a tin cup for a few quid or so when you're caught in a storm.

But I was always so nervous of lifting my face case there'd be someone recognise my dog more than myseln, from the police reports put out looking, so I'd not really get a wink of sleep, keeping Jip under his blanket. But nobody ever said if they did. I reckon the truth of it is there's more than one Magwitch out here wandering at any one time, each wishing to get clear of these death-cold flats.

There were other close times, like when I come face to face with a fella in a field one evening near Harvest, but he was so drunk he just carried on his way after wishing me a good morning. I did wonder it might of been that Huw who'd the shed before me. Or this one time when I cut my hand on a trap wire that deep I considered serious going to a hospital and risk being caught the pain was so bad. But I'd those antibiotics, and I got through. Another time, I ate the wrong mushrooms, saw the whole world in black and white hours upon hours for eternity. Another, ate a sick rabbit, the sweats for a week.

But these things, they only pushed me further into the nature of the place, as if I'd slain yet another dragon and got stronger for the battle. And so, I carried on, carried on. Funny what you can put up with when you have no choice.

Anyroad, seemed none in village thought owt about it the winter after, when the coppers come out all the wrong sides of moor looking for me with the dogs and the helicopters and all that since I'd made the dash. To them in village, I was plump, rough, quiet Glory, hefted, with the ginger curls, not thin little Hope Gleason the townie office girl with the bottle-blonde crop, small and frail and nasty.

That's why I reckon Mark never caught on. By then, the very skin of me carried the scent of the land.

When I first took to shed, I'd buy tins of cheap cider in village and get bladdered on me tod in the trees. But see, drinking doesn't make the trauma go way. It brings it all in at once, chaotic and without filters, focused on one terrible moment after the next seeping gaudy into each other, making this great burning monster inside your head. And then the worst would come as I remembered:

The monster is me.

One night, this big police torch comes shining in the trees. Skulled beyond belief I was, a reet embarrassment. I thought, well, that's it, woman, you're caught. A copper! I was so tongue-tied I reckon he thought me backward, the way I'd gone on. 'Mark,' he introduced hisseln. But he wasn't like one of them townie plods. More like a hand to this place, a way in him I was reet acquainted with. Only concerned for my well-being, he said, with his kindly face.

I muttered my first word in weeks, offering no hand. 'Glory.'

To begin, see, I thought, keep your enemies closer, lass, hide in plain sight, all that. But that's not why I was Copper Mark's friend as it went on.

Still, I knew straight up I couldn't do that drinking business no more if I was going to make a home there. I was terrified I'd wag my loosened lips and go and bloody tell him the truth for the hell o' it. I worried for ages if I hadn't gone and told him about me that pished night, frait he'd come back sudden to take me in. I couldn't let go my breath till when he sidled up to me in Sarah's, told me I'd nowt to be shant about with 'the thing in the wood'. That he'd a load of drunken moments he'd rather forget hisseln.

I'm not sure I smiled, but he touched my arm very light, felt sorry for me I suppose, and it was very sad and tender for me, cause I hadn't felt the touch of any person, let alone a man, since I run. Mark, I'm sure he sensed that, but given the way he was, said nowt further round it.

Not long after, he come up shed, told me Parish meeting had decided I could stay, seeing as they'd put up with this oaf Huw roaring bladdered in village for years. Mark had reminded them Huw'd had the pies off windowsills, ladies' undies off the lines for hell knows what purpose. They didn't want another of his ilk taking root. Apparently, there was some reet pearl-clutching round the Parish circle, only too glad to settle in my favour.

It was a great relief there was no angry owner to throw me out on my ear. The shed was on national forestry Mark patrolled, so he said to holler if there were owt I needed, and that's when he'd left me a walkie. He knew what loneliness was made of, I reckon, and he didn't wish it on his worst. It took me quite a while to trust that small act of kindness even so.

One afternoon early on, we were stood by the shed grasping for connection, and he'd said out the blue, 'Been meanin' to ask, yer pup?' And pointed to Jip.

I went all hot and cold. 'Oh, aye?' I managed, squirming in my boots.

'Thomas stead, is he, Breckton way? Been breeding merles fer donkey's, them,' he said, changing feet like a horse, awkward, a half-smile. 'Looks like.' He put his hand to Jip's snout. 'Eh, fella?' Jip wagged his tail so his rump went with it.

'Wouldn't know. Were a present from me mam,' I said quick, dizzy with it.

'Common breed round 'ere,' Mark said shy, scratching his nose, pointing to Jip again. 'Me da useta have a couple bitches wi' tha' merle gene an' all,' he said, smiling at the memory. 'One wi' tha' weir blue eye.'

'Common, ya say? Oh!' How I laughed with relief, and together we petted the bewildered pup for a while, hands catching shy of each other in his scruff.

Mark must of thought, daft caw.

I suppose we saw it in each other straight off, some mutual pull, and so it ended up a few times after those first bumbling exchanges on the doorstop that Mark would come by in his truck to see if me and Jip wanted to come out for the ride – for the air, he'd give over, just like I used to with Bill. But I reckon he fancied a bit of company, or else felt sorry for me up there alone. He was my first true friend in village, and I'll sore miss him.

There was one time a couple of months into it that me and Mark were sitting in his truck by the Wilson stead, watching for an idea of poachers, armed with a flask of bitter shop coffee. Snow was falling like scrunched paper on the blackened dawn heather. I couldn't help thinking how lucky I was, to of found village before the snows blew heavy in.

A copper from Keldston come over the police radio then. 'Any townies through your end of late, save me a drive, o'er?'

'None that stayed. All go 'ome soon as we get first frost ont fells, o'er.'

'No place fer the likes of that slip o' a lass, the blondie bitch, o'er.'

'Nay, she's hanging from a tree north o' here in 'er high heels if she ken what's best fer 'er, o'er.'

'Foxes got 'er by naw I reckon, if the hoar haint, o'er.'

We all laughed then, me with a big open mouth like a scream.

But that's just another example. Being hefted to the land, it hid me well. Sheep stock. Glory from Glaiswold. That's what they knew of me. And what folk round here ken, they understood in their bones like hereditary. Bloodlines run deep in the vast howl of this land. That's what stands as true in this wild place, your history, and nowt else shines so bright with folk, that truth I'd been born with, and it gave me refuge.

That next morning early, after them lights, the trees were scratching the message over us heads it was time to leave the shed for good. I borrowed the lad a thick fleece, dark brown and lined, and a dun green wool hat left by some rambler I'd picked up in Sarah's one season that didn't fit me. The lad was putting it all on, a bit of a struggle, staring about my animal carvings set by the bed. 'Who's that, then? The Devil O' Th' Moor?'

My mouth gan dry, I threw myseln fast as lightning to the little bedside table, where I thought I'd tucked a newspaper cutting in the drawer. It was sticking out. That's what they called Bill, kiddies round here. *The Devil O' Th' Moor.* 'If ya don't behave,' their mams would say, 'The Devil O' Th' Moor'll come cut off yer tail in the night!'

'Who's thar lady in the picture?' The lad must of seen my own mug on there too, all blonde and prim with my lippy on in that office photo at Barnes and Co. they kept using. 'And the kiddies? Who's them?' He peered about at it, all inquisitive but not touching owt, and I grabbed at the paper and scrunched it in my pocket tight. I turned to look at the lad, and his eyes went wide and clear like a brid in the wood. He looked so small in that fleece and hat, like he was already disappeared.

'Were just an ald waste of paper fer keeping me drawer shut,' I said quick, and I pulled his hat on straight, motherly like. I smiled as clear as I could muster. He smiled back, but I saw that line of fear in him, glistening. After all, he'd seen what I'd done to that devil back at cop shop.

'D'ya reckon me mam is still laying yon?' he said, obviously reminded, his bottom lip trembling, gan pale.

'I do, lad,' I said. 'When the ambulance comes, they'll take her to hospital down Eversdale, let us know what's what.'

The lad studied my face, a tear ripping down his own before he spoke again. 'A'ight,' he said, a sharp t, resigned already in his few year to being told things that don't much make sense.

'You'll be reet,' I said soft. 'Naw, fetch tha' tin opener off top fer us sack.'

'Where we off?' He brightened at the thought of an adventure, I suppose.

'A couple of errands vanna, then we'll go see about yer nan's farm.'

The lad nodded, fey round the eyes, not caring much with all the rest of it looming so large in his head. The wee scrap was worn down like a nail that keeps being bashed, all smooth and soft and spread thin.

We set off into the crisp new day, walking careful down the slippery inlets of the dried beck till we come out to the gully, deep pink heather running into the bracken flecked with scrags of grey-blue wool. The white stuff had naw melted away as if it had never been there at all, and the sound inside us heads was faded off, the magnetic scream replaced by an eerie sort of silence that reduced Jip to a nervy trot. The sky was watching somehow; the sun hid its new invisible stare, pushing blunt and heavy on the back of my neck, determined and slow as we went.

The lad was the first to spy the brids – so small and still in the leaves, they were, like rag dolls really, lying bloodied at the head. Gradually, we saw them every place around, as if us eyes had adjusted to a dimmer light. I suppose they'd fled village for the wild when it happened, only to find there was no end to it at all. Dozens of tiny bodies I recognised, and I spoke their names out loud by way of a funeral: there, the lemon-yellow necks of wagtails, the green-white streaks of an ouzel, the midnight shimmer of a raven's feathers in the low morning sun against the pale dip of the land's dry silt. Jip nosed them all about, carrying a big one in his jaw a half mile or so, a grim prize.

A fox, the lad found, its eyes crawling with ants, gorgeous great tail like a luxurious hat in the weeds. 'So big,' he said with reverence, poking it with a stick. 'So orange.'

'Young'un,' I said. 'A tod.'

'Wha?' the lad said, amused. 'Tod?'

'It's a he.' I jabbed my boot at its black balls. 'Big ald noggin on him, too.'

'Tod.' He repeated the word, rolling it in his mouth as he stroked its bloated body with his stick. 'Tod.' He wiped his hands on his fleece and smelled them. 'Like piss,' he said, swallowing a giggle. But his laugh was more a warning to his-seln at how familiar he'd become with me, and the fear and what I'd done with my knife previous must of reminded him then that he didn't know me at all. He frowned. 'D'ya think you can phone me da?'

'You know 'is number then?'

He shook his head deliberate like and squeezed his hands together, making his knuckles pure white with the thinking on it. Perhaps he had the notion that all adults have the num-bers for his mam and da to hand. It must seem that way to many kiddies.

It was then I saw it: a perfect circle dug over in the field some metres wide, lined with eighty, ninety of them dead brids laid out. A ritual, a wish. A dawn chorus. Ordering the world of the dead. I crouched to look. All the delicate bodies, feath-ers vibrating in the grass. Their heads twisted inward, eyes rotted black. Bite marks in each of their wings, a rip of flesh and feathers. Not animal, the teeth marks.

I thought of my nan then. Her childhood tales of the cunny women. Weir ald sows who lived out yon trees and crags, paid in meat and wool for love spells and bindings. She'd unearth remains of their curses in the fields where she played as a kiddie: crabbed little brid skulls sun-bleached and bound with blue borage, slim-boned beaks set pointing the stead to hell. And sommat, aye, about witches biting their poppets. Like pins in a dollie.

Jip whined, made feet around it. He didn't want no part.

'Who done that?' said the lad, stepping round the dead. 'Fairishes?'

'We can't know all the stories of the world,' I told him, taking his small hand to steady myseln more than anything else. And that rush of fear pulled at my belly. Madmen crawling cross this rotten place, gnashing at it, arranging it, throwing a curse. That was the notion then. I tried to remember how many inmates old man Dutton had said were housed up Bellemere. Touched my knife, and the newspaper scrunched in my pocket, and it sharpened my resolve.

'I'll wait fer you,' Bill had whispered, pushing his face to mine the last time I ever saw him. 'At the end of the world.'

'CLARK FARM'

Gelatin silver print, mounted on board

320 cm × 250 cm

He must of seen those grand ambitions on me, the lack of ways out. That was all he needed, Bill Gleason. Like a vampire invited over the threshold.

Eighteen, I was. A complete ninny! My life was so simple, is the point. Young Farmers of a Tuesday in the orchard shop hall. Sean's mobile disco twice a year, us lasses dancing round invisible handbags in clean blouse and jeans; the lads in the corner swigging greasy out a bottle. The steam fair of a spring, jumble sales autumn, petting zoo summer, for which I brung late lambs. Auctions of a Saturday, library. Church of a Sunday, us wending fields for a gossip to the roast after.

I'd worked the family stead all my life, knowing no different, and everyone, including me, had taken it for granted I'd marry local and carry on with the sheep. Maybe we'd merge a couple of flocks, my mam used to say, once I got hitched. That was the level of local ambition back then. How the great steads are made, my nan would say. History repeating, building on itseln without change.

But the reading of books had shown me the dangerous edge of the world. Books all the time, I was. Cause when you're a farmer's daughter, everyone's in bed by eight or nine, and it's as dull as ditchwater of an evening, let me tell you. My parents, seems, had never thought of having another child, being middle-aged when they'd had me, but I always craved the company of a sister. Being homeschooled, books were my sole comfort for being a child.

Mam must of known it of the life, and she would take me to this manky little library next to the village hall, one of them prefab things with a ladder up to a plastic door the council is obliged to provide for rural communities. Whilst she picked up a Catherine Cookson or her Mills and Boonses, I'd get out all the old novels by the greats from the wonky metal shelves: the dog-eared Brontës and the plastic-cuffed Virginia Woolfs and the snot-smeared Emily Dickinsons, the untouched Jane Austens and the darkened George Eliots, spines unbroken and never stamped.

Do you know them stories at all?

Well, I'd lie there of a night in my little scratchy bed, taking in the words by the lamp as sustenance of the soul. Most of them were stories written by young lasses just like me, trapped ont moor by their heritage, not a light cross fell by ten, and the thrash of a lonely squall in Winter's cold hand. I'd escape with them lasses through time and bring them in close, vanishing into worlds where swarthy ideal men would come for us, riding the stars on sleek black steeds. Scarred men with rare secrets, labouring through storms and snow to find true love at last.

When truth be known, most of these scanty lasses, these beautiful writers I loved so much, died young, and in pain, and some had been very alone, as if all God put them on this Earth for was them precious words to be cast precarious into it as wishing coins into a well.

But they were my downfall, you could say, when I met Bill. See, those books were sommat of a religion for me. I'd convinced myseln coming up that my very own version of Rochester would appear purely by the hand of destiny, as if just by the act of living I was turning the pages of my own book, prewritten in supernatural ink, a tapestry of fate that only required a quiet patience. Surely, I'd reason with myseln, the story will unfold in a perfect arc, plotting itseln to the final, natural, romantic climax.

Aye, I was convinced. My own handsome stranger would come to save me, and honest to God, anyone might of done, long as it wasn't one of them dullard Macks. Thought I was too good for the muck, did I? Such a stupid, stupid lass. Christ, I didn't know I was born.

Spring on farm, we'd sometimes find sickness creep about in the damp, when the flock's not strong. When the lambs come, some ewes don't birth right, or they'll cast over and die where they fall. Other times, the lambs come up funny, or slow, and need to be put down.

Anyroad, the farm was doing meagre after a spate of fly strike. It's where these horrible flies land on the flock and lay their eggs burrowed down, then the maggots eat their way out of the flesh. And it'd been raining a great deal; the weather had come far too early, so the fleece was heavy and wet. And what with the soggy grazing, they'd got all kinds before we'd even started with the stuff we'd usually give them for it, and their fleece would come off at a much lower yield after. Terrible thing it is, to watch a vet go round a shed finishing them off. And rare expensive. So they'd bring round the knackerman instead.

This knackerman would drive about miles in the commons, looking for us smits on fleece – pink ours were, a line sprayed through a circle like an ancient mark. We'd raddle ewes and the lambs in matching neon flashes of colour, blue or pink or orange, to tell which gimmer had birthed what slink, so some had two colours on their wool, and we'd pair them up of an evening come in. The knackerman, he'd be able to follow easy which. He was granted his own judgement to cull any of the don-fer ones and load the carcases in tipper and bring them back for disposal. He'd make a note of any that looked badly, and where they were, so my da could go up have a look-see.

The proper name for this profession when it's advertised is 'fallen stock operator', but nobody round ours would call it that over the fence. It was a job that required the strong stomach and pallid detachment of an abattoirman.

Often, the knackermen up ours were paid in render and fleece, or what we called pull, cause you pull a dead sheep's fleece, you don't shear it. Despite years of paying the Macks in brass for this service, Da went with Gleason's instead, a tiny new ad in the recent Yellow Pages that offered this option. Even naw it seems queer of him to of done so. It was not at all like Da to take on someone without a recommendation. There was certain a streak of devilry at play in the world when my da called on Bill Gleason.

But he must of regretted that decision sorely quick, seeing as word went round wildfire t'other farms as to what my penny-pinching da had done, and he'd to ply Jed Mack and the sons with quite a few ales to get back on his good side after that little betrayal. Christ knows regret can't begin to describe what he must of felt later.

But naw, I suppose, Da's with the rest of them, and he shan't be thinking on me again.

The first time I ever saw Bill Gleason he was walking with my da cross yard in his wellies, overall smeared with muck. His hair was all to one side, like he'd been sweating at sommat heavy, and he was jangling a large set of keys. He moved nimble, like a slape, edging the way, throwing glances at his flank as he chattered on to my da.

I'd never seen such a thin man be so quick and strong; the sinews on his neck like rope, jaw flicking against a sheer of black stubble like a burned field. Jewelled flames for eyes consumed his view, ravenous. He was older than me by a lot of year, but that straight back and swift way about him made my head all hot and drifting.

I reckon if Bill'd had an ounce of music in him, he'd of been one of them dirty rock stars with the greasy hair and the sparked-up eyes. Exquisite bait to any young lass. But he was tone-deaf as a pigeon, and so, forced to find a calling for this strange and godlike energy that sucked the air from a place as he moved in it, he come to rest in the dark.

Course, rock stars are bloody disagreeable, except to young lasses with no experience of what men are. And so, the rascallion sniffed me at the door, with my scrags of red hair and level face. I must of looked like a child to the man, stick legs in wellies, a great thick sweater over jeans all three sizes too big so's I could wear my johns under in the cold.

The farciest I'd ever get was throwing on a nice blouse and jeans for my Young Farmers dos; that cheap gold chain with a heart on that my nan had got me for my Sweet Sixteen. Never did I buy a dress till we moved off to town, and always in them few year I felt it indecent to be parading about the streets in heels pinching like mad, arms and legs bare naked, goosing in the wind. But there was sommat unnatural in me by then. Bill's claws had sunk and turned in the ripe of me, sowing that weed that engulfed some innocent part of my being, and choked.

Anyroad. After Bill clocked me that first morning, I'd be any excuse in that yard, sweeping or hanging about trying to look cool as a cucumber with my earbuds in, kicking clods by the gate, making out I was helping. You'd feel his energy wash in before you saw him. ''Ow do, lass,' he'd growl, a fag hanging from the corner of his mouth, and my belly would start up flitting. I just found him so damned exhilarating. See, Bill Gleason was the world out there, and all the possibilities. He'd slide in the gate, window down all weathers, an elbow on the ledge of his truck's window. He hardly gave me the time of day, but I felt it in my toes he was playing with me some kind of game, a challenge, a swirling of my insides, a calculation of sorts he was making to my character.

The sense was that I just had to be there, not doing owt special, just existing, and let him come near. I'd make out I was the shepherd, getting in a weir ram. Step by step cross the field, he'd come closer, curious of my stillness, till I'd grab his horns.

I never caught on, did I, that Bill was not the hunted but the hunter, preying on me whilst I figured him soft and no danger to me. I didn't flinch when he finally caught me, did I? Stupid, stupid lass.

But then it was all up in the air again. Da got his suspicions the third day in, when Bill brung another nineteen dead from far vanna. Pattinson, the hand, big fella he was. Like all of them, he went on his byname, just Pattinson. Don't suppose he'd of answered if you called him owt else. He'd been with us donkey's years.

Well. Pattinson was tasked with the counting off the tipper, the weighing and the pull, but he'd been ginger of saying owt on his misgivings, for it wasn't his place, so he'd come up house before tea to appeal to my mam. 'Missus,' he said, cap in hand, knowing her the most pragmatic of the stead, and after he'd got it off his chest, we sat up in kitchen with the Aga on for warmth to wait for my da, as if someone had died like and we'd to pass on the news, nursing cups of hot tea and a bit of scran in the quiet. Pattinson breathed funny, big ald barrel chest on him, and all we could hear whilst we waited was his big gulps of air and the constant wiping of his brow with his greasy ald rustling cap.

Da come in finally, steam rising from his back as he threw his boots, and the story come off at last with Pattinson. 'One of them kiddies throws stones up abbey, that Wrigley biy, Alfie, he comes over to the van and he says, that weir fella you had in knackering? He were wringing them necks, healthy ones, like. Saw him do it up hillock by Griffiths'. And when he come in, that fella Gleason, with the count on the tipper, I see least six with them necks done in, no signs of the fly stroke up them legs or face. One were from that lot you took in autumn last, them hoggets.'

'Tha' reet,' muttered Da, a calm rage brewing red from neck to muzzle. Da was only a small man, half of him a shock of grey hair, but he was full of blood. 'You and young Bagley, take the Rover wi' keys in, crack of dawn, follow the git about th' place, quiet like. Make out yous checkin' fences or sommat.'

'Should of gone wi' Macks,' my mam couldn't help floating, and Pattinson wriggled, for he must of agreed with her. Da threw her a look. 'Thank you, love. Very bloody helpful!' And he went off fuming with a scrape of his chair to wash his neck for tea.

See, on this land, we live by a constant, and us families, we go back solid as stone for time: dependable stock, no fussing. Slow in choosing, slower in changing. We ken us place. And naw, we'd gan too quick over and caught us shins, bringing in this unknown entity for the sake of a few pennies, and shit, if we weren't bloody paying for it straight off. 'False economy, see,' Ma rattled as she moved the tea things to the sink. 'Yer da would rather scrape mould off a spoilt apple than buy a pound fresh up' market a shilling.'

My pewr mam must of only blamed herseln when it all happened later. She was apparently on the telly soon after I run, filmed sitting there at that very table, and though I cannot for the life of me imagine why they'd blame her in it all, they'd gone and wrote about her in the papers in rotten terms; how strange and backward she was, how ignorant and gullible. They'd said about her red chapped cheeks and wiry faded hair, and how she wore a flowered pinny at the table as she served them lukewarm tea, weak as potatoes. They printed her age, sixty-two, and mentioned she looked much older, on account of the worry.

To have some townie hack rip my wee mother to shreds for the whole country to gawp at, and know she must of read it an' all? Even naw I can't think on it too much.

See, she'd told them newspaper rascals, in great trust, I suppose, that had it not been for my da being such a grubber them spring weeks, and her being such a doormat with money affairs, and seeing as I was such a 'good lass' before, I'd of not met the man to ruin me, and not a thing of it would of occurred.

But had it not 'gan on', as she reportedly said, I might not of had my freedom all these eleven year, albeit at a greater sacrifice than any woman on this Earth might deserve.

There was this time once, early on, in one of the bothies they had a payphone in the hall, and I wondered if I did call farm, if my mam answered, could I of spoke to her? I missed her sommat sore them months, and despite us never being close in the most common sort of ways of a mam and her daughter might be, we had us own understanding that formed in me a feeling of home. But then, I pinched myseln, give over woman! You call there, it causes untold woe. What would

I ever of said? God-fearing folk, Mam and Da. No way would they not of reported it to the coppers any way round. And so, I never did.

Oh, not that it matters, does it, us sat here at the end of the world, listening to me blabber on?

Let me tell you how we got romantic from there, Bill and me, with the hands out like hawks atop them crags, leaning over with binoculars whilst munching on my mam's cheese and pickle cobs, as if they were at one of them falconing displays.

Well, Bill caught on to their watching, and was purely entertained by it. Bill was more like an animal with his senses, tuned to the land. Beast-deep with intuition, he'd a strange core to his soul that knew Nature's songs. Any tiny change in the wind, a singular cloud skating, a shush in the grass, and he'd ken instant-like to move hisseln out way. And so, when I come up, he decided, I reckon, oh aye, I'll get this lass on my side; we can play that game. He'd caught some thread in my soul and recognised it there. A feral sort of magic, Bill had. And it was as if I could see all time around him, future, present, past; and in it, we were bound together.

Course, there was no reason for the Wrigley boy to fib about what Bill was doing to the flock, and well, it was true. But I couldn't let Bill leave when I'd only just found him. Aye, it's sad to say. I thought he was my Rochester.

Is that a smirk, my friend? It's laughable, int it. More like my bloody Heathcliff, I know.

But imagine, I went to Da, told him this cock and bull about how the only way we could know for sure that Bill was cheating was if I went with him on the tipper to help. Crafty, eh? Bill'd not suspect me, I said, explaining the git'd caught me looking a few times previous. Was it not agreed, I argued, the flock might be gan over by the week this rate?

Me mam, I recall, gave a great choke of a laugh, hands in the pastry at the table with her show on the wireless. 'She's not daft, 'er,' she said. 'He'll take she's sweet on him, or keen to learn. Reckon it's not a bad idea, Da.'

'Well aye, but ya not concerned, Mam, about 'is taking advantage?' he said, face redder than I'd seen it a long while.

'Well aye, but you got fellas agate crags. Watchin',' Mam said, pressing hard into the nakit, her cold rough thumbs through the dough. 'Got to do sommat, Da. Can't let this guy be taxin' under us nosies!'

And like the virgin put out for the dragon, it was agreed I'd go out with Bill on the pretence of learning. It was set twixt us nobody would say owt official like to the man, and I'd have to persuade him with wiles, hanging about being a nuisance.

And there Bill was next morning, rumbling up to the gate, just as the sun come up in a golden breeze, as if it had brung him along in its bright tail. His sharp-boned elbow hung at the window, a knuckle of meat in the shadow of the yard. I went blowing up to his door, heart beating, wellies and mac on, proper wrapped up, a bag of buns and a flask in hand. ''Ow do,' I said too loud. 'Don't want to be mithering, but d'ya fancy showing me a ride about? I'd like to breakfast up top, if it's the same wi' you.'

'Jump in,' he said, quick as lightning, hauling that great truck about so fast I thought I'd lose my nose. Perhaps he's

innocent of it, I said to myseln, seeing as he's agreed so fast
to me going with him. Maybe the hands are plotting with the
Macks, to get rid of this stranger taking their jobs!

His truck inside was dirty and smeared, black torn vinyl
seats all dusty with red earth. Greasy lanolined fingers had
pressed in the soft dash leaving bruises like they might on
flesh, a stink of the slaughterhouse about it: old blood, adrenalin, an edge of piss. But so sparse. Bill had to have his things
neat and tidy otherwise. Like a soldier, he'd say. Things weigh
you down, make your life heavy. Get rid.

But I wonder naw how heavy his life was already, and the
heavier it got, the more fastidious he was to the point of obses-
sive. When we were later living in town, he'd sit there and
read a page of a book, then rip it out and burn it in the hearth,
as if the words had been written for him alone, and naw they
were used and done, and he had no further use for them. Make
of that what you will. I can see a psychiatrist having a field day
with that little snip of information.

Between us in that truck leant this mighty wrench like
you use for a tractor, as big as his arm and weighted. A little
smashed green notebook and the nub of a yellow pencil swung
mad on a bit of brown string from the mirror where others tie
crucifixes and rabbit's feet, lucky heather.

I've heard them crime experts wittering on in interviews
over the years about Bill's little green notebooks, going so far
as to comment they were chock-full of the wildest poetry to
rival Ted Hughes! They see them scrawlings as the insides
of an evil genius at work. It makes me titter, that does. I was
privy to Bill scribbling in them books many a time, and he'd

write down what he saw and that, nowt more, just to keep it fresh to come back to later.

He wrote on that first day with me, *Sun bright. Wolf in the wood come / Keep keen ears for the waste o' him, the fox.* They all made a lot of that one, I can tell you. Was I the wolf? The sun? The fox? Truth was, none of it was about me. That was merely Bill noting the path of the massive fox in wood that spring that'd kept on at the rabbits and the brids, cause it was quite common that Bill would be able to pick up a raw dinner of a morning lying torn in the scrub, some sorry beast or other played with and abandoned.

See, Bill viewed the edges of this world like no living soul should, and it gave him this rare turn of phrase, sommat romantic and startling that, course, appealed to me from the first. And so, them sadistic southern bastards, with their silk ties and rooms full of paper and half-smiles like they'd got their soft, fat paws in their pockets fiddling on the subject of Bill Gleason – well, they'd taken a fancy to that rot, had they? Like a fine wine or cheese, they studied the precious permutations of noble damage.

That first morning out in the tipper I'd sat gawping like a schoolgirl at Bill's things all around, as if I was surveying the innermost workings of the man's heart. 'Job must get you reet muddy.'

'Bloody,' he corrected, and stared at me, close yet far off, with them rare eyes as deep as lakes.

Bill's eyes, when they caught mine, were like when you see hills in the distance, and you try to measure how far with your gaze, and you could swear them so near that you'll walk a few steps more and be touching. But then you realise it's miles yet and the hills are so very far, and the sky darkens, and it was only a trick of the light that made you think you were so close. And yet, still you go on.

That's when the rush of Bill come over me in a great passion. It was the first time we were alone, and it was like being with, oh, I don't know, an angel come flapping in with giant wings all overwhelming and fierce; or a tiger, friendly and beautiful, but baring teeth ragged with meat at the edges. Being with Bill was a rainstorm up high when you're far out hillwards staring back at the face of the land, its colours dark engulfed by its own adumbration, and over and over the lightning strikes, and you're dizzy and nare sick, but the power of it keeps you looking. How unnatural the natural can seem! Imagine how very exhilarated it turns you, how eager you are to continue; how pliable to any amount of looking and learning despite the very real danger you sense in the unknown.

Bill was always the unknown to me, make no mistake. The core of him, where the animal lived, where he knew to run or stay down flat or kill – that was in him like venom, and I knew not to question it from that morning in his truck without being told.

It was glorious, that first sun I seen with Bill, rising over the rubbed ridge into the land, unveiling all that was night-hidden in fresh light. There, the hazy outline of the helstone, Black Dog Pyre, the ruins. The blue of yon hills a pale sea of shadow cross the dawn. Content as fed lambs, we were, parked up top, warming us faces in the new day together.

But when the brids took up their chorus, so thick and loud, it was frightening to me, as if they were screaming to warn me of a great beast on the prowl, some monster I couldn't yet see. I put it down to how open I felt that dawn, everything tingling and hurting with joy, and bigger and more profound than I'd ever felt it all.

And danger sang in my soul bright black, its warning left unheeded.

For all that, I loved Bill Gleason from the moment I saw him cross that yard, cause everything in my life was completely known and mapped out. I could of looked down the line of time and seen how I'd be on farm, day by day, hour by hour, wed to a Mack till one or t'other of us was buried in the ground. I could almost feel my hands chapped and hard and cold in that same nakit of dough on that same ald kitchen table, listening to that same ald show my mam loved on the wireless. At first, I'd only be listening to it cause I missed her, exactly like she'd done with her mother, but then I would grow to like it as much as she did, the harrs growing grey in my nostrils all the while.

I could even see my young'uns at the table clear as day: a daughter, plain but hardy, taken to nursing the lambs like myseln. Little lads, ruddy blonde Mack genes down to their bones. Maybe two or three tykes, taking out with their da in the winter dark, me hoping for five minutes' peace to read a page of a book but never getting it, and smiling anyway for the love of their little homely faces in my lap.

But I never believed my mam's smile neither, with them dead, tired eyes, and it worried me any time I saw it on her.

Well aye, I could see it all: there I'd be, in that great draughty house forever, up them same creaking stairs with the same faded *Hay Wain* print at the top in the broken gold frame; the stacked matrimonial bed I would sure sleep in – my mam and da's bed naw, with the dark wood headboard and the broken foot never mended. The same bed where I'd been born, where my own kids would be born; the same bed where I'd likely die, fifty, sixty year from naw, gods willing, if I stayed put.

And then there was the savings account that sent me flying down the road to Damascus.

See, there'd been this leaflet at the library, a new course of Creative Writing at the community centre in town. A proper writer coming to teach it, an' all. It cost a few hundred quid to enrol, and it would of given me a certificate. I always wanted to be a writer of books when I was coming up. Used to make myseln learn grand words I found in old books, their meanings and uses, improving myseln, so I thought.

Over tea that evening, I asked my da if he could give me over a bit of cailo for it, seeing as I'd been working all year without a penny coming my way. I showed him the leaflet first, and he fingered its smooth ink as if it was blasphemy, going red in the face at the table, angry or insulted, leaning back in his grubby shirtsleeves on the chair, his very own bloody throne of Solomon. Then he started up laughing as if I'd told him a really good joke. "Ere, Mam, get this, it's a good 'un!' he called through to her as she washed the pots. 'Yer daughter's claimin' she's going to college up town, to be one of them snooty book writers!'

'What's all this?' Mam come in drying her cracked red hands on her apron.

'Says it's three hundred quid! Just fer them watchin' ya write down farcy words!'

'Mam?' I said, hoping for an ally. She did read books, my mam, after all.

She picked up the leaflet and rubbed her face, both us eyes on her like lasers. 'Nay brass in it, lass. Books.' She stared some more, then laid it down respectfully on the table like a tiny animal that'd just that second died in her hand.

'Them women writers, all rich spinsters, they're,' chipped in my da. 'Or else, lesbuns!' He gave out a shout of mirth, tapped the table.

'Like yer second aunty, Paula,' Mam interjected. 'Wi' th' short 'air,' she whispered, mouthing the words sacred. 'Lived wi' another woman.' Her tired eyes grew round. 'A nurse!'

'Mam, you've short hair yerseln,' I started. She lightly touched her perm, worrying.

Da let out another whoop so loud the dogs stirred in the yard. 'Funny caw, 'er. D'ya remember it, Mam? Paula? Wi' milk?'

'Aye,' Mam said. 'She'd only take sterilised milk in 'er brew.'

'Sterilised!' shouted Da, entertained, banging his hand on the table.

Whatever become of my second aunty Paula?

'You've to be born to it, to make a go o' books, pet,' said my mam, ever so solemn, laying an uncertain dough hand on my hot sure fist. 'Sommat like that.'

Da picked his teeth with enjoyment. 'Hafta be, fer three hundred bloody pounds in cash!'

'Oh, oh, oh!' I gave over, pulling a sulk. 'It's like a blummin' double act in 'ere, int it!'

Mam was burying her face in her neck so to make chins. 'C'mon, lass, you'd have no time fer work! That's hobbies, that is!'

Da pushed the leaflet back at me with a reverential finger. 'Daylight robbery, pet.'

'Daylight robbery?' I was pushed over with the ignorance of it. 'Well then, just like yous got me working fer free, I suppose I'm a slave an' all!' And I stormed out, crying bitter on my bed with a chair pushed under the knob. Was like I was no older than ten or twelve and I belonged to them! But course, what it was, they couldn't see fer looking why I wanted to leave my own farm.

And I never went on the course.

It was only a few weeks later that the thing with the folder occurred.

I'd been helping my mam clear out her bedroom drawers, looking for this blessed brass ribbon brooch with pearls she thought she'd lost and wanted to wear to church. And there, under her cheap nylon petticoats, I spied this bright blue plastic folder, and on the front it said my name, HOPE CLARK, and my National Insurance number all set out.

I opened it up in the drawer, my back to Mam. Folded inside, reams of printed-out savings account statements in my own name, dated over my entire childhood. Almost four thousand pounds when I was born, put in by my nan. But as

I ran my eyes down the pages, the ledger begun to reduce by a hundred there, twenty here, forty there, over all the years I'd existed. Till winter previous, when there was nowt but *29p* stamped there in black.

'Mam?' I held them up in a fist, my hand trembling with sommat like rage.

She looked up, distracted, and on seeing the folder, barely shrugged. 'Yer nan left it ya fer yer eighteenth, but Sheila at bank said donkey's years since she'd let me myseln take it out fer farm, seeing as we needed things about the place o'er the years like.' Mam folded a pile of jumpers on the bed as she spoke to me, not meeting my eyes. 'Seeing as ya 'ad no use fer it anyroad.'

'But the three hundred fer the course!' I said, my face reddening like my da's, and me mam never responded, except for the slight tilt of a lip she gave off when sommat was too above her to say owt.

And she folded another jumper in the quiet.

Christ, I could of screamed blue murder! Trapped, I was! The entire passage of my life was set out like pegs on a line, as sure as when I put one foot in front of t'other on the Hawthorn road of a Tuesday morning, and the bus would come at two minutes past the eight o'clock hour, and the same three people would be on it, hook or by crook, with the same baskets and caps and scarves, and the same conversations going on about weather and eggs, and I'd get on to the same chorus of ''ow-do's and 'nowt but middling's in return. No different versions of it from season to season, year to year, no changes nor errors or omissions, as if there existed an eternal script in this land folk here had to stick to with us queer rituals, or else. It seemed to me that all I had to do for the rest of my miserable life was wake up when the cock crew and do my bits around farm, and all would fall into place forever and ever without my so much as blowing on it.

Till I met Bill.

Bill shouldn't of ever been in us lives, when you think on it. I should of been sat there doing my bits with one of the Macks. But there I was, and this vastness in me was being woken with the finding of the savings account. Exciting, it was, as if my life had just started up all shining from under a dark film of muck that'd been stifling me, like the heroine in them old tales I loved so much.

And so, as me and Bill sat there together in his truck that first dawn, sipping stewed tea and looking out on that vista that was all and only ours, that sense of danger was a sweet taste of recklessness, unknowing, a path dark and strange. This man, my escape, by any means possible.

And at that moment, Bill sighed long and melancholy, like he'd felt the change in me, and knew. He spoke through the shadow of his own haunted eyes. 'All that beauty. Makes you want to die, don't it?'

They say Bill was a solitary sort before I met him, as all monsters are. Alone in the empty, fighting off them unholy instincts years. I'm not sure I would of recognised the signs even if I'd known, but I felt them sure in my boots. Darkness is mysterious, cause you cannot see what lurks. In the beginning, that unknowing excited me about him.

After we'd gone out that first morning, Bill called for me all week to go with him in that tipper, into these great grey storms that'd near flooded us farm off from the world that month, helping us none at all with the problem with the flock. But we'd still go out, cause that's what I wanted, and my da was frantic with the loss of stock, so it was just Bill and me, and everyone else could do one.

How it went is that I'd spot us smits, and Bill'd tell me to wait in the truck, and he'd go out to the animal and check it in the wet on his own. Took that great wrench with him, and a rope.

Sometimes, he'd come back, and I'd roll down the window, and he'd lean there, his hood to my face, rain pouring down his beautiful nose, explaining the condition of the beast as if it were a car broke down in the mud. 'Reckon it's don-fer?' I'd say, just thinking of snogging him, gazing at his words as they come out his lips, rather than thinking about what he meant by them.

'Reckon, aye,' he'd say, thumbing his nose all casual, a grim expression round his mouth like he wished the contrary. 'I mean, we could try wi' it, bring it to vet, but then yer da loses money, I lose money —'

'A'ight then,' I'd cut him off, sad, but I wanted to please him like young girls do with men. I'd put on the radio and look out the other way up the hill whilst he did it, and the rain bleeding down the window seemed like all that flowed in me, pure and urgent.

He often waxed on when he returned, about the ways of the land, as if he still felt it necessary to justify his kills. I wasn't entirely sure if he was speaking to me, hisseln or some higher force. Sometimes, he'd scribble in that little book on the string after he'd done it, and sometimes, he'd hold it open and read out loud a previous day to me, his cool hands still wet from washing off the blood, and it was beautiful, I suppose, like poetry. But as I say, it wasn't.

Course, Da didn't believe the numbers, and nor should he of, seeing how many carcases were coming back clean, and he pressed me for what the devil was going on. I'd sit there of an evening at the table with them, and he'd ask about every single kill that day, red in the face and worried, and I told my da stories that might suit him, sat there all amiable and nice, Pattinson's reports overruled by virtue of my being the daughter.

As these interrogations went on, I begun to think of my nan, who'd believed when she poked the eyes out of a rabbit with her mouldy ald finger before skinning it alive she was blinding the beast to the agony as it struggled on the hook. She told me there were lines through the wild that we followed, and some were brutal cold.

It must of been near the end of my life on farm that I'd not much patience for it one evening. I turned to Da and declared with all the arrogance of youth, 'You find it hard to believe this is happening cause you don't allow yerseln to consider nature's cruelty to the extent it affects us lives.'

Da looked at his daughter sitting there gloating with her speech, her rude feet up on his bench like a stranger chewing on his bread and his eggs all cocky and selfish, talking in this new unnatural way, and he said, 'He's had a great influence on you, that mucky fella!'

'He has, Da,' I said back, quick as lightning. 'And he knows a shitload more about the world that any o' yous lot!'

I slammed down my plate to cracking in the sink and stormed off, my da half pulling off his belt to take to me so disturbing it was to him, growling after my newly sharpened shadow naw fully informed as to that bloody savings folder in the drawer. 'Never have daughters!' he grunted. 'Never have daughters!'

Da must of known then he could never prove Bill was stealing his sheep, cause I'd gone in it too. At the end of that week, he waited at the gate of the evening to tell Bill thanks very much but we's done here, touching his cap as was his habit when he was nervy, but that was that.

I watched from behind the net at my bedroom window quite tearful as Bill prised a final brown envelope from my da's tight grip and was ceremoniously turned away by the staring hands at the gate, shovels at their sides, making out they were taking a minute from mucking or digging. Deep down these loyal men were made of giants' blood and Vikings, fists the size of his face and a foot or more on him. But honest, they'd all taken frait with scrawny Bill Gleason in their bones like superstition and wanted him gan.

Mam come timid upstairs that afternoon, tapped on my door like a servant. 'Love?' she ventured, barging in to find me laid out a pancake on my bed, cradling an old teddy. They must of known what had gan on. She sat on the edge of the bed and patted my shoulder, tenuous like. Not ones for touching, none of us lot. 'Best he's off, pet. No good woulda come o' it.'

But early that next morning, I was sweeping in the yard out of habit or duty, I suppose, or maybe some sense of what might come, when I heard Bill's tipper, and my heart went queer.

'Hope, love!' he called from the road, the gate being locked on the north side.

I went over squelching in wellies, swimming with excitement.

'Reet nithered, eh?' Bill said, moving his jaws against his tongue, looking me up and down slow. I felt in that look I was wholly made of womanly things, I can tell you.

'Me da don't need you no more,' I said stern, leaning on his window, brushing his great elbow with my hand. 'Says you was too – thorough.'

We shared a smile.

'Aye, but I need ya,' he said, the light in his eyes the double meaning. 'Wanna come out on another job wi' me?'

'When?'

'Naw. Far out, though, almost to Glaiswold.'

'That is proper far,' I said, not focusing on much but Bill's wonderful eyes and mouth and thinking of kissing it hard like a slut. My da would have me slaughtered. I bit my lip and tasted the blood. 'Hold thar,' I said, running back to get my flask.

I'd come back in less than a minute, scared they'd look out window. I got in, slammed the truck door, grinned triumphant. Bill laughed at my excitement, genuinely delighted hisseln that we were sure on the same side, and we set off quick. 'What did ya tell 'em?'

'That I were off to town fer a bit wi' Nicola,' I said. 'Me mate from Young Farmers, but she's on holiday in York, so.'

'Oh aye,' Bill said, and smirked. And I'll admit naw, that certitude of chaos, that wriggling from the crook? I was all snout and tooth.

And we sped along fast as you like, north of there, towards the Viking road where the black tombs of warriors crack in the wind, and into the narrow fogged rocks of the crags.

'KILN NARROW'

Gelatin silver print, mounted on board

160 cm × 250 cm

Us little band reached the top about four mile off village. A strenuous climb, it was, and the lad did well considering, egged on by Jip weaving about between us as we went.

The day was coming in gold, so we took a moment to rest us legs and look down at the land's empty majesty, the sun streaming in shadows through clouds that striped the green below into irons and blues with the tiny pins of steeples of churches, a drift of smoke on the breeze from days-slow smouldering stubble below. We breathed it in, a slight rasp of burned chaff in us noses like new bees. So open it was to gaze upon all that life that it felt like the way out.

We would live.

The lad sighed deep, tears choking his eyes. 'Just me luck,' he said, near comical like. 'I were proper lookin' forward to goin' seaside wi' school next week.' He gave another big sigh for effect. 'Never did go.'

It occurred to me as he said it I'd not set eyes on the sea in all the eleven year I'd been at shed. When was the last time

I'd been? Probably when I was a teenager, even before that. Sudden more than anything at all, a new sense of freedom come over with such force I found myseln making a promise to the lad. 'We'll do this thing naw up Bellemere, then after when we're done wi' it, we'll go seaside fore we head off to yer nan's.'

The lad didn't much react; he just kept looking at the clouds, blinking. I suppose he'd meant sommat else. Maybe that all his friends were dead, and his mam too, and the pier, so exciting in the photos he'd probably seen at school, would naw be full of stinking bodies anyway, and the slot machines wouldn't be the same without all that hustle and bustle and the machines all dinging and music blaring with that edge of golden happiness when you win a line of paper tickets; that smell of sugar coming off the laughing girls' mouths, and the throng of it all he'd so been looking forward to that someone had most likely told him all about already.

Any doubts I was having about Bellemere were fading fast listening to the lad. Well aye, I might of had my freedom again in the worst possible way, but it was nowt but a prison if there was nobody to share it with. Once the lad was dropped with his nan, I'd inherit a vast desolation – and the sky. My fingers glanced off the newspaper in my pocket, the only photo I'd left of Bill, and it felt sharp and torn. And that rush must of got the better of me, and I was after thinking, well, aye, Bill would of likely changed on the inside as I had out here, all that time passed. We were so alone naw, after all.

The land had in it that feeling of being heavy as the three of us trudged tired through the rusted barrens, ankles catching in the scrub, keeping off the easier-flagged paths laid through it to be sure of us solitude. Underfoot, larger grey stones come loose from the hills tripped us and bruised us heels with their sharp parts, but we kept on with it, inspired by the sky's glaze of harsh blue, its banks of thick cloud like an ocean rolling west as if pinned to the horizon. It was sommat to strive on.

Truth was that we'd no chance of merciful shade afore the sparse edge of green fir some mile down, distant black strings of branches like shadows in gold earth, and we were to burn like beetles under a magnifying glass till then.

'Lass,' said the lad. And there in the next field over, I spied a young woman, townie looking, blondie, a bright orange anorak, blue toggles, sun-yellow pockets as if a conscious attempt had been made to make the thing as ugly as possible. She was poring over her unsuitable bags, hair in her pointed city face. 'Fella,' said the lad, and with that, we three edged over, movement unspoken between us, some flocking instinct drawing us in. We stooped by the hedge, dawdling, Jip sniffing, to catch on what had occurred.

'Offcomers,' I whispered.

'Aye, that,' said the lad, and we stared.

I focused on the young fella appearing from the thick hedge where he'd been crouched in a matching orange anorak. We watched quiet as he walked over and zipped up her bag, wheep. He offered her a flask, which she batted away. 'Sod off!' she yelled. 'Just get out of it with your stupid fucking warm drinks!' Southerner, course, hiking far out when the sound happened. Bewildered, she was.

'Lucy, come on,' the fella said, trying to take her shoulder in a smooth hand. He was a nice young chap. Then I saw the dried blood at his ear. He rubbed the side of his head; it was aggravating him.

"Ow do,' I said loud then.

The pair of them turned sharp and stared as if we were aliens. He managed a smile, eventually. 'Hi,' he said, gave one of them little finger waves the townies have. 'Rambling,' he says all proud, as if it is a grand achievement to put one foot front of t'other.

This skinny one Lucy flew to the hedge between us, breathless, fingers in the brambles, grasping. 'Sorry, does your phone work out here?' Posh caw. She pulled out a great gold phone, started bashing on it like they do, nails pink as pigs. 'No reception out here. For days!' She smiled quite hysterical at me, flat brown eyes, somehow ashamed to mention the clear problem for manners. Pale, she was. Sommat wrong inside. She looked to her companion. 'Ask,' she said quiet, tugging on his jersey. He stepped away from her, hands up. Not much strength in him for arguing left. 'Assk!' she hissed, glancing at us. But the bloke just stared at the land, emptied thin.

'No phone on me, lass,' I said then, interjecting to save the time. 'Where yous headed?'

'A bit deaf,' she said, waving her hand at her ear. 'Since that noise.' Smiling fake. She had started to gush at the nose.

'Bleeding,' I said, pointing quick.

She got out a flowery scarf from a pocket, started dabbing. It was already red through. 'Gah!' she squealed in frustration, holding up a hand for us to wait.

'What *was* that?' said the fella in my general direction. Nice blonde hair, he had. 'Does that sort of thing happen much out here?' His eyes were spinning a little. 'I mean, terrifying, right?' He smiled a little broken smile, begging for comfort.

'Aye,' I said, kicking at the ground. 'That it were.' I shoved my hands deep in my pockets.

The man stared, lips moving, but nowt come out. He grasped at his forehead.

The lad nudged me. Jip sat at his feet, looking on. The good-hearted mites wanted to help. But the last thing we needed was these offcomed'uns tagging along. 'We're off down coast,' I said finally, with a nod. Aye, a flock will scatter at the first sign of danger.

These two were only a few mile off village, anyroad. I mean, I did wonder about any more lunatics wilding about the place, but, so. I kept it to myseln.

'Have a lovely afternoon!' the lass said all chirpy, scrambling the scarf back to her nostril. I suppose she took us as a sign all was well in the world, that we were off to beach, that we looked well. The fella stumbled against her, losing his balance. 'Asssk!' she hissed more urgent to him.

But we slipped off before he got up the courage to ask, whatever it was.

By the time we were sat in them cool green lichen fronds some mile yon, the lad was all flushed cheeks, and Jip had his ham tongue stuck out dripped panting onto the mustard moss-ringed blue of stones. I felt my own head swimming with the sun, but there was nowt to be done, so I shut my eyes for a bit, and that helped.

After a fair swig of water, we took to peering through the shade at the bright land the front of us, sweeping up and over into the heat. 'Miles an' miles an' miles,' said the lad.

And no bloody shelter, I thought to myseln.

As we caught us breath, I begun to make out the shapes of strange-looking hay bales in each field that didn't belong. Stretching on these shapes dotted, some clumped together, some far spread, but that silence I ken so well was flooding everything around us. Ya, tan, tether, I counted these shapes. Then I figured it: the bales were the flocks, dead where they'd fallen from the sound. We must of been near a farm for them to of been out like this so early in the morning, or perhaps they'd wandered out in spite of it, and perished.

'Sheeps,' the lad said.

'Sheep,' I said sharp. 'Collective noun.'

'Eh?' said the lad.

'Don't fret, lad.' My heart was pounding. To think of my da's flock dead like this was more upsetting to me than the people we'd seen.

I reckon it's true what they say about those afflicted with my kind of outlook: that we identify with animals more than we do other people. Maybe cause we're more like animals than folk. Bill once said to me that most humans can't bring themseln to answer their natural callings, cause it feels too base to them to let go. After all, a beast shits and eats and mates and kills without a thought for those of his species around, and that's not too Christian. I tend to the notion that folk may be animal in their biology, but we're not animal in the head. We've been given the ability to choose how we behave, and that's the difference twixt man and beast. That would of made Bill very angry if I'd said so back then out loud, but that's how I feel about it.

Then sudden, a sound of motors come from the south, carrying on the dead cloy of wind through the trees. 'Wisht,' I said to Jip, and the lad got down too, and we squinted to the far road that ran white from where we'd come. A pair of military trucks rattled down it, smears of dark tin on the sky, headed for Morton Hill. 'Them soldiers would kill us, naw we's infected,' I lied to the lad. See, the trucks were swerving all over road as they went. Sommat off.

'Infectied?' he whispered louder than talking, a sudden panic in him.

'The sound in the night that killed 'em in village. I reckon we're sick naw from't,' I said, not knowing if what I was claiming was the truth or no. But that pull, to get to Bill before they did, drove me in them moments.

'Ya think it were the Mericans did it to us?' He gave a small cough. Smart lad, really.

'Probably they'll see them two townies on their way,' I said then, more cynical than intended.

'Oh yeah!' said the lad, cheered in his charitable little soul.

I thought on the sonic booms we'd sometimes suffered in village when the American jets went out on exercises. Always without warning, they'd shake us from us beds, bring plates down off the shelves, clawing us eardrums till we'd all think it was World War III about to start up. Terrifying us all like dragons, they come nose first speeding to the ground before swerving back up high as you like, but I didn't ken sure if that meant it was owt to do with it. I thought about them lights, and what I'd seen, just like Mark had said. Had the lights been what them pilots were practising for?

'Lad, when it happened, did ya hear? The sound?'

The lad rolled onto his back, thoughtful, sweating in his fleece, but I suppose it was too much bother to him to ask for a hand to get it off. He stared into the high hushed branches like an older lad might, chin all muddy. He spoke careful, thinking. 'Were like, say if ya got a punch in the eye, but the punch stayed in yer face fer like, ten or twenty counts.'

I nodded plain. Little lad shouldn't of known yet what a punch in the eye was like. 'I don't get why you didn't die.'

'Or yerseln.' He looked at me square. 'When me and me mam was in the jail, Copper Mark said it were the padded walls that protected us, y'know, cause they was to stop the criminals using their mobiles in the lock-up. That maybe it was them walls after saving us from the sound, fer that.'

'Well, aye. Reckon Copper Mark and us was out o' the range o' it somehow,' I said. Oh, Mark. I can't think on it much even naw.

The lad said, 'Copper Mark says it must of come out them big new masts, the noise feeling.'

There'd certain been a stink about it the summer last, that great new mast they wanted up Morton Hill. It had some super-capacity for linking to satellites in space that was meant to make the web pages go faster, but folk round here, who weren't much for using the computers in any case, said they'd rather stick to the mast they'd already in Shoreton, case this newfangled one was polluting the atmosphere or doing their heads in funny with its microwaves. They were worried about the flocks losing their way like they'd heard somewhere brids do when they migrate with that modern technology all abouts in the air nawdays, sending them off course.

And there'd been that yarn going about concerning a mysterious kettle of hawks out at sea, but that sounded like a load of poppycock, seeing as hawks don't go nowhere else for winter, and not a soul I knew in village had been to sea neither to witness.

Anyroad, the patchy reception with the Shoreton mast had not gone down too well with them American pilots at the base, nor the young'uns, Sarah told me, for the gaming they do naw and all that new 'content' on the Web they like to stand about gawping at, so they'd seen to it that it went up, despite the petition at the shop making the rounds. 'Dull enough round here fer youngsters, them that don't be interessed in sheep,' she said, nodding to a gathering of acned teens by the graveyard as she had her cigarette break at the door, all of them in great bright plastic winter coats up to their noses, devices in front of their faces. They were like aliens from a different climate, making do.

'Lately, feels like all anyone wants to do is forget the past, don't it?' Sare said.

A smirk to myseln. 'You're not wrong thar, pet.'

But just looking at the pack of 'em, these young'uns, I was disturbed. Maybe they'd been sensing that low shift in the air an' all. The way the sky slunk grey and slow; how water fell thick from the tap. Nobody talked about it, but aye, it was there alright. Made you feel like none of it was ours, this land, the keeping of it. And yet, we were part of it all.

'God bless 'em,' Sarah had said then, shifting foot with her fag in one hand as she examined the youngsters. 'Like a hole in the ground convinced it's the entire world.'

Truth be told, like in ancient tales of the gods who take back what is theirs, I reckon in village we'd all felt it coming long ago, from the sky, the sea, that crackle in the earth. We were flies on the back of a horse, being shook off. The strangest thing? We *recognised* it, did we? That hereditary, shaking us bones. I could see it in them kids that day: instinctual, it was, an en masse nihilism, as if the whole planet was about to break out delirious and we couldn't stop it from happening.

'I were never bored when I were young,' I said to Sare, lying royally to make me point. 'Loved it out here, in the fresh air.'

'That's you though, Glore. Don't make 'em like that no more, derthee?'

The lad closed his eyes as we sat resting. 'I'm blummin' famished, Glore.' I handed him a crushed mint cake from my sack, and we all had some water, Jip drinking from the dip of a flat stone.

I took to explaining what was happening. 'We hafta get to that hill yon. Bit of a trek yet, lad. The one wi' the brown tower sticking up.' It looked not more than a matchstick from there, perched on a tiny jut. The crematorium chimney for the prison. For Bellemere. 'We'll walk quiet along edge of grough all the way. Should be not too bad.' But I could see the lad was faded and would not walk much more; crumbs of tired sugar hung round his lips. 'We'll do a few mile round, then rest up fer night,' I said, some sort of compromise to put an end in sight for him. After all, it was least seven more mile, and I could see little strength in him left. He'd probably spent his days in village with the telly and one of them great bags of crisps they have naw for supper, by the looks of his puny white legs. My, at that age, I was browned in the wind all year and eating apples off the grass; my strong young feet could walk twenty mile in a day through fog or sleet looking for a ewe gan over. But not this wan lad. I worried then.

'Listen, pet,' I started, pulling my knife out from the breast pocket. Clean, it was naw, and he caught the flash of it in that pale light, eyes given over to shivering. 'You'd better have a go o' it. Let me teach ya how.' I turned the blade to my hand, proffering the handle.

The lad stared at it like a lost thing. 'Wha' do I need that fer?'

I set the knife down on the sedge for a moment to drain the fear out of him, drawing him close by his shoulders. Hot, they were, padded with the fleece, a faint line of pulse dancing frait through little veins. His pewr lips were all dried out, tiny freckles puffed at the sides, them bright blue pools for eyes clogged from crying hisseln to a state. 'If owt should happen to me,' I said firm, 'or if ya reckon I can't protect you no more, you take this knife from me and use it.'

'Where ya goin', Glore? You gonna leave me?' Panic coated his eyes.

'Nay, nay, lad.' I tried a little laugh, shook my head. 'Only so as you know.'

'In case?' he said, the lip trembling naw. He sniffed tears back.

'Aye, lad, that's it. In case. Naw, take it up nice and careful. To that tree thar.' A birch stump in the dry earth, some five foot up, long cut over, its rings in their hundreds, bark all plated and grey. Earwigs scuttled shiny in the heat. A notion crossed in me: insects for protein. Then I set to the task with the lad.

He took up the knife as if it was poisoned, finger and thumb first. But by the time he come over, Jip making feet all tongue at his side, boyish ways had kicked in and he was stabbing the air like a little soldier. 'Good knife, this, Glore!' he said like an expert, making the best of it, I suppose.

I picked up a stick from the ground, broke it to the length of the knife. I made a motion upwards to the side of the stump. 'Pretend this is their body, and this is their lungs, and heart here. Remember, the body has these big veins you can get. If ya break one, they'll die quite quick.'

'Art-terries,' the lad said, nodding sagely, pursed lips.

'Bingo. Best to stab on their left side, in the soft. But the heart is here. More in the middle.' I tapped my own chest. The lad watched careful and quiet, knife held high in his left hand, like he was waiting for his dinner. 'You left-handed?' I said.

'Me nan tried to make me write wi' the other one for a bit, but it come out funny.'

'Well aye, good ya left-handed. Easier for a little lad like you. Strong cross-stab, like this then.' I showed him a couple of times, drawing the stick cross my body and up. 'And pull it out quick, fore the body has time to tighten on the blade. Ya want the blood to come out.'

The lad stabbed up at the tree a couple times. With a few adjustments, I showed him how to use his height as an advantage. 'They can't get ya, see, cause you're too small. So if anyone comes at ya, just keep ducking, light on yer feet, don't let them grab ya.' Cause, I wanted to say, if they do, they'll cut your throat, strangle you to death, suffocate you. Worse.

He did well, striking upwards, a little grunt each time, then a cry when he hit the tree, bark flying in chunks. 'Well done,' I said. Jip jumped up at first, but then I called him to heel for safety.

Soon the lad was yelling, smacking the tree with the blade 'Ya, ya, ya! Fock you! Fockin' arse-all! Die! Die!' Them moles were all up black, red cheeks puffed with the effort of it, or the rage, perhaps making out the tree was the man killed his mam. Making out like he was me.

'A'ight naw, lad, very good, that's the size of it, you got it, they're dead fer sure!' And I wrested the knife off him, all wriggling about, and he took instead to kicking and punching that pewr dead tree till he had no sound left in him at all, a wretched foam of sobs and spit formed at his nose. He dropped to the ground, knuckles stripped raw, and took up calling out for his mam again.

Jip went over meek and low, one guilty eye left behind case I objected, licked the salt from his hot little face. But I said nowt on it, muttering under my breath, impatient as usual, the knife back in my pocket, and went looking out rabbit holes for a bit, and when I come back empty-handed, the lad was quiet and still, Jip's head on his knees in the sun. He had the water bottle in his hand, gazing listless cross the vast land in front of us. 'You'll be reet,' I said, and scuffed his hair.

'Yar,' he said calm, and he squinted up to me, grateful, I suppose. 'Can't get the top off this water.'

We crept slowly along the grough another couple mile, the lad dragging sommat awful and given over to constant moaning. The sward was seamy and sparse through the roots and unpleasant on the tread, peat crumbling sodden into strewn drystone, and the sun naw set to shimmering red in us eyes. Sometimes, we'd step over the bodies of sheep, their dear black faces rancid and bleeding with flies, legs naw useless pins under huge fuzzy coats. 'Sheeps are massive!' said the lad, and I wondered sadly if he'd ever seen one close up before that day.

And so we dragged along, dried out and tired, through one dull field to the next, as if the fields were empty rooms with walls of moss and stone, and through each wall we stepped like ghosts in a house after everyone's gone away, after all has been locked up and they've bolted the windows, and only the cold wind of solitude bangs on the doors for company.

There come a point in that day when we had to take Kiln Narrow, a yellow-stained fog from the morning clinging to the brown weeds that darkened and rose around us. The hills come up brant and orange either side, the path rust macadam underfoot: the crumbs of an ironstone site lining the edge of Morton. When we were kids we'd run in the sodden fairy rings here, ghost-stemmed mushrooms marking the lines where witches run widdershins at a wolf moon.

Like many gullies ont moor, the beck is naw a dry, hollow vein since being forced in to wash ore a hundred year back. Works burrow the steeps like a pestilence where they dug out the soul of the land, abandoned kilns black like risen ghouls;

smashed furnaces spilling toxic flakes of blooded rust to settle in the like-coloured mantel. One day, these relics of destruction will melt entirely back into the land it raped as nourishing rot for the soil.

Was an eerie place to tread, the sick trees hissing and the echo of us deadening up the shorn-parched banks, desiccated rocks cracking like bones as the wind battered its faces. The steppes of long-smoothed turf cast shadows like bodies on the ground as we crept, bright blue as oil on dirt. And I saw Bill's face as we went in the colours, smeared with the dark and the fury.

See, in that monotony of razed wild, somewhere buried, there's a boy lost.

In the first months after I run, I'd stopped at a rest near there, and they told me the kiddie's cry had carried from far vanna, and they'd gone off with torches and dogs and sticks looking, and yet found not a harr of him. A full moon the night it happened, and those who went out said they felt followed.

And naw, in the same damned place, we weren't alone neither. The strange kobold texture of stone and silt sings its own language there, not caring if you understand; a howl somewhere in the wood. You are a stranger here. The world goes on. This is what it says.

'Don't like it 'ereabouts,' said the lad, heeling me close as crumbs. Jip trotted ahead to sniff at the interesting minerals in the whinstone, or maybe, like me, he ken where we were.

'Me neither,' I said to the lad. The last time I'd been there, the same yellow fog had dampened my hair, slick smoked air coating my lungs with a taste of blood off the rock, making me retch. Bill and me, struggling into the kilns. 'Naw, get lost,' Bill had ordered me, and obediently I'd slid back down to the truck with the empty pink flannelette blanket folded neat on my arm.

Jip stopped, front paw up, sniffing rapid on the road ahead. A crackling noise, sommat banging in the breeze. Pinks and yellows bleeding through the haze, till we got close and I could make it out proper. A grand bouquet of flowers tied to a fence, cheap ones with lots of chrysanthemums and that papery babby's breath stuff that seems dead already. Petrol shop cellophane with fake lace edges, a stiff blue ribbon clattering like a broken wing in the quiet.

I knew straight why they were there. One of the mams, leaving flowers, an offering in vain to the land to bring her kiddie home. They must of known the grave was close, but never found it.

We stood looking for a while. The flowers were well battered by the elements, cloyed petals all wet and see-through where mice had been at the middles for the pollen. A sorry red plastic candle propped up a sign: handmade, childish writing in felt pen, *Bring Davey Home!* A cheap black rosary dangled over an ugly prayer card of St Anthony, the sort of tat you can buy at church if you put a pound in the box. Eleven year gone, fancy coming up here still, I thought. To this horrible place.

The lad studied the little grotto from afar, not touching owt. 'The saint of missing people, that Anthony,' he said, pointing at it. 'We's Catholics, so.'

I gave a cynical grunt. If this little lad's mam'd been Catholic, then I was the bloody Virgin Mary.

I'd startled the lad. He looked to me proper frait, thick lashes going. 'D'ya reckon we could go missing on this road an' all?'

'Nay, lad. Them things don't happen no more.'

'Phew!' said the lad, like he was in a cartoon. Cause, Jesus, where were we? And he wiped his brow like in a cartoon too, but I caught him looking sideways at me all sly, checking I wasn't the Black Dog come walking on all fours to bite him.

Just then, from out in the gloom, we heard the ringing of church bells, so clear and sweet they could of come from just cross the way, but I knew myseln there were no church bells five miles least, and that weir sound pinned us down heavy with confusion and not just a drop of horror as we trudged with its relentless cacophony, till the lad started up laughing, saying, 'No worries, Glore, tis only a recording set to go off by itseln, carried the empty land wi' the wind!'

'Aye, lad, that, sure.' And he did relieve me in that brackish hole with his clever conclusion. Sure, he was probably right, for there was not likely nobody left to be ringing them in such harmonious fashion, but it wasn't a Sunday morning neither, when you'd likely hear bells, and for that it was queer to have been set off at all.

In that moment, I was tickled rotten by imagining a band of bell-ringers had lived through the sound just like we had, and were at that moment in a belfry going through their bobs and courses and grandsires like mad to call survivors to the church. I burst out giggling, and the lad took a wary step back.

I grabbed his hand firm, for reassuring the mite I hadn't gone totally doolally. 'Nay, nay, nowt to worry about,' I said, but not sharing my thoughts, for it might give a young lad hopes of finding comfort where I was sure there was none. He was right, it was too regular and perfect-sounding, a triggered recording, and soon, it stopped as abruptly as it had started.

I dragged us out of that hellish place fast, for it was nowt but misery and memories, and we'd certainly enough of that to go round already thank you very much.

When the sun was too low to go on, burning us with its fire even if we tried to look away from it elsewhere, we come cross a tall black barn at the end of a burnished meadow, two dead slapes chained to the side just like my da's dogs would be naw, and I felt sorry for Jip as he sniffed their coats with a whine, looking for stories in their fur.

In the barn, there was nowt but dead rats, so in the knowledge they'd not be nibbling us socks in the night, we slept solid through, concealed warm in the bales with us feet touching naw and then, the lad being too exhausted to care too much where we put us heads down in the dark.

I thought about going and looking for them lights once more, but it creeped me just to think on it, and what good anyhow would it do me, I reasoned, and found there was no answer.

So I pulled out that little newspaper clipping from my pocket, and I looked hard at Bill's photo till all I could see were the dots of ink. But as I held it to the light, I noticed for the first time the word 'Mack' backwards in the moonlight, printed on the other side of the scrap. I turned it over, and I'll be blowed, if there wasn't a line in the Births Marriages Deaths about Josh Mack getting engaged to my old mate from Young Farmers, Nicola Hodden. Well, I had to smile to myseln.

I must of fell asleep thinking on Bill, cause in my dream, against all best advice, I was trying to feel that rush I'd get when he kissed me, like he might kill me too. I remembered in that same dream a detail of his nails I'd forgot, always with blood lined in them, running over my naked body and scratch-ing inside, and my own blood fresh drawn would mingle alive with the newly dead.

'Run,' he'd said with his hot mouth over mine the night before they come for him. 'When this is over, when there's nobody left, we can disappear.'

Then I dreamed I was with Bill in the old house, and I said to him, *it's over naw, Bill, the whole world has disappeared around us just like you said it would.*

And when I opened us front door, there was one bright star, watching in the dark.

'ABBEY'

Gelatin silver print, mounted on board
160 cm × 250 cm

The abbey was razed by a king long ago. But further back still, they say it was a site for witches, a temple for high priestesses reared up in tribes of queens who could talk to the land and learn ancient truths. They scattered their great stone circles along miles of the ley, surfaces pitted with cupmarks, tattooed faint with lines and marks in prayers and spells no living person can read. When I was a girl, I'd run my fingers cross them stones as if it was some weir Braille, and fancied the stones spoke to me, telling me secrets, filling me with the earth's power.

On the morning me and Bill first drove towards Glaiswold, the ruins of the abbey soon come into view, jagged blue-shadowed in the orange of morning. I caught movement past its broken walls, flicks like white gossamer that seemed to jump between the high slitted windows that still stood in them crumbled flint walls. And Bill caught on to it an' all.

See, when you ken a landscape like we both did, you catch the quickness of flight out the corner of an eye, the slowness or heaviness of unnatural movement at un-animal heights, like machinery or folk messing, sometimes a beast struggling a trap, mantling its prey.

'Scower tha', kid,' Bill said, pointing to the ruins with a knuckle over the steering wheel. I flinched at the kid part. But then Bill often called me 'kid'. He was a lot older than me, after all. I gazed at his jaw, stretched like gorgeous canvas over bone, a pulse in it. The ferocity of it made me all nerves. I ached for that pulse to be about me.

'Shan't mither stopping,' I said. 'Probably tha' Wrigley lad grassed on you to me da, throwin' stones about, skiving. Allays thar, 'e is. Bit touched, I'd say.'

I laughed it off, but Bill stopped sharp, weighing a determined arm on the back of my seat, and reversed at speed to the stile at footpath. He pulled on the handbrake till it creaked. He said, 'Best introduce me to the little shit.' And a cloud come over his face.

Alfie Wrigley was on his tod, flinging bits of peat at a carving in a pillar, a grubby figure of Mary Magdalene with her gold cloth long tarnished down to scraps here-there of glittering stone. Alfie was dressed in his school uniform. Posh school, it was, but he never went. He'd wrenched his little green tie to one side, arrogant strawberry blonde hair piled in curls for his mammy. His jacket had these intricate green velvet buttons like you get on a marching band's uniform, and against the gaberdine's grey it was a bloody smart kid to be mucking about like a gypsy's boy. He'd his tongue out to one side, concentrating on the flinging.

'Oi!' called Bill, striding over kneeless in blue overalls, fists made tight at the front of stiff arms like he was going in for a bruising. The way his skin tautened took my breath away, its shine of sweat on tanned dirt, the way he moved his hot mouth, all wet, anticipating.

Alfie looked up with a bored expression in his piercing green eyes. 'What do you want?' he said in his little prince's voice all lazy, balancing like a conqueror on a pile of grey stones, one leg up, an elbow resting. He flicked a look to me. 'Ho-ope,' he said in two syllables, by way of a greeting, as if he was a man already, and better than me; not a shred of respect in him whatsoever.

'Alfie, what ya been sayin' to big Carl Pattinson about Mr Gleason?'

Bill stopped at the Mary Magdalene, glazed over staring at the lad, the stone eyes of a brid of prey.

'Nothing that wasn't true,' the lad said cocky, slightly put off, kicking at the green moss that ringed the stones. It was hard to tell if he felt sorry for tattling to Pattinson, or just didn't care.

'You bloody lost me the job at 'er da's farm!' Bill yelled. 'Three hundred quid, about!' A pulse in his neck was beating hard, some parasite woken in his system rushing around hungry.

Alfie shrugged; he didn't give a toss. Then he mumbled his retort just so as we heard it, but so as we could of heard it wrong. 'Shouldn't have done it then, mister, should you?'

The three of us stood in the thick silence of that ruined abbey for a moment, the only sound Alfie Wrigley's impertinent shoe thudding at the moss.

Bill's eyes lifted, heavy cannons in his head. They were dark naw, scrawled over with a violent ink. 'Go wait in truck,' he said flat to me, frame bristling. 'I need a word wi' Alfie, man to man, about manners.'

Alfie shrugged again, one shoulder after the other, and it made my skin boil how rude he was, so I left Bill to have his word, and went back to the truck with a skip in my step, pleased to give Bill a chance to tell the lad hisseln that tattle-tales don't get far in life.

That night, this great thunderstorm come over from the sea, a black mass of sky like devils running and spitting. An arc of truck lights had come screeching up my ceiling through the streaks of rain just as I was falling asleep, then an urgent banging took up on the door. Fred Wrigley, it was, drove up from his stead. I recognised his desperate voice when it flew up the stairs, gabbling loud to Da. Looking for his biy, he said. Lost ont moor, haint been to school. And naw this storm. Folk were out with torches and dogs, mumbling in congregation, stood drenched by us barns.

I couldn't say owt about what had gan on with Bill and Alfie that same morning. If they knew he'd given the lad a stout word up abbey, they'd blame him for the lad's running off.

Instead, I pulled my nan's warm quilt tight over my head and shut my eyes against the night, drifting in the stars with Mary Magdalene. As the thunder bellowed and shook my windows, I put my fingers to myseln and touched the soreness where Bill had been that morning, rough and new in the back of his truck. I ran hot thinking of his boned, scratched hips and silked dirty hair; the taste of him like fresh meat – nay, it was more like fear, but not his. The thin blood of his profession in his nails, the ridge of one cold ear.

All the while, I gripped the single green velvet uniform button Bill had pushed in my hand at the truck's door, by way of his good evening.

Before I run, that copper had questioned me as to why I supposed Bill left me alive that first time he took me to Glaiswold in his truck.

I told him it was cause Bill loved me.

The copper snorted, mocking me. 'Pewr caw,' he'd said, under his breath.

But I reckon I bought myseln time with that answer.

'MORTON HILL'

Gelatin silver print, mounted on board

300 cm × 250 cm

The moors are soaked in bones and blood, not as old as the hills, but made from them. The burial mounds we call howes litter the land with pieces of cracked hogbacks still lodged in the sod, sacred gravestones carved by the earliest Vikings, of bears and wolves and gods that died long ago here.

Sometimes as a kiddie, I'd climb their great pagan curves, patterned like the back of reptiles or the weave of leather strapping, a tooth or claw like a pebble come loose. I would weigh it in my small child's hand, feeling for remnants of the fierce, battle-torn man, or woman, that must of hewn it for a friend, a child, a lover, a god.

Bellemere Crag hangs over a great dried lake of bronzed mud in cracks, its ancient face a flat gold plate of barren weeds foamed thick in mineral-rich holes like the mouths of the mad who dwell atop. It used to be quite the thing that folk would come with metal detectors and kites of a Sunday, to dig up old coins, bits of ancient daggers, slung clay pipes. They'd scrape up leather parts of the drowned, unearth the fossils of spiky fish. It seemed they were after destroying sommat hallowed in the place, bringing up what had already gone into the light. But after the first of them old Viking bodies was discovered in the peat, nobody come there no more, for fear that whatever had befallen these great battle lords and captains all them thousands of years back was catching.

See, I believe sommat echoes natural in folk: they ken that death can soak through the spirit. It was sure no place for a kiddie to fly a kite no more, and gradually, the site was taken back into the tomb of nature, its violence lost in the living groan of the soil.

The Vikings are long gone an' all, carted off to museums and whatnot for preservation. Instead, HMP Bellemere naw cuts into that crag.

I heard it's the most remote High Security Unit in England. From its roof on a clear morning, you must be able to see the whole county and next over crisp as glass. You'd spot a rabbit from up there. A maximum security hospital for the most dangerous men they catch: Category A psychopaths, paedophiles, serial killers.

Bill is deemed all three.

They said at the time he'd be accessing the best therapy, to help with his 'extreme behavioural issues'. Apparently, they built an arts centre inside: non-toxic poster paints, felt shapes and plastic scissors, as if they were tots and not adults at all. And a music room with recorders enough for every 'client', and triangles, a piano bolted to the floor!

Well. I am yet to picture a man like Bill Gleason painting his deviance away, or tootling on the recorder to forget his urges, but I suppose the facility created jobs for those in the area who had nowt better to do for money than placate devils in the barren.

The building of it come about cause of that Willy Fregg, a feckless lunatic who'd escaped the holding unit in the town of Glebedale, raping and killing a further three women on a rampage lasting less than two days before being captured in a visitors' car park at Bassenthwaite in a stolen vehicle, blood smeared cross his beard with his victims' half-eaten underwear on the passenger seat. I remember reading about it – I think I was expecting at the time – and Bill had found the whole episode supremely hilarious, laughing heartily at the paper whilst shovelling eggs in his gob at breakfast. He kept saying, 'Good on ya, Willy Fregg!'

'Why good?' I asked. 'He's a reet bastard.'

'So what? He really did the system up!' And Bill beamed as if he was proud of the man.

I didn't see it myseln, but that was Bill's logic, so I kept my lip buttoned. Any police or community service to Bill was evil and controlling; and anything random or wild utterly entertaining. It didn't worry me too much, for it was only his opinion after all, but when they started clearing the old slaughter yard at the Crag, he was furious. 'That were a beauty spot, previous!' he'd say, smacking his cutlery on the table.

He forgot I knew full well that's where the steads brung the flocks for dipping and spathing three month before the shear, and had done since my great-grandfather's time at least. So whatever Bill was going on about, Bellemere Crag was never no beauty spot, for the dip's poison had long soaked into the ridge and killed all the foliage down the side, and the name that means 'pretty lake' made little sense naw. It wasn't 'belle' at all, and the 'mere' dried up in Saxon times. My grandfather used to say, 'We'd drink the dip when we was young, and we's still here, int we?' But he died in his sixties of throat cancer. So much for his saying about what's right.

By the time the place was finished, they'd had Bill in custody a fair time. In the papers, they said he might be sent down South to one of them farcy London places where all the 'big boys' went, and I remember I sat down heavy and cried when I seen that, for although I wanted to hate what he'd done to me, and to the others, I loved Bill Gleason in some desperate romantic way for ever such a long time after, and the thought of him so far off from me was too much of a loss after losing everything else.

I suppose I felt in some way that me and Jip, we belonged to Bill, and like a slave set free with nowhere else to go, I took to wandering, aimless and heartbroken. It sounds completely ridiculous I should imagine, but the truth is that for a long time after, Bill was my home wherever they had him, and for that, I wanted to be near, come what may.

When I read he was to be in Bellemere, I remember being sort of relieved, for if I wanted, I could come out to the heights of the moor, stand straight up, and catch sight of that tiny brown chimney smoking the dead in the distance, and know he was there, secured in a place we once ran wild like animals in love.

Despite its looming presence on the skyline, the prison could not hold many inmates. I can only find out these things, course, by asking in local chit-chat, or looking at the papers left out in village, or hearing sommat on the wireless. So I'd asked old Dutton casual as I could what become of that dipping place up the Saxon lake, and he told me it was become that big new ugly prison for kiddie fiddlers. That the sheep was taken into the commons at Saxely naw instead.

'That a big prison then?' I said, all innocent like.

'Eighteen, twenty of 'em monsters, abouts,' Dutton had said, puffing on his pipe thoughtfully, wood bowl rested on his beard, white hair tanned with nicotine.

'Not many, that,' I said. 'Fer such a big place.'

'Not many do them diabolical things to fill 't,' he said.

'Not many get caught, anyroad.'

'Aye, woman, that be the truth o' it.' And he puffed on his pipe, and we stood a while in the quiet, considering the view that frosty morning over to Morton Hill.

And see, the barrens were still a few mile yon, and a nasty wind slapped us clothes into us bones despite the blaze of the sun. With a breakfast of stale cobs, me and the lad clung to the hedge, pushing on, Jip limping scorched paws, for the scrub in this weather's hot as eggs.

Just as I was thinking on trapping for us next scran, we come upon a handsome flint farmhouse past the low drystone. I decided straight we should go in, get cleaned up, look for food. I went creeping first, hoping for the use of the toilets and sinks. 'Wisht,' I said to Jip, and he sat with his head cocked on the path. The lad stopped next to him, swaying from one foot to the other, tired out in his school shoes. 'Stop 'ere a minute,' I whispered. 'Shout if anyone comes.'

I went in quiet, feet flat to the red tile. First by the stairs, a little guest toilet with climbing rose wallpaper. A bar of soap on the glossy white sink with the scent of lavender I slipped in my pocket. It was so clean and nice it broke my heart. There was still running water from the little copper tap, and the lights worked normal. I avoided my own eye in the mirror, stepping into the hall. 'Lo?' I called out. 'Anyone home?'

The silence was that same dreaded answer. Nobody breathed there.

I found the farmer and his wife in their room upstairs: a pair of ruddy big'uns like caws in the bed. Then two bloats of girls in twin beds in a pink-painted room with all the trimmings, manes of blonde hair spilt over lace-edged pillows.

I called to the lad and Jip to come in, and apart from the rot singing with flies, the house was tidy and clean. Normal, I would say.

'Cor, stinks!' said the lad, dramatically holding his nose and waving his little hand about.

'Aye,' I said. 'Take no notice, lad.'

'I'll need a dolly peg fer me nose!' he said, smiling some and lifting his little chin, trying to make light of it, bless him. A brave little lad really.

We plonked down together on the big floral couches in the living room, worn out naw we could rest, and the smell wasn't too bad in there. I turned on the telly, and on some of the channels they had old Westerns playing, and some of them silly reality programmes I wouldn't follow, but the lad told me the real test was going to be the news, cause a lot of other programmes, he told me, were pre-recorded and running automatically.

'How d'ya know such a thing, lad?'

He shrugged, kicking his school shoes off at last. 'Watched about it on telly, how they make the shows play so tha' if there was a war or sommat, they'd still be on.' He wiped his face from the few flies that had sauntered downstairs to bother us.

Funny, int it, how the insects didn't die with the sound? Must be sommat about the way they hear, different to us beasts.

The lad slumped his head on the sofa with his knees up and shut his eyes quite sudden, and I let him sleep.

A clock chimed somewhere in the house. It had a deep brass bell so comforting that for a moment I was taken back to my own farm, and my mam and da. How it must of been for them the night of the sound, how by naw they'd be all blackened like them up in the rooms. I'd seen, had I, exactly how they'd be that minute, same stage of rot as most everyone. There was no way they'd of been anywhere but asleep when the sound come, given the farming hours they kept. And that was sommat of a comfort to me, to wager they probably wouldn't of known a thing of it.

Maybe I'd go to farm after all this, I thought. Bury them in the field at the back of the yard where the fallow would of come up glorious with them daisies and foxgloves, like last time I was there; all colours of butterflies and moths supping on it with their patterned wings like fur. Let's face it, I'd been a demon of a daughter to them, but I could do this one last respectful chore.

There was one tiny scrape in me wondering if they might of survived for whatever reason, like I had. Then, don't be daft, Hope, I said to myseln. You ken they're dead. You can sense it, how they're gone from the world. Be honest, lass.

With a lump in my throat, I looked through the telly with the doofer I'd found hanging in a brightly crocheted bag on the arm of the chair, much like my nan had made for hers. It was sad being in that house knowing they were all of them gone at farm.

Jip was curled next to the lad head on paws, and I thought then, after all that dog has lived through, he seems tired of particularly this, and disturbed by it. But then maybe that was me putting my human perceptions on the animal.

Worn down myseln, I shut my eyes an' all. But I shouldn't of, cause with me, the stains of death rub off into dreams and write new stories of it.

I woke shouting, infernal images flooding away into the hell they come from. I'd caught hearing a woman screaming blue murder outside, far off, a man's voice shouting, 'Lucy!' and wasn't that the posh caw in the orange anorak's name? Or maybe it was in my dream. Jip and the lad were zonked out, so I put it down to imagination. Wouldn't Jip be up barking, if someone was out there in danger?

I picked up the doofer again without much hope in me. None of the TV channels had any live news, and instead they had images of coloured bars and codes on cards, digital numbers running down where the news would of been. So, nobody left to turn on the programmes.

That's that, then, I thought. It's everywhere.

I turned it all off and went upstairs to scout things out. I'd earlier spotted a thin beige cable running into the girls' bedroom, and I was hoping for an internet connection, though I wasn't sure how to fix it if it wasn't on. I'd not used the internet in my job at the office much, only for emailing the Excels to my boss once a month, and I'd not had the interest in learning it more than that.

The stink was true ghastly in the lasses' bedroom, so I pulled the front of my sweater over my nose. I opened the big bay window that looked out onto empty paddocks and leaned on the sill. They had a display on a cork board of dressage rosettes, in blues and yellows and reds: 1ST, 2ND, COMMENDED. A horseshoe nailed over the window for good luck. My nan had reckoned a horseshoe hung like that would stop the Devil getting in.

The things we let usseln believe.

I found a laptop on a small pink desk in the corner. It was falling apart, white and scuffed, covered in them scratch 'n sniff stickers I'd had myseln when I was a lass, and glittery name tags, JENNY and EMMA.

I liked that the lasses were not so spoiled as the alien teenagers in village; their having to share one old-fashioned computer warmed me to this family. These girls might of stayed on to work the land. They were so like me at that age it filled me with sorrow.

I opened the laptop and it sprung to life. I could view and click the strange collection of things the girls last did online: a photo of chubby Jenny or Emma in a white bra taken in a bathroom mirror sent to a lad called Kyle; bee earrings bought online; a fan club notice for a Korean pop group who looked like girls; a video of teens in tracksuits having sex up a wall; a search for *best place radius 15 mile Pakistani food*. A search for *end of the world signs*. But there was no way of getting a connection that I could fathom. I pressed at the wire a bit, hit some of the buttons, but I didn't proper know what I was doing.

I spied a phone chucked on the floor. There was a photo of a pretty bay pony taken at a petting fair on the screen. The notion crossed my mind that this pony must be dead naw, and if it wasn't, did it have a person survived, like I'd survived to mind Jip, so it wouldn't starve to death locked in some stable somewhere?

If I thought too long on all the pewr animals we'd seen on the way, and all the others we were due to see going out, it would make me go silly in the head. But worse, I realised with horror, if all the animals were dead, I didn't know how we'd come to eat later when there was nowt left fresh in the shops or houses. We'd have to plant. But who knew if the soil was any good, what with that white seed stuff coming down after the sound?

Wandering the land them winter months when I first ran, I ken how important my catches had been to my survival. Sure, there were mushrooms and certain wild plants, berries and roots, but when the body is pushed to extremes, such as exhaustion, cold and stress, fresh meat is the only sustenance to quell the panic in the veins.

I imagined the rabbits might of done alright, burrowed deep in the ground away from the sound. There were probably

other creatures, like badgers and voles. I'd not want to kill a
badger, I thought. More like a dog they are, with their patches
of black and white, and them big eyes like teddies, the grunt-
ing. They could carry TB, an' all. I couldn't remember if you
could eat meat infected with TB. Then I started wondering
about garden centres, where they'd have compost, and seeds,
planters, all ready to go. How long does it take to grow a
potato? A tomato?

All these far-off thoughts, milling through me apace.

I come to that I was suffering some sort of fever dream, a
rush due to all that had occurred. I took a great breath of air
at the window and centred my energy like Bill had taught me.
One thing at a time, he'd say when I lost it. Make the ideas
line up, like a list.

The phone wasn't locked; I could get up the dialling pad.
I took it out to the landing, away from the dead, and dialled
999 to see what would happen. After all, we could always
make a dash for it and be a mile off before anyone come if
I changed my mind. But I needed to know what was left.

Out on the landing where I was stopped, I found I was in
front of a printed picture in a large plastic gold frame, a copy
of the exact same oil painting from the 1960s my Uncle Vic
used to have on his landing when I was a little girl. It's all in
shades of green and brown, and I used to stand there studying
it after washing my hands in the guest toilet when we'd go
there for tea of a Saturday.

It's of a young woman, her long dark hair pushed to one
side, very tan skin she has, and I'd imagine she's naked, like
Eve, but only depicted from the shoulders up, so we'll never

know. She's leaning her hand on a tree and looking at the viewer, black eyes longing, with funny buck teeth and perfect lipstick. The nakedness sends some otherworldly quality, as if she's in another time or place. It makes her seem exotic and yet still of the land; maybe the person looking at the picture was the stranger here. I liked to think I understood who she really was. There was sommat magical about the picture that had always resonated with me.

The woman in the painting is called Tina, as printed on the bottom on a little gold label never peeled off. But my uncle used to call her 'his Rosa'. I'd not seen a copy of it since. But here she was again, Rosa of the forest, peering at me from the trees at the end of the world. How funny it is, the things that align like stars when you least expect them to.

Well, aye, Ms Elgar, just look at us naw.

When I pressed Call on the 999, the phone rang for a really long time, and I stood there, staring at Rosa. I was just about to give up when I was connected to a recorded message. *Please try again later. We are experiencing an extremely high call volume at present.* Then a tone, dee-dee-dee. It repeated a couple of times. Then I was cut off. What did it mean, an extremely high call volume? Who was left in the world, to make the calls? It worried me, who was where, calling? Maybe a lot of people. Maybe none. Maybe it was an automatic message, triggered when there was nobody to answer. Disappointed, I realised I'd not established a thing.

I looked through the numbers on the screen last dialled, and noticed a number that said ROB MORTON HILL. I pressed that. Surely someone at the American airbase might know what had gan on, if anyone was coming. There was a click, and it put me through to an automated message, a woman with an American accent: *You have reached Morton Defence and Storage Two. Please enter the extension you require after the tone.* I pressed anything, and the phone rang again, for only a few rings this time. A man answered, local accent, young voice shaking and insistent. 'Em, thank God, you okay? I were stuck, but the bloody door's open naw, so.' A cough.

'Rob?' I said. There was a pause. I'd confused him; he didn't ken my voice, and so he hung up. I tried to find the number again, but I was too unfamiliar with phones to get the number to appear on the screen again.

But it meant there might be others alive. Perhaps the world would start up again, like it had after other terrible plagues and floods and wars we'd lived through. In living memory, there was that bad one few year previous, then you hear about other things far off, don't you?

I mean, that's what we're doing here, int it, Ms Elgar? Hoping we're wrong about the end of the world. Maybe though it's only cause we can't imagine the shape o' it. What could be.

With a sink in my belly then, I realised the inevitable would come to pass. I'd have to hole up again, this time with uncertain supplies, and nowhere safe to go. The shed felt no good, considering the lunatics who'd plundered village, and them lights come in so low. And I'd always had an almost irrational fear that someone, or some *thing*, might set fire to the shed for a lark with me and Jip inside it. 'Rosa, what naw?' I asked the picture. But her name was Tina, and she didn't reply.

I looked round the house at the other pictures on the walls, and it was evident that Rob was the big brother of the two lasses, some special engineer for helicopters; photo after photo of him – so proud of him, they were. A shelf lined with trophies for flying model aircraft along one sill. A framed certificate for excellence at work in another. He was a skinny lad with a mop of blondish hair like his sisters, thumbs up, flying various machines with the headset on, some taken in this very house at Christmas and that. Another lass, long brown hair, tall and slim, better bred than us round here by her features stood next to him, smiling. His girlfriend. Made sense he was at Morton Hill, if he'd been such a high achiever.

I found the kitchen, a cosy bricked country-style with a high beamed ceiling and a big old oven with iron plates, so I made us up some proper scran whilst admiring the crackled green tiles, the dimpled copper pans: eggs and bacon, thick fried bread, tomatoes fresh from the fridge, all cooked in lard the mam had dripped herseln into a round red clay jar with a great cork for a lid.

I could of had all this, I mused as I cooked, a nice farm kitchen with the tiles and all that. Bitter of it, I was, in that moment. I ran my hands over the shine of them, the round polished kettle, the hob. But then I let in the truth of it. I would never of settled to this sort of life. My mam always used to say I was harbouring sommat wild in me, even before Bill.

And it started up like a fever in me that morning, the not knowing. Where he was, if he was still alive. You have to understand, I needed to find out.

While Bill was locked away all them year I never thought of his movements day to day. I suppose I knew he was safe, that the land was safe. But since the sound? Every moment took on a new and urgent weight, and if I'm honest, I couldn't separate that urgency from my own wantings.

I heard the tap of Jip's claws on the tile as he wandered in. He was grateful for the big bowl of stale cat food and the milk I'd poured him, wagging his tail.

The smell of cooking must of roused the lad an' all, and soon the three of us had stuffed us guts ready to carry on. 'How much further?' the lad asked, wiping egg from his little cheeks. Honestly, I didn't understand his mam being so rotten to him. He was easy as pie to be around.

But see, I was somehow disturbed by that. Compliant and sensitive, he was, clever eyes constantly watching patient for instruction and guidance. I caught the glimpse of the dark history in me and clapped my hand to my face to drive the bastard out. 'Five mile, maybe less naw,' I said flat. That glimpse was a warning, was it? That where I was headed no young lad should be following. 'Why don't ya stop 'ere with Jip, till I get back tomorrow, then we'll go seaside, to yer nan's?' I said, sunny as I could.

The lad was alarmed at this suggestion, his small hands fanning at his face to protect hisseln from what I'd proposed. He almost shrieked it. 'No-wah! I'm not keepin' on me own!'

I gave him a look, to make him do as I say. 'Listen, lad. When a dog barks, he's saying, "This is where I am! Look at me, all brave and dangerous!" He'll go on barking at anyone who passes. But stamp a foot, he'll run back the way he come, crying. He can't defend a thing. Nay. The one that's the danger is in the shadow, quiet and alone, the one who hides till ya really get close, and then, snap!' The lad jumped back, trembling, and I got in his little face, close. 'You've heard of The Devil O' Th' Moor,' I snarled.

You could see the thoughts leaping in his head. 'Mam says The Devil O' Th' Moor is witchies on all fours wand'ring, biting the sheeps to death like the Black Dog in the night.'

'They say that, aye. Quiet, she is. Ya reckon she's docile. Ya won't know she's waiting, till least you expect it.' I snapped my hand close like a jaw and held it there. '*Be you ware, wary there.*'

The lad searched my face, drowning eyes looking for the sense in what I'd just told him. 'So, the bitin' one's the danger?'

I rounded the table and grabbed his shoulders, pinching. 'I am.'

A quiet keen come from the lad like an animal caught in a trap, and so I let him go. See, when we imagine monsters, we give them a face, and naw with my riddle he was too frait to argue. And so my downtrodden charge took to the sofa, whimpering to sleep.

I gazed on him curled with the pup, the slumbering inno-cents, and my mind fell down a path so familiar to me, and yet so dark, that my heart started up like a brid. Merely the idea of me and Bill together was to summon an ancient presence I'd felt many times before. And naw, it was wending with fast and hungry claws, searching out the call.

The stink of death in the house got the better of me then, and I rushed to hurl in the nice little guest toilet under the stairs; a painful blueish mass of rabbit and phlegm come from me like a demon. *Blue. How is that?* I must of thought. But it wasn't a very strong thought then, hardly heard above the din of all others smashing about in my skull.

I went to the kitchen and leaned on the sink, washed my face with the nice little soap, and found myseln staring out the window into that great empty wild. I could see all the way to the barrens. And if he'd gan over like them other lunatics? Well. I touched my knife at my breast.

I set to packing a bag on the counter as practical as I could; cereal bars and the like I found in the cupboards. Sudden, the lad ran in glaring pale with Jip barking at his ankles, and the sound of gravel moving outside told me I'd not considered the voice on the end of that phone coming back here. Course, it was bloody obvious!

'Who's comin'?' the lad asked, almost screaming with fear. 'Is it th' men?'

I told the lad to go upstairs hide in the bathroom with the bolt on the door. 'Take Jip,' I said. To the lad's credit, he dragged the pup by the collar without messing, and ran like crazy up into the rot.

The front door rattled with a key, and I braced myseln in the dim hallway ready to fight as the door swung open. The son, Rob, nineteen or twenty, boiler suit with the boots all polished, crew cut, a slack jaw of pimples. Behind him on the driveway, a great black military vehicle sat with the motor running. 'Who th'ell are you?' he whispered, voice cracked and ashen. He broke out into a hacking cough, spitting black blood to his bluish lips. He must of heard it close enough, the sound, I thought, being up airbase. I noticed the black trickle dried from his ear.

'They're all dead, yer family. I'm sorry,' I said quick, noticing he was jiggling the car jack in his hand as a weapon. 'I just come 'ere wi' me kid, shelter the night, is all.'

Rob looked at me from the step with his pale face and blinked. He didn't try to enter his own house. 'It were you who called me then! From us Em's phone,' he rasped between breaths.

I nodded aye. 'How comes you was the only one answering up base?'

He leaned against the jamb, the jack too heavy for his weakened fingers. 'Didn't find no one else alive.' He sighed with a single nod, tears reaming a tight cheek. 'I were deep in this pipe underground, fixing a duff cable. Emergency. Sommat weir, flight tracking, and I were the only one on shift knew owt.' He coughed, almost collapsing with the effort of the story. He gasped to carry on. 'Felt the jolt o' it; ears come over strange, so I went into tunnel, and me crew was all just layin' thar, blood out them ears, all fockin' goners.' He threw the jack into the gravel, like it was useless naw by way of the story, and he shut his young eyes. He could hardly catch a lung. 'Me sisters, I thought, when ya rung... I'd been trying 'em fer ages, see.' He ran his hand through his hair and gave a whelp.

'Is anybody left to rescue us?'

Rob didn't seem to hear. 'Automatic door thingy. I were trapped, 'tween corridors, all me mates dead!' He wiped his face over at the memory of it. 'But then it come back on, the power. Like...' His eyes grew wide. Terror spread from his skin to mine.

'Like what?' I held his thin arm, and he looked into my eyes.

'Like the base'd been jammed for sommat to happen. Sommat we wasn't allowed to know. Out thar.' He peered over his shoulder to the land, as if it was coming at us growling.

'It's over naw, lad,' I said, trying to be kindly. I didn't mention the lights I'd seen flashing. It would of only brung that fear we could already taste drifting in even closer.

His eyes were bloody and searching. 'I hear the phone going far away, so I patched in. Were you, then? Callin'? Only, I couldn't hear too well.' He rubbed at his ear with a palm.

I nodded. He still couldn't believe it wasn't his sister who'd rung, I suppose.

'Took ages!' He collapsed into his scratched hands, a whimper like a girl, high-pitched and wanting. So dismayed he was, that his young life was drawing to a close, and that all he loved was gan afore him.

'Sorry fer getting yer hopes up,' I said, and I was, truly. He looked up, saw clear I was the last one left to him. He was grateful for the words. 'Why not go up to yer family, in the beds? Have a lie-down.' I slid my knife from the shirt. He watched as I unfurled it and rubbed its edge on my thumb, and he bent down sudden against the porch and let a long spit of dark blood fall from his mouth onto the tile.

'I'm dying, am I?' Rob said to me then, the reality like dust in his young blue eyes.

'Aye lad,' I could say with some certainty, having seen it time before. I mean, we've all been affected, like with this blessed cough, but bleeding ears signal the death sentence.

'Were meant to be married next year,' he managed, as I put his limp arm at my neck. 'Katie.' It was already a memorial, her name, the way he said it out loud, the way I'd said the brids'.

'Bless you,' I said. What more.

I took him up to the bedrooms with my arm firm at his slender waist, but the stairs were a task of their own, as if he'd already set to dying from the feet up.

Once we reached the landing, he gazed at each door. The rooms behind contained nowt for him naw, his overalls sagging like a body bag over his chest. He was giving way as I forced him on to a narrow green door that had to be his. 'I don't want to die today,' he whispered close to my face as we went, like children do, his eyes so glossy they were like mirrors.

'There's nowt to be said fer it,' I told him as I pushed him on with my knuckles. 'We all die.' And I got the door open, and we went inside, and Rosa looked on from the trees.

I laid Rob out on his child's bed in that box room, his aeroplane models hung from the ceiling knocking his sad head as we went.

I drew the thin blue curtains to, pulled up the quilt patterned with more planes to his bloody cheek, and he stared at the pale sky through the gap in them curtains, plotting his course into the above.

By the time we'd got in his motor to leave he was dead, I reckon, and I take comfort that he went from whence he'd come, in his own little bed, amidst the silence of his own sisters, and his mam and his da, and not in that hellhole deep under Morton Hill.

'THE CRAG'

Gelatin silver print, mounted on board

160 cm × 250 cm

Bill Gleason. I would still taste his tongue hot near mine in the night, the moment before his deep kiss, all them eleven year. I don't remember sex so much as kissing. It seemed all about us mouths being open and alive and wet, and everything that come from that wetness: us skin and limbs and the heat in the room in that dead little house, dust motes in a sheaf of sun or the blue of moonlight from between curtains as we creased and buckled like a crushing car. Us bodies would fall into each other's materials, hard and soft mixing and collapsing in magnetic forces, ripping open and separating and flattening, then rising again in the collision, in the destruction of one into the other until there was no longer two, but only both of us melded and bent into a smaller space. It meant we were when together more intense, denser in thought, in happiness, in love, in hate, in fury. Two of everything swallowing great clumps of the world, spitting it out twice as fast and hard.

But in that process, that falling in love, I reckon parts of me and parts of him were unfairly recovered in the crushing.

There had occurred a physical diminishing of both what we were alone but whole before, doubled or swamped or reproduced in the other's quality, till what we were together was distorted, stretched, made thinner or more heavy, yet less, and not either of us two people at all existed more.

How I live with what I saw, what I did, what I did not do, is to believe that in some way an outside agency beyond us had taken control. We all do this, do we? Essentially, becoming passive in the action of us wrongdoing, however small. The car went off the road. The keys have disappeared from their hook. The glass slipped out of my hands. It might come with farm ways, the cycle of life and death, that acceptance of the constant changes of states and seasons, but I don't reckon on guilt. It seems alien, out of my hands, like that glass that smashes on the floor.

'Guilt is to do wi' religion,' Bill told me driving back after one particular difficult evening. I was weeping in the van, my skirt soaked with blood. 'Latin verb, *religare*, to bind to. Latin noun, *religio*, an obligation. Mass social conditioning, is all.'

And so I reckon my conscience took on that it's more natural not to feel it. After all, the fox feels no guilt for killing the chickens when he's not hungry, leaving them strewn bloody in the coop. The cat claws the mouse for sport, and is keener for it.

The lad was quiet as we drove to Bellemere Crag. I could see him in the mirror, clinging to Jip's thick fur with white hands. He finally looked away into the fog and said flat, 'You a witch, then, Glore?'

I'd almost forgot what I told the lad when I got in that mard about him coming with me to meet Bill, and what with him seeing me use the knife at the cop shop, I reckon he'd naw had time to think on it awhile and didn't much like his conclusions. 'Nay, lad, I were jesting wi' ya!' I said, letting out a laugh – a false laugh, but one that might set him at ease.

The lad become very red, biting his lip, and the moles on his little face come up black. I wondered if he'd heard about Bellemere, if it was stewing in his imagination with all the horrors he naw knew. Anyroad, the day had straight proven too much for the little fella. 'I want me mam,' he mewed between sobs, the usual cry. 'I want me mam!'

I said nowt to him more, cause there's nowt you can say that makes them feel better in that state, and we carried on.

I finally swung the motor onto the cement path to come round the back of the hill, the brume fallen so thick and white that morning was naw cleared like smoke blown off, and the land sudden rose in a great wall of silver rock, whistling through its cracks with a fusty breeze of golden dirt.

With the lad finished with his snivelling, I tried pointing out the tombstones from the Vikings, all the pretty knotwork carved with tongues and wolves and the faces of gods, and finally took his mind off with that. 'They was there to mark where great warriors went down, all the Vikings in them big horned hats,' I said. 'Swords as big as you are tall, and blades like on a harvester.'

'Went to Hadrian's Wall, I did,' he said, looking about desperate to connect to any living being, and finding only me. 'Wi' school.'

'Y'know about the lookouts, then,' I said. 'How the Roman soldiers watched for hours from the Wall fer them tribes from the North?'

'Aye, they 'ad all blue faces,' said the lad, grasping onto Jip, who obliged, nuzzling his pockets for biscuits. And I thought, Christ. If anything went bad with me, it was hard to imagine these two sweet beasts surviving alone.

The chimney of Bellemere finally rose over the ridge against the white of the day, darkly smudged as if drawn in its own soot. 'Chimley,' the lad remarked. I didn't correct him.

I was breaking out proper nervy as we neared Bellemere. 'When we get there, yerseln and Jip keep watch from in 'ere, and if ya see anyone coming, beep th' horn once, quick, and I'll come running.'

'I don't mind,' said the lad, worn out and sad. I saw his heart break a little more then.

I ruffed his head, and his hair felt good and silky, and I said, 'You're reet wi' me, lad,' but I couldn't say if I was sure of it.

I'd slide in first gear to the back of the place, park on the road. Shimmy down Crag into the mere and go through that way, just as I did when I come there as a kiddie. It seemed likely that the entrance to the crematorium would be less secure, given the ones coming in that gate would not be much for escaping. I could try and get into the prison proper from there. The townies who built this place didn't ken us ways, but they needn't of worried. Not a soul would of tried to break in.

I parked us on the siding, where they used to when bringing flocks for the dip. The lay-by, naw overgrown with nettles, dropped direct into the pit of the mere, and if I was careful, I would be able to climb down the mossed rock.

I fixed all the doors of the motor with the lock, and I told the lad to get under this scratchy-looking grey army blanket with the pup. 'Get some kip,' I said kindly like, covering his scared little face, glad to have an excuse to do so, tucking in a bag of crisps from the farmhouse.

'A'ight,' he said quiet. 'I'll beep if a man comes or sommat.'

'You'll be reet,' I said again. Pewr mite. It was the first time in his life more or less that Jip would be apart from me an' all, and I could hear him crying a bit when I shut the door, but he settled with the lad and the crisps, for he was pretty quiet after.

I went round the side and looked down the sheer to Bellemere. Nobody was about. I listened, but all was still. The flat zinc roof was built level with the road, so folk couldn't see the place as they drove past. Don't suppose they wanted a reminder as they made their way home that only two steps from the road, lunatics sat rocking, chewing their own legs, muttering to the Devil, chained and buried within the earth.

But as I say, this cursed lot was familiar to me. I'd played there as a kiddie, and seeing as they hadn't moved the Crag itseln, I soon found the old way by slipping between the back of the gutter and a wire fence till I was standing on the brown looking up at the great iron security gates blocking the main entrance. Except naw they were open wide, and between them, cut rough into the hill, rose the prison building, a dark cement square with mirrored slits for windows like a helmet, an obelisk to cruelty, a charnel house of mad kings. Where Bill Gleason had hisseln been interred for them past eleven year.

As I stood in the shadow looking up at the place, I saw the great glass doors were smeared with black. Rotted blood. My breath started up like bellows. What was I doing here, leaving a feeble lad and dear Jip behind me all alone when there were escaped madmen about the land, to enter this pit of devil knows what? If any harm come to me? I couldn't answer it. All I know is that it called, pulling me in further.

I'll wait fer you, Bill had whispered. *At the end of the world.*

I gazed at the devastation, heart in my mouth. Scattered about the concrete yard were bodies: guards, doctors, inmates; perhaps six or seven with them green wristbands, all bloody and crawling with death. Just the same as in village, that silence washing in.

Six or seven here don-fer in the yard. Then the two in village made nine. Not more than twenty inmates by old man Dutton's reckoning. I would still have to be very careful then. Cars weren't allowed to be parked at Bellemere no more, and the staff come on bus each shift. I hoped to Christ that bus had not been at Bellemere when the sound come, or we might later meet the lot of them driving about on the road, escaped, hungry and cold. Undermedicated.

I kicked some of the bodies over to see their faces, muttering to myseln, but their faces had gan. None of them was Bill. Maybe I wanted one of them to be. Then again, I did not. Each one I turned over, a cool tide of disappointment and relief run over me, in equal parts and absolute, cancelling the other out, till all I felt was numb.

Wiping my boot toes on the backs of my shins, I touched my knife and slipped to the doors, swinging wildly on great black hinges in the sudden caught wind. I took a breath like diving and stepped into the dark hall beyond. The stink told me enough. That I could go on.

I read in the papers that Bellemere is built on a panopticon model. 'A great curved amphitheatre of bad actors', some mouthsworth called it on the radio. The cells circle round, facing the guards' viewing post at the front, each door and window and wall made of thick unbreakable glass. A mirage of freedom, but a total loss of the thing that makes us most human. Privacy.

See, the inmates at Bellemere were forced to eat, sleep, shit, piss, wank, and sometimes die with an audience of their captors, bright strip lights on twenty-four hours a day, no ventilation, no heating, no physical contact with any other person under any circumstances. Medieval, that slow torture, old Dutton had reckoned, but then again, it could be argued that the monsters who lurked at Bellemere had forfeited their basic human rights by previously gorging on them.

An amber light roiled the dree concrete walls at the entrance, a sign the doors were left open. I was hoping to tell if Bill was still there with a glance through the window, instead of having to put myseln in grave danger by checking the cells one by one. 'Bill,' I said out loud, as if he was a god listening, 'please show yerseln, if you're still alive!'

I'll wait fer you. At the end of the world.

His words echoed in my memory as I careful put tread.

There were no guards in the reception booth, security doors all open inside, so I crept cautious through the metal detector and along a narrow white corridor, following a red line on the floor labelled THIS WAY TO MAIN HALL. All I wanted was to be sure of Bill, to have it done.

To have what done exactly? Well aye. That was the question. On one hand, I felt that pull as a tide, and I imagined how it would be, caught in his arms once more. But then I'd touch my knife, and that tide would wash out, and I'd know we couldn't roam the wilds together, especially with the lad. Bill could be crazy as an autumn bear, all I knew of him naw.

But I'd loved him so long. Just cause he was capable of evil things don't mean he wasn't capable of love, of being loved. It's confusing, cause of the misery, and at times, aye, he'd treated me shabby. But we'd seek each other out in that dark like any man and wife, and found the seams lain glittering in the cold.

As I entered that hellish place, I thought on Bill's hot mouth, a flash of his weight on me, an exquisite intangible that only existed when the two of us were close. To explain it clear is impossible, but it urged me on, that idea, hardly there at all, but everything flooding in a longing of before.

I thought too on the lad, and pewr Jip, all hidden and trembling in that blanket in the motor, relying on me to keep us safe at the end of the world, and my heart keened at the choice of it.

As I followed the red line, a great banging of metal and glass went up in front of me, shouting and tapping, and it occurred to me that the punishment of this prison was not just the glass rooms and the lack of touch, but the cacophony that comes up in such a place. It scared the living shit out of me, tones darting and smashing against each other, creating alien frequencies not unlike the swoop of the sound, and I listened still for a moment, my back against the wall, to make sure the lad wasn't beeping the horn or bashing owt to get me back. But the noise was inside, up ahead.

Deeper in I went, along the straight line, till all signs of sunlight and fresh air phased out, windows metalled over, cracks plastered in. Long corridors lined with concrete, garish padded fabric stained with spit and blood and other stuff. Alarms on every wall, six feet apart at elbow height so as you could ram them in a fight. Defibrillators. Fire extinguishers. Everything bolted down, swiped in, rounded off, glassed in. Bright greenish lights poked harsh at my eyes.

A door come up as thick as a castle wall, sixteen or sommat bolts inside its frame like a great clock, then a door on the other side of it, this one's glass run with chicken wire: just a gesture of a door to give you the luxury of feeling safe for one second more. I pushed in.

The main hall takes your breath away. The energy, vast and bleak, is like a ruined cathedral, a forgotten burial chamber. A great glass beehive, five or six floors high against concrete, set in transparent niches for each man's entombment, sparkling its crumbling surfaces in refractions of artificial light. If it wasn't such a grim pyre of a place, constructed for some other purpose such as a church of glass or a glittering fair attraction, it could be thought extremely beautiful, a work of dreams and men.

The black dripped down the upper glass floors like syrup in the chill from fallen shapes in rags, hunched against walls or laid out on glass floors as if suspended mid-air. The cells were otherwise empty, doors flung wide. Glass staircases either end of the circus had seen a bloody stampede, by the looks of the prints on the steps. Bill must of fled, I hesitated to conclude. Hadn't I searched enough?

But then my eye caught unnatural movement on the ground floor, a level that didn't seem to be catching the light like the other floors, as if even the guards had no stomach for looking at these offald monsters, hiding them in the shadows instead.

A deep male voice rose sudden from my left, steeped in the noise of glass that come from farther off. 'Good story, this.'

'Who's there?' I cried out, nervy as all hell. For I didn't know what was waiting for me in this world or any other no more.

A thick glass door to my left was wide open, and in the shadow, my eyes followed the voice and adjusted to where it had come from: a massive skinheaded fella in his forties, pocked as ald meat. He was sat on a wooden crate reading a book, mighty content, great dirty feet up on his bunk, eating an iced bun of all things with tattooed White Power fingers. It wasn't jam on his cheeks, but old blood, the way it was smeared.

He looked up from his page with level eyes and smiled at me calm, gold teeth in black gums, as if we were in a summer park and all was pleasant. And he went on with his reading.

'D'ya know Bill Gleason?' I said, my voice trembling and thin.

'Ha-ha,' the man said flat rather than laughing, as if he were reading the words from his book.

I crept off to peer in the cells that were lost to the light, and as I got closer, I made out a short figure swaying a little, his shadow catching the strip overhead. He was still locked in his cell. 'Hello?' I said. Asian he was, this fella, dumpy and short in a red jumper, but then I realised he was there with no pants, hands over bloody ears, cheek and penis marbled white pressed flat on the glass like bloated offal. 'Christ's sake,' I muttered. Sickening, it was.

That banging went up again louder, more insistent. In darker, under the stairs. Within the maze of dirty smeared glass, a gaunt figure huddled with his back to me, thinning hair matted in spiked silhouette, catching on the dust of filthy air. He was banging the glass walls with a scabbed fist: bang, bang, bang, but patient like, rhythmic. Wrapped in his prison blanket, brid-thin shoulders and sallow cheeks, just like them pictures you see of prisoners on hunger strike.

I went to the wall to study him and caught my buckled coat on the glass, announcing myseln. He spun on his heel with the echo. 'Get th' fock away!' But then his tiger's eyes widened in recognition, flashing panic. Like, could I really be there, or was I a dream from long ago? He couldn't trust his mind. I mean, nobody would, in that situation. No matter what you might say about him.

'Bill?' I said.

He whimpered, that wet mouth open as I had left it, but naw full of black teeth and a yellow tongue. He hugged his blanket to his chest and shuffled to the door of his palace to peer at me with them still-flaming eyes. 'Glore?' He put a boned hand flat to the glass, breath steaming the surface, eyes searching my face for reality. 'Is it truly the end of the world?'

'Aye, reckon, Bill,' I said, dizzy with looking at him. Time had stopped, and we hung there for a moment, me and him, just sinking in the past as it was made.

The skinhead broke the silence, peering over at us relaxed like, ogling through the walls. 'I told you so, brother,' he said matter-of-fact. 'All finished.'

'So it is, Clive. I fockin' stand corrected.' Bill nodded solemn, eyes deepening as they wandered away to this Clive, distorted far through the walls. Then that gaze floated back to me, the face drawn in pits of charred water.

This was supposed to be Bill, but I couldn't quite focus on him proper, and I could tell he was struggling to see Glory in me. We were looking at imaginations of years, instead of the faces we had in front of us naw. The matter of flesh and skin and bone was less or more in stranger proportions than the sketches we'd held of each other all that time, and us minds couldn't work fast enough to tidy up the disappointments we found in the wrinkles and sag.

I suppose that's why he started gabbling. 'When that noise went, and they all keeled over, this greet lairy bastard, he were out bein' walked back from solitary. Went berserk for a time, he did – did you not, Clive – but not so long after, he left th' doors open, and any who'd not dropped dead, that he'd not seen off, they run fer it, into moor. But mine didn't open, see. And then Clive says to me, he says, and t'other one, wi' 'is kegs off, he says, yous pair of nonces can stay, and starve till they turns up, he says, int that right, what thou said, Clive?'

'Tis, son,' said this Clive, rocking on his box. 'Verbatim.'

Bill seemed to hang on Clive's words as if they were poetry, some great truth. I'd seen it before.

'Who did say that?' I asked Bill, reeling from the state of him. His face was not Bill's face to me. Rather, it was Bill's face with all the evil stripped out, as if the evil in him had been what had made the beauty, and naw it was gone with no demons left, he looked only normal, and plain, and this was deeply disturbing to me.

'I did say that,' said Clive, eyes red with mad blood. He had a funny accent, a city patois that didn't belong in the land. 'Them pair, this wormy bastard and George there, they be nonces, see. I jammed them buttons or they would of, you know. Gone back out looking. Trust me.'

'Yer a nonce an' all, Clive,' said Bill. 'So don't be callin' me no nonce.'

Clive nodded slow. 'I may well be, Bill Gleason, but nobody's going to take me up on that now, is it?' He gestured to his giant form and chuckled, as if he was the cleverest bastard this side of Gateshead.

'Useta kill little girls wi' one hand, feckless sod,' Bill said, smirking, trembling a little. 'Don't go denying thou haint told us all about it!'

'Why not let them go, Clive?' I asked him, feeling less brave than fed up. 'None of yer bloody beeswax what they do, after all.'

'I likes raping.' He stuck out his tongue and waggled it at me like a kid might, then he turned back to his book, casual. I couldn't scan it. Was it a threat? After all, he'd already slaughtered those naw dripping down the walls.

But nay, it was more that this big lump Clive was waiting for rescue, like a massive great babby with a wet nappy on his arse. What did he mean, *till they turns up*? So hefted to the system, he was, as to be completely relaxed doing what he always did, without no other instruction forthcoming. Read, wait. Eat. Why hadn't he left otherwise?

But then I thought on the lad's mam an' all, and it made me weary, the idea of this feckless giant striding about land doing as he pleased with them what survived.

The big ald bastard leaned huffing to the floor with some effort and took up a tiny can of pear halves he'd had away from somewhere, quipped it open with a great bloodied thumb, and poured it down his neck.

Bill glanced at me and slightly frowned, a sense of disapproving. I'd not remembered Bill so weir-looking, with them scrags of eyebrows and strange straight eyelashes that caught the light and turned blonde, fringes round empty holes. Had he always looked so soulless?

Bill jabbed a finger at Clive. 'Reckons someone's comin'. Fifteen years served, not used to havin' 'is own mind.' He rolled a finger at his temple and gave a bridie whistle. Bill seemed high or drunk to me, or maybe he'd always been this screwy. I couldn't work out if I was disappointed or sorry for him, or plain shocked at myseln for ever loving this clearly unwell man. But all of me wanted to save him from Clive.

'They'll come,' said this pink bugger with a finger by way of a salute. He was so chuffing sure in his world. How sure had me and Bill been in ours? I felt pure vexed. 'Till then?' He nodded at Bill and the other one, waggled his tongue about.

The other one started screaming like a child. I looked over Bill's predicament. If I left, Bill was tight wrapped in that blanket, starving in his box, at the mercy of this maniac.

'Nobody much left out thar to be "they", far as I can tell,' I said, storming to the guards' box, where they must of viewed the prisoners through the wide glass screen. 'What number room you in, Bill?'

It was strange. The decision had actioned itseln the instant I saw Bill was in danger.

As I say, all the other prison doors were open, so I pushed into the booth, stepping over a body in uniform. I spied on the belt a baton, long black rubber, which I slid out and weighed in my hand. It was much heavier than I imagined. It felt like violence. Sex. I fluttered up and gasped, gripped the baton hard. It turned me on somehow.

I hadn't thought of sex proper for a long ald while.

'Three-o-two!' shouted Bill then, his voice bouncing off the walls sharp, like a demand of many Bills. He was shuffling into the far corner of his cell, eyeing Clive.

I scanned the situation from the viewing box. Clive was making out he was still reading his book, laid-back like. I located the wall of emergency releases. 203, not 302, and 204 was jammed with folded playing cards to never push in. I soon punched them with the baton, savouring its heavy rubber, and an alarm of three beeps went up in duet as the two doors unlocked with a clunk.

I saw it in slow motion, Clive getting up. Bill's door sliding open. That viewing box was well made. I was on Clive swinging my baton before he made it to Bill.

Clive gurgled with the shock of my knife. The way it looked, the handle stuck from his neck as he fell, I didn't understand for a moment. So short and delicate that blade seems, which is why I keep it so sharp. And I see Bill's fingers come away covered in blood. I wondered vaguely when he'd stolen my knife off me, but with so much in play I didn't register the meaning of it proper.

'Glory,' he said, smiling, coming over all relieved, laughing really, as Clive's great heft rolled about on the floor groaning. Then Bill lifted a black cold toe and pressed the handle of my knife hard into Clive's gross form. Clive rolled with a shriek, and blood hurried cross the floor. Bill laughed with the wonder of it. 'Nonce,' he said soft, and my body bled inward, all fast. I closed my eyes for a moment as the energy that leaves with death flew past me, rancid as demons.

The other they called George was laughing silent in his box with his hands over his ears. A proper queer scene, he was. Bill went over to this George, pressed his face to the glass, and hissed, 'Last time you fockin' spit at me tapioca, eh?' What an incredibly odd time of it Bill must of had in there!

How I felt about Bill then, if I'm being honest? Well, aye, he was there in front of me in his stained blanket, hair matted and patchy, white streaks all through as if he was fading one strand at a time, triumphant over tapioca. His face was thin and leathery, teeth done in. They were Bill's eyes, sure, but they were the shining, maniacal newspaper eyes of the Bill Gleason I had known only for a short time before he went down.

And he'd got my knife off us in a whisper.

All them years I'd been imagining Bill as the almost rock star figure I'd seen in the photos, an actor's velvet voice turning Bill's best words to art in the radio plays. That blurred but relentless national ghost of my husband, flitting under that coat between car and court in a suit bought for him by a starstruck solicitor. A suit I'd only ever seen in the papers, in black-and-white print. A townie suit with a sheen to it I didn't much like. And that's all I knew of it, not the colour, nowt. My sum of Bill Gleason, these past eleven year.

He'd been reborn, I reckon, somewhere between being named in the press and being sentenced. Acknowledged by the world for all that he had done. He was a vain man, after all. He languished in that short fame as the dark prince he'd aspired to be. Adoration or hate, the attention was all the same fabric to him, and he consumed it like fire, and it made him strong and new. For a time.

To see him naw was to see that persona broken down, a china cup smashed where you can still see the pattern, but you can't drink from it no more.

They say if you stop believing in monsters, they fade away and won't bother you again. I believe that's what I was seeing in that moment: the raw material of the man I'd known and loved, and all that was left was the pathetic spindle of his soul, whittled down by his own bad deeds.

Bill finally plucked up courage, stepping over Clive's heaved form like a sulken wether. But we didn't embrace; his arms had flashed back inside the horrible ald blanket. Instead, he grazed me lightly, sharp stubble catching both cheeks, a continental habit he'd nurtured long ago to seem grand.

But I felt that heavy press of him as a pain in my skin. The smell of him, piss and dirt and old sweat. It was overpowering, feral; the breath of a dog once they've finished their meat, a fired gun. His presence was only inked in where a man should of been, a scribble over a mistake, dark and torn, hiding the meagre person Bill really was. He seemed so ridiculously frag-ile to me, like an ancient book they keep out the sun to stop it from crumbling to dust.

We left that madhouse with George's glassed screams ring-ing in us ears, the final grunts of Clive sticking in my mind, and I kept thinking of his big chapped strangling hands cling-ing onto that book. Bill giggled nervously, shuffling in his blanket like a really tired Jesus. 'He only had three pages to go; it was a whodunnit!'

'*You* did it. Naw, come along.'

At some point in that yard, I must of thrown that filthy rotten blanket off him to the ground as he squinted in the sun, and I found underneath that he was wearing a yet filthier dark blue shirt and trousers, and one of them green bands at his scrawny wrist. He had on no shoes, but he did have on thick wool socks, so I reckoned knowing Bill Gleason, he could climb nimble up Crag.

I was in a daze as we went. All I could think how all was bloody surreal alright. We'd dreamed of being the only two people left on Earth, and here we were, Bill and me, almost alone but for a few stray oddities. And the lad.

And the lad.

Bill looked about the courtyard, confused at first, staring at all the rotting bodies. He was panicking, Adam's apple moving up and down in his unshaven scrawny neck. He cowed to me with faded eyes, wrung dirty hands. 'Look at all this! Not normal, is it?'

I mean, if he'd been one of my da's slapes, the state he was in, I would of had no qualms taking him to the side of a shed with a length of wire. But instead, I found myseln feeling sorry for him. Trouble was, it was that dangerous sort of sorry you feel when an animal is in such a state that even putting them out of their misery seems more distressing than letting them live another little while.

And I loved him, certain, soon as looking at him. He was my only remaining family, after all. 'Are you over it all naw, then?' I said in that yard, lining my doubts with hope. A woman and a child alone, as I said, not much of a prospect.

Bill saw a crack in my defences. He brightened. 'Wha?' He was smiling in the back of his face, smug or sommat, as if, what in the world could I be referring to.

Faint, coming up in the sky, there was a rumble. We both stood stock, listening. 'A motor, Glore,' Bill said slow, looking to me for answers. 'The authorities, no question.'

Well. 'The authorities' had long been a swear word twixt me and Bill, the night wraith come crawling into my sleepless shed. I weighed the options. Fock getting caught on account of this one slowing me down. Could we leave the lad behind instead, in the middle of nowhere on Bellemere Crag, inmates not accounted for, on the off chance what was coming was help? It was insane when I played it out.

The sound of engines was coming at us straight, more than one vehicle. I thought on what we'd seen driving gammy

174 · CATE BAUM

through the barrens. No way I was sticking about. 'Did they give ya therapy, fer yer urges?' I asked him, agitated.

Bill was entertained. He always loved a struggle. 'I suppose, aye. Therapy. Not thought on it really, some eight, nine year.' He shrugged, hands up to the sky like he used to when he told me a lie, when he would swear on his mother's life; his mam being dead never stopped his evoking.

Christ, he looked just like a beggar standing in that yard, like when they chant, *Spare change fer a brew* when everyone bloody knows it's for skag. But see, if it tells you the sort of person I am, I always used to give them blaggards the pound coin an' all.

I sighed at Bill's answer, forcing my brain to consider things. It was hard to gauge a person's sanity so long faltered. It was like reading a book a second time eleven year on. You know the story, and what's being said, but not till after you've read the words. I had to put it all out, to see the ley of it. I found myseln blurting the whole of it then.

'Look, I've a little lad wi' me, neighbour's child. She's deed, like th' rest. Taking 'im to seaside fer a breather, then on to 'is nan's farm, up Pettingrew.' My accent had thickened in the land, hefted to Bill as I was. I looked in his eyes and saw that know-it-all grin I'd clean forgot, all ready to burst over that weir skinny face of his. 'He's not fer you. Get it?' I said, clear.

Bill's face dimmed. 'Wha' the dickens ya saying, Glore? Not fer *me*? Who d'ya fockin' take me fer?' he spat.

'I take you fer Bill Gleason, The Devil O' Th' Moor.'

Bill started up laughing like an old motor hisseln, a piss-take sort of a laugh, as if he was bitter insulted, but also pleased with the shape o' it. I remembered that little habit of his then, from when me and him was first living in town, and I'd disagree with things he'd heard about from his townie mates that were nowt but opinion, but declared as fact. Only, naw I was strong and grown, whilst he was stuck sounding like a child, giggling all defensive like that. 'What're you naw, Glory? A complete lesbun bitch or sommat? Wi' yer fat arse and th' ginger harr?'

It was true that when I was a young'un, if he'd called me a fat caw or ugly I would of crumbled in tears and begged for mercy. But it dawned on me that Bill hadn't been able to grow up in that prison with them grotesque man-children all around him like brids pecking their own shit, and so I dropped his comment hot without acknowledgement, putting my feet square on the stones up Crag, offering Bill not a slip of help. 'If ya gonna be that way,' I said over my shoulder as I pushed up, aware he could get a full view of my fat ginger arse. Fock 'im, I thought.

But truth was, naw the game was in play, and a smirk come on as I pushed myseln up the crag.

'A'ight, Glore, only teasing. Jeez,' he muttered, still following me like a lamb, sucking them rotten teeth as if he'd told a really funny joke and I was being a complete focking bitch about it.

It was familiar to me, that sucking of the teeth and the muttering to hisseln, and I felt heavier in my body and a chill up my back, but as we climbed, I realised the chill was my husband, newly escaped from the madhouse.

My husband, who, eleven year gone, was convicted of the rape and murder of five little children and two women, all buried and lost ont moor.

'HOUSE'

Gelatin silver print, mounted on board
160 cm × 250 cm

We moved to the two-up, two-down, as Bill proudly called it, after we got married swift in the registry office when I found out I was up the duff. To me, it felt that carrying was like being haunted from the inside.

It's etched in my memory, them waving me off from farm as I was driven away by Bill Gleason, a petulant king who wouldn't even shake my da's hand nor come in house for a brew. Smaller and smaller the little mam and da got as I watched out the back of the truck. Standing by the door, they were, figurines in a clock, faces all set with worry and sadness, and me all shrugging it off with my things in a box on my lap.

I was only young.

Bill's mam when she died left him her ugly little terraced house in town, built atop slums out of cheap red brick and crumbling tile on a street of houses that looked exactly alike. Kiddies with jammy mouths would ride their bikes up and down soon as they were off the breast seemed to me, screaming profanities and playing their music loud out the windows. Their mams huddled in doorways like coffins, mouldy ald cardies and slippers, yelling to each other about this and that in a fashion my own mam would of found common as muck.

The garden, as Bill had called it when he'd described it to me 'wi' grass and trees and that', turned out to be a cracked concrete square just about big enough to hang a plastic washing line, with a tumbledown shed full of nettles where an outside khazi used to be. There was a patch of yellowed wormy grass at the edges, some bright-smeared litter from the kids next door chucking over their lolly wrappers for however many years, naw rotting into the fence. A kicked-over ball, soft and dented and blue, never retrieved, and later destroyed in a fit by Jip. Not a tree in sight.

Kid, what have you got yourseln into, I thought, looking on it that first time.

I can't say I hated it; it was my first proper home with Bill, but my parents detested everything about the relationship, and that made me all righteous like. And I was pure sour about the savings folder I'd found in the drawer. But mostly, I was simple too proud to admit it was a mistake to go with Bill. And so, I carried on.

Around that time, Bill met an old acquaintance in the pub, just come back from somewhere or other, who got Bill a job away from the land. This ginger streak of piss, Steve Wilshire was his name, I despised by no more than looking at him. Later, course, I figured they'd met inside. But I was so naive back then you could of held me to the sun and seen straight through to Morton.

Bill started working in an office over a factory in town, Barnes and Co., running sales for feed, making three times what he made on the knackering, so he was well chuffed.

They've changed the name of the place since. Had to, I suppose.

I found out when it all come down, that the reason Bill'd never been able to get a proper job away from knackering was on account of his previous criminal record, but this Steve Wilshire's cousin was the gaffer, and he'd a soft spot for convicts trying to make good.

Chuffed with this stroke of luck Bill was, getting me work there soon after as an accounts girl, which compared to farm made me feel farcy for a bit, till I got too fat and tired with my bump to even sit at my desk, and then I went on Maternity. But, course, I never went back.

When we set up in that grubby industrial town, I become further and further detached from my old life in every way, and by then, Bill had started catching these funny ideas I tried to shake off, but they stuck like burrs on a cat. These blokes he'd met in the pub, Steve's mates, they were neat-looking union types in cheap suits and shiny ties, and he started dressing like that too.

Bill frequented them awful townie pubs as if he was earning from it. Loud pop music and football on the screens, all the yelling. Tiny portions of posh grub served on slates round ours we'd use for roofing. Everything with coriander, which to me tastes like the soap you wash your arms with after birthing a ewe.

Up us way, see, women stop in the family lounge, torn bags of salt and vinegar in the middle for the kiddies whilst they carefully nurse spritzers, tapping their fingers to a nice bit of Mario Lanza. But these townie lasses, they mixed with the men, all high on themseln. Hunkered on draughty pews ripped from old country churches for the benefit of their fat pagan arses, demanding great jugs of snakebites direct from bar never asking the men to fetch it. But them men would never offer anyhow, rude pricks. I'd watch these lasses, with their purple-stained tongues flicking like turkeys in a slaughter-house, banknotes planted between nails long as flags marking it was theirs and they were ready. My da would of called them blowsy brids with nattering beaks, getting in men's business, pecking. I couldn't find one pal amongst them.

So I stopped going to them pubs long before the bairn come, and Bill'd leave me on my tod in that manky ald house to watch telly or read. There was a library in town, and I'd lose myseln having a look through there of an evening, gazing at the writers' photos on the jackets where I'd such a longing to be. I felt too jealous to read them, and I'd put them back on the clean little metal shelf, a bitterness in my fingertips where words could of been coming out, stopped by the thoughts of defeat before I even begun it. A writer? I'd mock myseln: *you don't have one bloody story in yer sawdust head worth telling, boring caw.*

And so it went that I didn't enjoy my books about dashing heroes sweeping a lass off her feet no more neither. They felt to me naw childish and silly, and so I put them aside, and instead stared out the window each night, waiting for Bill to come home in a reet drunkard mood, shouting about for his dinner, or pissing on the bathmat, or wanting rough sex, stinking of booze.

I'd tell myseln like a motto: he's a job and a house. He don't hit me.

And I'm not on farm.

For a while, I tried my best with it. I had my hair cut too short in a hairdressers near work, dyed it a bright blonde. Bill thought it was wild-looking. Said I looked like his 'little whoor'. I took that as a compliment at the time. I thought I was keeping Bill's interest, dressing like them slatternly women in the pubs. I don't have to tell you what Da thought of my new hairdo. Christ on a stick!

But I liked the way it made me feel. Dirty. Free.

The bairn Bill called Cheryl Ann, registered after his dead mam, no discussion. He was so very delighted them eleven weeks she lived, and doted on her every chance he got, really showing a kindness I'd always believed was there. He'd not change the nappies, mind, or do the mountains of laundry that had suddenly appeared, nor help with the head-wrecking night feeds. Nay, that was firmly his agenda, to keep off all that lark. His house, his rules, and I didn't have much to say in it.

He informed me quite early in the pregnancy, like some disclaimer he was entitled to, that he wasn't interested in changing around his own life to be a family man. But he also said once, 'I'm so made up I'm a father, love.' So tender in them weeks he was, when we were a family for that short time. I think he was as close to satisfied as Bill Gleason could ever be, even if I was straight miserable with it.

When Cheryl Ann was brung home in a flurry of pink flannelette from the hospital in Da's car, Bill become sulken with me, taking to sleeping in the box room. 'I'll wait fer yer figure to come back,' he'd say, pushing a spiteful finger hard into the slight fat of my thighs, monitoring me when I buttered my toast.

I'd find him four in the morning lying on the little camp bed with his shoes still on, reading them new books about Chaos and Magick with a k. Sometimes, he'd go out all night, then come back slamming the front door huffing from the cold, washing hisseln in the shower singing, waking up the bairn with his racket all hours, mud and other strange wetness tracked through the carpet and on his slung-off shirts.

Other times, I'd find him weeping in the dark, inconsolable, full of sorrow. Or empty of it.

I noticed after a while that he'd got the hang of it in his speech patterns, the arguing ways of these other townie men, and the vain talking over each other they did; a wriggling out of bad ideas so it seemed like his own unformed ones were better, and he'd make a case for one of these queer notions he'd come onto, and I'd just nod and agree he knew better than me about it if he asked for my support on the matter.

See, he had a way about him, Bill, like he ken things he'd never been taught, as if he was born knowing. An old soul, my mam said of Bill. She believed ghosts float about moor with no place to go, turned out of heaven, searching for those bairns that are born empty. Then, in they slide, with all that ancient knowledge, a cuckoo's egg in the dunnock's nest.

Course, I'd only come up a shepherd's daughter. As Mam reminded me often, I ken nowt of town. I got up half four in the morning all weathers, boots on at the door with the hand-me-down wax jacket and out with Da to the sheds, great bowls of kibble in my hands to where the slapes were chained at night, and I'd do my tasks. All I knew was the land and my silly romantic books written more than a hundred years ago by loveless, lonely girls like myseln.

On farm, Mam did cheeses and eggs, and I helped with the wool and newborns. Sometimes, a mammy would get lost, or caught on a fence, or else they just cast over. I reckon there's nowt on this Earth sweeter than the breath of a tiny lamb reared in your arms on the bottle, the way its thick greasy coat makes your skin itch and you've to hook it up so it don't wriggle away and bruise your belly; them dear black knitted faces like another little beastie inside its soft wool case. And they'd chew on my hair, me squealing for Da to prise them off.

And once they'd been out a while and found them little legs, I'd scratch their noses in the fallow and name them such-and-such – against all better advice from my elders. I'd go to the dales and there'd be this little dear lamb coming pelting over to nuzzle my hands in recognition, and my delight was pure and whole.

Then one day, inevitably, I wouldn't find them again, and I'd see my da with the big truck coming back from the other farms, and my heart would sink to my boots. And I'd think on how cruel the world is, when those lambs to me were priceless, and Da had sold their warm, precious, sweet little bodies for eighty pounds apiece.

I'd weep about that quite often, how very cruel was the land I loved so much. Even naw, I can shed a tear for the babbies I reared, if I let it in. But then I hear Da, or Bill. And they say in my ear, *Come o'er, pet.* You ken nature is cruel, and that's how we live on this land. Everything must die to make way for more life.

Seeing as I'd had a knack with the lambs, it was some shock that Cheryl Ann had nowt about her resembling them newborns. She was instead a hollow plastic doll in my arms. Sommat too fragile and empty in her body, like she was already sick of living before she'd barely begun. I didn't understand the maternal bond the midwives bleated on about. I'm not sure I ever called her my daughter.

Simply, I'd birthed away my childhood, the consequence in front of me kicking, constantly needing. The bairn was the symbol of my last chance lost to not end up like my mam. And naw there I was, a mother at nigh twenty, trapped by my own set of irons much as I'd tried to outrun my fate by being off with Bill. It confused me how it'd gone. But I felt obliged to go on pretending to be as delighted as everyone else when they dressed her in ribboned hats and cotton frocks with her dribble down the front.

But as much as I tried, Cheryl Ann never felt of me at all, staring empty with her plain ald face all wrinkled and serious. And just as I did, she sensed we were strangers in some way. She felt to me weak and wrong, not kith of me and Bill, but instead like a blurred photograph of the both of us that should never of been taken, a reproduction of the deep-felt innards that we hid away but was naw on the outside, come out into the world in the form of Cheryl Ann.

I can't know if I was depressed like some women are said to get after they've given birth, but the labour had been hellish,

184 · CATE BAUM

and I bled a lot after, and they couldn't find Bill in the pub till near the end, which made me resentful straight off I suppose, when he'd turned up half-cut with an argument in mind. It was not a good beginning.

Quite soon after we'd brung her home, I'd caught sight of myseln in the mirror, exhausted in the middle of another screaming cold night with her great ugly mouth hollering and fussing and slobbering. And I'd wished with all my soul that she didn't exist – a horrible, wistful prayer you don't really mean.

My parents made the effort with Bill once the bairn come, trying their best to get him round for Sunday dinners and that, but it was no use, cause he knew straight they were only interested in seeing me and the bairn, proper set on using that time to persuade me back home. My mam would ring up and ask me what Bill's favourite meat was, or his favourite pie. I'd tell her, get Chinese or a curry, but that just sounded impertinent to a woman like Mam.

Bill wouldn't visit farm. Too proud to let it go about when Da fired him for the sheep. 'It's water under bridge naw, Bill!' I said to him one time, trying to persuade him over the edge of his blessed Satanic book to come for Easter lunch.

'Yer da is nowt but a bloody spiteful bastard,' he said, turning the page with a sharp nail. I didn't remind him what we'd done to my da. He would only of had a story all ready to rewrite the past, and make it anyone's fault but his own.

And so, I'd always go visiting farm on my tod with the bairn. My da would drive up and meet me outside the little house with the neighbours gawking and muttering, and Bill wouldn't even come to the door to say 'ow do. My parents were decent folk in their own small way, but I loved Bill dearly also, and it forced a dilemma that made me reet stressed.

My mam asked me one of these afternoons I'd gone up on my own if I wanted to stay for a bit with the bairn 'fer a holiday', was the way she put it. I suppose she could see it was doing me in, all that pressure, and I burst into tears. 'I shan't,' I said to her between sobs. 'Bill wouldn't like it.'

'Too much like yer mam, is your beef,' she said. 'Proud as a Toby jug and no mind o' it.' And she sighed aloud, like she was the one supposed to be crying.

Cheryl Ann died a few weeks after on a Wednesday, the same day of the week she was born, the same day of the week the world died naw.

There's that rhyme says what happens to them babbies born on a certain day, but nowt about the day they take their last breath. You know it?

> Wednesday's bairn's a child of woe
> But she learns life's solace so
> She shall learn by broken toys
> How to mend life's shattered joys.

Christ. What a prediction for a child.

Bill and me, we'd been having a drink with his new mates in the front room. They never brung their own women to keep me company. I mean, they didn't look the sort to marry. And so, I was made out as the stick in the mud every bloody time they come round, taking over my house like a bunch of sorry philosophers wandered into chambers.

She must of gone blue in her crib that damp evening as I sat downstairs nursing a brandy over a jigsaw of the Silver Jubilee in the corner, trying to find a little peace whilst Bill and his mates squabbled noisily about Stalin and Hitler and Aleister Crowley, and how them in London had no frigging clue what the North was like.

I'd been listening to all this babble like you might listen to the wireless when you're doing sommat else. Just a noise to keep me company as I sat. And then, from nowhere, I had the strongest sense, this bite running through me in a jolt, and I stood up knowing she wasn't there no more. Up the stairs I'd gone, deliberate and careful. Up the stairs to her room. Then down again, to Bill.

I'd had to wait to catch his attention least five minutes whilst he yattered on and on, aggravated by my tapping his arm in front of the men, snapping at me when he peeled off into the kitchen for me to say. Right till the ambulance come to take her away, I reckon he didn't fully believe me Cheryl Ann was dead; that it was some ploy I was creating to keep him from his mates.

Cot death, my mam called it. Da was quite philosophical, reminding me of the lambs and nature, how they'd perish in the field all quiet like, far off, if they weren't made right in a part of them we couldn't fathom, despite their tiny dead bodies appearing formed perfect, lying there on the tipper after. Not one kindly word round it offered, when I was the one borne the child all them months. The one reached a finger through the bars of her cot and pressed her little fat arm and found it cool and still, and somehow thickened. The one peered into her tiny blue eyes as they gazed past me glass-like into the beyond, lids half closed due to that sudden and inexplicable lack of breath.

Hell, I was her mother!

After it happened, a notion took to nagging at me constant that the mix of us, of Bill and me, was sommat unnatural, and that any child we bore would die from some sinister defect made of those parts of us that should never be repeated.

And I had to wonder what brutal god had answered my prayer.

At the time, with finding us dead bairn shocking me so, and Bill taking it as a personal insult from God, the pair of us set to convincing usseln as some cold comfort that mortality was the proof we're no more than beasts, and can act like them so. I was such a clod taking Bill's word for a lot of things. Maybe I was keen to impress him, make it up to him. Else I'd let it alone cause it was easier.

The first night I was in it was soon after, when he come in ever so late, banging and sliding, howling up the passage wuther-like. I crept into the moonlit hallway to the bathroom, where I found him heaving on the tiles, clinging to the side of the bath, mouth full of shadows. I turned on the light and he was all soaked in blood, a deep red from his mouth to his knees. He seemed drunk, but instead of booze stank of iron, piss, adrenalin. I ken that smell from farm. Flinched.

'I can't get it to die!' he was wailing. This strange, deep voice I'd never heard on him, wolf eyes roaming the walls. 'It won't fockin' die!' he whispered conspiratorially.

In my dressing gown, I kept my distance, slippered feet froze on the threshold. Throat all dry. 'What won't die?' my question rattled in the night.

'Out thar!' he hissed, covering his head with his sodden jacket.

I spied the knife then, lain in the clean white of the bathtub. Scrags of blonde hair and sommat thicker that clung to the pool of scarlet. At that moment I must of crossed into some other reality, as if Bill had drawn one of his magick chalk circles and I'd stepped through. Then he pulled from his pocket his truck keys, held them out to me, eyes begging.

And, well.

That sunless dawn, Bill slept naked and feverish on the landing all wet and twitching like an animal done hunting whilst I burned his bloody clothes in that grubby concrete yard.

And I turned my eye to the dark.

I've heard some call it grooming, what he did to me. I remember having a certain understanding of it, when I was more in tune with his insanity. I can't say I feel the same naw, when I think on what we did with my da's flock, or up abbey with the Wrigley kid. Long before Cheryl Ann. See, Bill's manifesto wasn't the measure of his deeds, but of his justifications. It was a storm in me back then is all I know, passing through beautiful and terrible, sudden and heavy, but it rolled fast away, and all that remains is the damage.

I still see Cheryl Ann in dreams sometimes, her tiny, curled fists there in the grey of the moonlight, hard pale fingers coiled like fat worms in that blessed pink flannelette. And then I'll feel that silence from when I found her, as if death had fallen everywhere in the room and covered it like snow, muffled and chill.

I've come to ken the silence that always enters after; it sticks to the air for some time as the soul is waiting to leave, to take its place elsewhere.

'LANES'

Gelatin silver print, mounted on board

160 cm × 250 cm

Looking back, it was proper daft not to of thought more about the lad these last days, cause it was straight clear that Bill wasn't hale in the head and not cured at all. I wondered if they must of put him on sommat to keep him down, like they might an injured wolf so it won't bite. 'They 'ave ya on owt in thar?' I said as we stood on the furze catching us breath from the climb up Crag, hoping the bravado on me he wasn't used to would get a straight answer.

Bill sighed. Switched down a gear, some prison muscle kicking in. 'Were supposed to get me monthly Depo injection in me arse, couple days ago. But the bloody world ended! So naw it's fading off.'

'What were that fer?'

'Stops me cravings. Sex an' that.' He huffed, a bitter laugh. 'As if I felt sexy in thar.' He shook his head like he'd been cheated of sommat. He rummaged in his trousers. 'And this lot.' He drew fistfuls of various pills like sweets from his pockets, held them high, displaying them spilling from his dirty fingers. 'The little ones were fer the injection, side effects, heart, so won't be needing them no more!' He chucked a handful over the Crag.

'Nay!' I yelled, as if it was Bill going over and not just the meds. I knew some tablets make you funny if you stop sudden. And Bill was funny enough already.

'Them ones, make me piss foamy.' More pills flew in the air, blowing away in the wind come up, the mud scattered with them. 'Make me sleep all the bloody time.'

'Bill,' I kept saying, for what else could I say in a situation with a madman thrown his medications off a cliff?

'Chop, woman,' Bill said. 'Else they'll catch us up.' He dusted hisseln down, as if he'd scattered a person's ashes and said his goodbyes.

And I suppose I was thinking on how easy it'd been for Bill Gleason, even in this pathetic state, to take down one of them lunatics so swift, and wasn't that why I'd come to look him out? Protection? At least, this was the reasoning I was speeding through on that crag.

'Me motor's thar,' I said. My throat turned tight, expecting any second to see that convoy come charging over the hill. Bill dragged behind like sommat stinking on my boot. I squinted over at the lad's pale face peeked out from under the blanket in the window.

'That's the laddie then?' asked Bill, pointing as if he was a brid.

I didn't answer at first; it would of felt like giving permission. Instead, I gave the lad the thumbs up, took Bill hard by them wood shoulders. God, he stank sommat rotten. It reminded me of before. 'I'm glad to of found ya, pet.' Did I mean it as a goodbye? Was certain true.

Bill caught the whiff of my indecision. 'Wha's doin', Glore?' He shuffled about, losing that skin of his for a moment, none of the fight in him. 'Eh?' He tilted his head, looking ill in the dun light. Underslept, a hunger in his skin. He'd no strength for urges yet, but old Bill was there, awakening, stretching forgotten muscles, like the vampire had a taste of me. 'After all this way, ya leavin' me at the mercy of whoever's comin' over that bloody ridge reet naw?' He looked about, sniffing, as if the very air was making him sad.

I swallowed bile. It was terrible. I was trying to focus on the lad. But then I'd see in my mind the way Bill's jaw had hardened when he pushed in that knife in there, and sommat else come up in me.

'Could I have me boots back, least?' He sort of laughed, pointing to my feet. His laugh turned to a cough. He wiped his hand on his chest. It sudden felt like rain.

I looked off to us motor. The lad was watching at the window like a ghost, and I could hear Jip start up whinnying faint off. I stared down at them boots of Bill's that'd kept me so warm and safe year on year. 'They're mine naw, Bill,' I said, studying my toes in the leather. 'Won't fit the shape of yer feet no more.'

Bill frowned at me, square as you like. The wind changed direction. 'See, Glore, I'd say that whoever's cleaning up this mess, the army, the government – cause by Christ, thar's bloody goin' to be a they – that's who's comin' reet naw. They don't want no madmen runnin' about moor, derthee?'

'Good point, Bill.' I meant it. He'd no idea, after all. 'As ya say, probably them.'

Bill smiled nicely, lips together. Did I hope he would fock off back into Bellemere naw he'd sniffed the air, wait for 'they' to fix him up like that Clive had been? I can't say even naw. 'Well aye, Glory, Hope, whatever you ruddy call yerseln naw-days. Wife.' Bill grinned black, and so quiet it was on that crag that I heard the spit on his teeth spread into the ruins. 'When "they" come, wha', I'll be still 'ere on me tod, will I? Me an' that maggot George?' He was laughing at me, like it was a daft joke.

We stood bearing off in that awful quiet, whatever was coming up the road louder, louder, a change of gear, and revving, them thoughts swirling with demons come to play at us heads. Grasping, I was, but whenever I caught the edge of Bill's point it slipped away, so lithe and sleek. That feeling between us was so familiar it come in as an unexpected comfort to me. I looked to the sky and found nowt but gathering cloud.

Bill said, 'Off ta seaside. Then out Pettingrew. To a farm. In this military van. Number plate not too hard to spot neither. Let's see.' And he moved round the jeep to take a note of it. 'Probably a tracker on it, an' all.'

My knife wasn't in my hand, and it wasn't at my breast. And then my eyes grew tight when I saw Bill had it, pointing at the motor, fingers dextrous and strong. He must of pulled it from that nonce's neck in there and I'd not given it a bloody thought! Bill leaned down and tapped the number plate with its reddened tip, one hand behind his back like a gentleman viewing a museum vase.

It was as if all the energy I'd left for seeing him off had gone into him as new blood instead, and naw he was thriving on that tiny drop of power. He twisted the knife skilfully in his dirty paw as he come back over, then bounced it back round to hold it by its blade. He offered it to me. I took it.

Aye, Bill. I see.

'I'll find other boots,' he murmured, finding my eyes. 'And knives.' He nare strolled over to the motor in bloodied socks.

And like that, the ruling was made.

The lad looked so vulnerable when I went rushing in front of Bill to open the door. He'd been weeping again by the state of his cheeks, crisps mushed in his trouser front. 'Glore!' he cried.

'Lad, this is mine husband, Bill. He's coming along to seaside.'

I think the lad was a bit confused, but so very pleased I'd come back at all. 'Hullo,' he said, his voice all cracked and nervous. I didn't say owt on the motors we could hear. The state he was in, it would of frait him awful.

'Lad,' Bill muttered, scuffing his pretty hair. The lad didn't much like it; Bill was doing it too rough, almost spiteful. 'Glad to make yer acquaintance.'

Jip growled low at Bill then, snout digging out from under the blanket. 'That Jip?' said Bill, a wide smile on his already smug face. 'Fock me, biy! You made it all them year!' And he went past the lad with his leaning in, a grubby thigh sliding close, and he started scuffing up Jip's bib same as the lad's hair. 'Me dog!' he said to the lad.

And Jip went all stiff when Bill pet him.

See, there are events from with Bill that I've clean forgot. Rotten, hellish things I blacked out so heavy cause I'd not been able to carry them. But Jip must of had foremost in his little mind what constituted Bill's essence all along, markers in time like the bones he buries in wood, left there in dirt to take on a certain flavour. Bill was sure in Jip's senses same as that earth, his festering stench on recall.

'Get in, Bill,' I said sharp, opening my door even so. 'We needta get off.'

You'll probably think it disgusting when I say 'forgetting his past acts for a moment', but let's do that here, cause it's what I did at the time – forgetting his past acts for a moment, Bill turned very friendly and sweet for the most part on that drive out to seaside said afternoon, specially with the lad. I started to think on what a bitch I would of been if I'd left Bill for that motor to find. Or worse, abandoning the lad.

At one point, Bill took a little nap, and I had to smile when I noticed he'd some of them pills he'd chucked all smashed into his socks, and it dampened down the energies that'd built up in the last hours; almost pleasant to have him there next to me once more.

Later on the road, we ate some of the butties I'd made at the farmhouse, and Bill fed cold bacon scraps to Jip through the seat back. Jip, always obliged to accept bacon, begrudging took them from Bill's grubby fingers, and after, licked his chops. 'Reckon he remembers me, Glore!' said Bill.

'Aye, fer sure,' I said, but that didn't mean what Bill thought.

The lad was whooping by then, rushing on Bill's high, which I'd also forgotten was a thing with my husband, this mesmerising kiddie energy he brung to the table wherever he went. It lifted us up as we went along, and it seemed to me the farther we got from that damned jail to coast, the more like 'Bill' Bill become. He caught my eye as I sped the empty road, and I sudden perceived his face as it used to be, sort of filling in the blanks a bit easier. Then his own dark eye come into focus, bright and alive looking on, and my heart jumped seeing it. 'My wife,' he said, just low enough to make me purely love him in that moment.

I looked away out the window, blushing not in shyness, but ashamed. It felt obscene. The land was flat and dark with not a soul cross the brown, shaven territory where the sun dogs glare white in low hours of winter.

You know, the first time I saw three suns in the sky I nare screamed with the oddness of it, till Bill had explained it was a sun dog, a mirage; what they called a parhelion, a trick of the light.

Why dogs? I asked him, and he said that the 'dog' in the word is not the noun, the animal, but the verb: to hunt or to stalk, and that the other two lights were hunting the true sun. 'Which is the true one?' I asked, and he never answered, cause maybe he didn't know neither, and we stared at all three till we fell blind. I scarred my left retina that day, three little dots burned in that never properly faded. When I close my eyes in the black of night, I still see the three dots in red. Bill and me, we're never finished…

'Love?' Bill said, bringing me to my senses, and I noticed the sky had changed a little, thickening in at the edges with the damp, and I knew it was time for the lad to start smelling the air and looking out for the sea.

'Th'way east; you'll catch the sniff o' it first,' I said to the lad, who was curled up like a nut in its shell with Jip between the tools that Rob had left there. Jip was sound asleep, and I thought to myseln, funny for Jip to sleep like that in the day, and I worried if the sound had done him in. I thought of the tod in the grass. *Tod.*

The salt wind washed in black and tarry at last, bringing the water to the lad, and he cried out, 'What a queer smell that is, eh?' a big grin on his young chops, and he kicked his skinny lad legs in them school trousers hard in anticipation, Jip at attention sudden with his harry ald nostrils to the window, and I was glad to see him perked up an' all.

Sure, I felt the heave of it, the familiarity I had with Bill, us bond timeless as a page of poetry left in a grave, never moving, never changing meaning, just rotting into itseln darker and more hidden. It made me water in the mouth, like when death comes in. Like when I get turned on.

He spoke, seeing me pale. 'Thinkin' too much on it,' and his eye pinned in me as I drove towards the bronzed cliffs. I let my own eyes blur a little so as not to see him sat there so hard-lined, but even the salt air was full of Bill, his animal sweat and beast need hanging, a code for me to acknowledge.

I ken what he was saying: he reckoned I was calculating how to do it this time, with this laddie, making it too intricate. But I wasn't that evil bitch no more, and Bill had no cause to be Bill neither.

But then I heard that wet of his tongue in his hot mouth like sex, and I jolted. 'Not that, Bill,' I murmured slight, just how I used to before in times like these. 'The lad's fer a day at seaside, then we get 'im to 'is nan.' The wheels were kicking up sand in the weeds, and the windscreen blew with fine, pale dust. I stared into the blank of it, not wanting to conjure any memories. But too late. Demons bucked for the hollow in the gloom of me. They obliged me with a show.

The blue paper kite come to mind, flying in that purple summer sky you get over this land. That summer after Bill took to reading books about magick with a k and psychic mind control. Devils and dictators, and hell being real and amongst us naw.

We had been picnicking on the hill out by abbey that day. No kiddies went there by then, on account of the Wrigley business, so we had the place to usseln. It was a picturesque spot for canoodling and a few nice cheese sarnies on a hot day, and so quiet you could hear the wings of white falcons from far off maybe a second after they lifted in the still air, hovering over some mouse or jay in the lilac heather. Then they'd dive down fast, mantling the creature below, a scuffle in the brush, and sometimes, a cry. But not often, said Bill. For the brid rips out the throat of its prey first, as a kindness. But I knew of brids and nature, and neither are kind. Falcons take the throat first to easier crop the flesh.

The paper kite had been a shade brighter than the sky, hovering all over the wooded horizon, first sinking then tearing along, high again, wobbling, its bunting tail tentative in pink like a babby dragon over the cream-white dots of the flocks vanna.

'The kiddie's flying it hisseln,' Bill had said, mouth full of meat. 'The way the kite's sinking. He keeps having to run wi' it. No grown-up to hold it fast.' He took out his silver hip flask and swigged, knees up on the rock in his ridiculous dark suit, trousers too short on navy-socked ankles. Fancied hisseln a regular Ian Curtis, with his dark greased hair and army-brown shirt. 'Must of biked it, that far off,' he said. 'How far from civilisation would ya say, Glore? That kiddie?'

'Five, six mile.' The sarnie in my mouth was sudden ash, near choking. I spat it into the napkin in my lap. It tasted sudden of the blood in the bathroom. 'Up past lanes, by almshouses.'

'The sea! The sea!' the laddie went screaming, and the line of the bay come at us from the sky, leering high and sparkling. Jip wagged his tail, pleased at the lad's happiness, and the memory of Bill throwing that bloodied blue kite into the grave flashed and faded as fast as it come.

I took a good lung of salty air to steady myseln, and we climbed the cliff line in the motor. Bill wound down his window and made a great show of sucking in air and breathing it out, as if it was a massive inconvenience I'd wrought upon him, playing up to me, squinting. His energy had shifted, but I didn't rise to it, keeping on till we could see the coast town ahead.

Aye, I thought, this burden I remember, like he owns my mood. I didn't like the feel of it much after so long without him. It was like trying on an old coat you'd long forgotten, to find it don't fit too well and that's why you'd put it off.

It tipped me to sadness for Mark at that minute, a man I'd never kissed, but would of, I'm sure, given time. Copper Mark

200 · CATE BAUM

was so easy to sit with and say nowt of an evening, to gaze into
the dark land and see it as the same place of beauty, just without light. Bill saw the land as a great theatre that shifted its
set each evening, and where the trees and heather and stones
had once stood, the penumbras of demons trod night instead.

'Reckon it's safe, do ya, goin' coast town?' Bill chewed on
his nails, an old habit I'd forgotten of him annoyed the shit
out of me naw.

'Thar's this farcy hotel they refurbed since you been in,
called The Diana. Thought we'd go thar, get a suite.' I grinned,
a theatrical sort of face, a plan out of nowhere that I knew
might bring Bill round. 'Like posh bastards!' I added. A bit of
anarchy went miles with Bill. He chuckled sour and looked
out the window, a sign he'd graced me permission.

Fock me, I thought. But we carried on.

Seemed to me likely coast would be empty; any folk survived would of been taken off to some safe place by whatever
authorities were left, or off to that hospital up Eversdale, and
that would of already happened, and there'd be nobody left to
see us come in.

Least, that's what I thought.

I'd the sense to look for ships, any that might be military.
But yesterday when we come in, there was only the empty
wide sparkling sea.

The coast town's many tiled heads craned up from coast
in front of us, and the gleaming white obelisk of the new
hotel beckoned. This town's not too big, I suppose, but to
us, coming off land, it seemed massive; thirty, forty thousand
residents thereabouts. 'Huge, int it?' said the small voice of

the lad, peering between the seats with sticky hands like he was us kid.

'Aye, lad,' said Bill, patiently, as a teacher might, the spit on his black teeth full of charm. I watched the lad in the mirror, face set as he studied Bill. And I mean, Bill's breath must of stunk.

There was a scatter of dead gulls in us path, maybe fifty of them, bright legs up stiff, and sorry though I am even naw saying it, I had to run over them to make progress, so many there were in the road. The crunching of their tiny bones was course not a pleasant sound, but Bill kept imitating it, 'Crrrunch!' he squawked over and over, miming hands wringing a tiny neck, and to my horror, that's when he bloody well hooked the lad in, who giggled besotted every time Bill said it.

I kept myseln quiet, glancing back to Jip, who had disconnected, blankly looking out at the sea in old habits. He'd been with other little lads in the backs of other cars, and by the end of it, he'd started to refuse to get in a vehicle at all.

I detest that's why Bill got Jip in the first place, to have a pup for them to coo over and lure them in, but I feel closer to Jip knowing that's why. We were the bait, were we, me and Jip? I know that's no defence, and trying to explain why I stayed doing it, I can't. It was all part of the spell.

We drove along the bridleway into town, through the back allotments where I'd sometimes walked the summer holidays as a kiddie, pulling sweet, hairy beans off their canes as I'd gone along with other sprats; a seedy blackberry hung in us faces, sometimes bunches of shining elders, and we'd pretend

we were all rich, and they were little spoons of caviar like one
of us had seen on the telly, their bitter, dark juice fizzing in us
teeth.

We saw very few bodies about up there, and I put it down
to the sound happening in the early hours; townies didn't rise
early like in village. That was lucky, I thought to myseln, for
the stink would of overpowered us coming in. But see, I didn't
catch what them circles of brids were when we drove in here
so full of hope.

I took us down a steep road past terraces of narrow white-
washed houses. Their tiny square windows gave nowt away,
but we all three must of thought on it, the folk inside tucked
in their beds, dead as doornails and bloated like the family in
the farmhouse, where that Rob was rotting an' all.

'Funny,' said the lad, 'nobody else like us 'ere.' He meant
alive. A silence was fallen on the place, that silence of the
dead, and we felt it in us bellies like a yearning.

We come over the roundabout that led to the beach, and
then the high-rise of The Diana was off to the left, so I spun
up that way. Bill was tapping the dashboard with his dirty
chewed nails as if we'd the radio on, and I touched his hand
then, only gently, but we ken each other in the skin, and we
pulled together like a tide to its moon, soft and under, with
the hush of the tow. Bill gasped, a sexual sound I'd forgot of
him, wavering and sharp. 'Glory,' he said under his breath; the
utterance filled me. I was the first person to touch his skin in
eleven year, and he, just about, mine.

The Diana is some fifteen floors high, like a great cruising
ship off the ground. When it was built, there was worry it was

the start of a rushed-in tourism. These flashy types from the city, putting on silly modern art exhibitions – no offence to thee, Ms Elgar. Pop stars and jockeys buying mansions on the spit, pushing up property prices for locals who wanted to keep it quaint and decent round about.

But here it is, named after the princess who died the month it was finished, built by Arabs brung in with the horses. Stables and studs were the new sheep, Sarah reckoned, but I couldn't see it myseln. A single racehorse costs thousands to keep, and if they get injured, that's the lot. Dog food. I've seen it. Then again, like this crappy modern art all abouts, horses are a good way to move money, and the Arabs must of liked that.

We drove in slow and smooth, keeping an eye out for movement. But there was none then. 'Looks like abroad,' said Bill, who'd never been abroad a day in his life.

'When we went Keswick, looked like 'ere abouts,' said the lad. 'Me and me mam, and 'er bloke fore last.' He jumped up a bit in his seat at the window. 'They got one of them big pools 'ere?'

'Got two or three, I reckon,' I said, pulling into the drive of the hotel. I hoped they did. It made me smile to think on it.

'You got one great bloody pool down thar, look, lad! Called the sea!' Bill chuckled unkindly at his own quip. But we didn't know what was in that sea, did we, decaying and unusual?

We parked on a white-lined square of tarmac. A beer terrace to the side, dusty plastic flowers in faded pots. Smart black canvas sidings flapped torn in the wind advertising lager, decking revealed as the canvas blew in flashes of the dead: those who'd been drinking late, hotel staff flirting after work.

The fire exit was stopped open with a brick of milk. A young lad in a green waiscot leaned bloody-eared and seeping against the door. His cigarette had burned through his polyester trousers where his hand rested, the butt of it still in his fingers, a perfect black circle in his flesh.

'Close yer eyes, if ya like,' I said to the lad, reaching for him.

'I'm a'ight,' he said, turning from me, staring at it all as if he was at a museum, passing through the exhibits. He grabbed cold fingers at my hand, and I pulled him along a little, cause he kept stopping to gawp. Jip muzzled us hands as we passed into the side passage of the hotel, past a granite staircase with a gaudy purple carpet.

I pushed into the main foyer ahead of Bill, who was hanging back, overawed but trying to look *nonchalant*, his favourite word. 'Yo!' yelled Bill sudden into the high place. His voice echoed abouts.

'Stop it!' I hissed, for I was terrified there were others hiding. My heart went beating through my chest as I made ready to confront whatever come at us. Bill just laughed, and Jip took up barking for a bit, settling into a growl.

The atrium ran with metal bannisters all the way up, the sloshy music still on, lights all sparkling in golds and pinks. It was built like I imagined one of them new country golf clubs you hear about, no taste to it at all: orange wood panels and concrete, too many lights so the drunkards can see where they're going of an evening. 'Lovely in 'ere, int it, Glore?' said the lad. Bill scuffed his hair, thumb lingering. I watched.

There were no bodies to see, but above us heads a cloud of velvet-blue flies gathered in a reverie. Bill jumped over the counter, rummaged for keys. 'It's them cards, like what we had in hotel in Keswick,' the lad piped. 'Ya bleep the card on th' door. Bleep!'

Bill frowned. 'Cards?' He'd been in prison a long time. Not like I'd ever been to a hotel neither. He threw up his hands, worn out. 'I dunno.'

The lad lost interest, started dinging the silver bell on the desk. I went round to a stack of little plastic cards in a dish with the hotel name written on, and a swiper, and when I swiped one of the cards in the thing, the computer lit up and gave a list of rooms to select from with a click of the mouse. As I fiddled, I'd a flash to another time, when I was blonde Hope Gleason, accounts administrator for Barnes and Co.

Bill couldn't stand I knew how to do it all and he did not. He'd never clicked a machine in his life. All ledger books and paper lists in that sales department at Barnes's it was, chits the men shoved in little notebooks, wetting a pencil stump with their tongue. They'd bloody use chalk for the leader board, as if it was the war. More like a bookie's, the energy of that floor, then me and the other lasses had to make sense of the scraps of paper they carried up of a Friday to do the orders, all covered in cigarette ash and biscuit crumbs.

Course, Bill had to be the lord of it all naw, so he started pelting the great tinted hotel windows with posh boiled sweets from the counter whilst I struggled on with the clicking. The lad giggled, nervous of it, pushing his little hands deep in the sweet bowl but not joining in; more like he was holding on to what was left. Jip took to yapping, half-heartedly chasing after

206 · CATE BAUM

the sweets, but it was a funny little yap, as if he didn't want
Bill making a mess of the place.

I got on with the job in hand. I shook off the recognition
of being well used to ignoring Bill as I was doing sommat or
other. But the pit of my stomach took to hardening.

Bill hooted. 'Well! I never imagined I'd be 'ere wi' thee
today, Glore! In this fockin' great 'otel!' He come round and
pointed at the computer screen with a yellowed nail, crunching on the confounded sweets with them rotten pegs of his.
The matrimonial suite, he wanted. Two rooms, air con, Jacuzzi,
four-poster bed, single fold-out in the other. I could stop with
the lad, I argued to myseln out loud, and Bill winked, cynical
like. We both ken the truth of it.

I clicked, and the computer told us the suite was called
Penthouse 2, top floor, and I swiped the card through the
machine.

Was I enjoying myseln, or playing along? There was a part
of me that'd obviously missed Bill, missed being Hope. Not
thinking, we fade into us patterns, for patterns are the meaning of it, are they not, the rhythm of us own seasons locked to
existence, in how we rise and fall and sleep.

The lift was still working, so we hopped into its glass shaft
feeling all glamorous, as Bill quipped, and that music come
piping in, comforting like. Jip jumped heavy into the lad's
arms, and we went up the top of the building in silent wonder,
gazing as the floors receded, any dead bodies passed met with
grunts of contempt for spoiling us fun.

It was all of it exciting, to be out and about, free of everything,
and I'll admit I'd started to have the feelings for Bill I'd lost

over them last few year. For the old days were far and long ago, and somewhat in the haze. Given the sheer magnitude of what had occurred in the last while, a shared experience of sorts, it might of felt complacent and arrogant to indulge in sommat happy, but we did it. I was high, being there with Bill, after all the times I'd dreamt about it and wept; let myseln fantasise how it might be if only me and Bill were left alone in the world. My defences relaxed just having him there. Like the slave who can only rest once the master is home.

I gazed at the glittering pale sea through the shining windows gliding by, a dream I would of stopped myseln from dwelling on before. I hadn't let myseln imagine much in the shed, for the comedown was too hard. But there we were, so I allowed myseln a heartbeat to enjoy it. 'A luxury hotel at the end of the world!' I said to Bill.

He smiled to hisseln. 'Not the end of the world. Just the end of theirs.'

The lad took to humming off-tune and all jittery, pressing his knuckles white. I threw him a glance, not turning my head, slape-like. He was unsure, rustling. How dirty we all were in us rags and mud, the whiff of us stale and cloying in that tiny space. The things we'd seen inland were clung to us; stories followed out from moor. I vowed we'd get straight to the bath, wash away all the horrors we'd endured, find some scran, fresh clothes.

Imagine how my head was put together yesterday, me thinking this was us new start, the four of us. Me, Bill. Jip. And the lad.

'PIER'

Gelatin silver print, mounted on board

320 cm × 250 cm

Penthouse 2 was all black gloss and mirrors, silvery flock velvet up a wall of flowers; a splash of that neon pink all the young'uns in village wore on one another. A colour you never see ont moor, that neon. I reckon that's just why they all liked it.

All this farcy decor appeared rather unnecessary, us all having lived so plain, and we started gasping and chuckling rather sarcastically at the sight of it. We'd an enormous lounge, floor to ceiling windows looking out on the vastness of the water below. Great swooping glass balconies over the cliff, plastic palms in pots, sunbeds through sliding windows that made you feel like you were on a ship. We were so high in the air it was like floating. A silvery table was perched in the middle of the way with a brass bucket for ice, an unopened bottle of pink champagne of all things in the melt.

The lad was dashing about in circles with Jip, room to room squealing. Bill just stood there, gawping, hands out like a marionette, goggling at the chandeliers, the flat-screen TV over the fireplace, the views. 'What a palace, eh, Glory?' he said quiet, intimidated by it after all them year locked away.

I slumped on the couch made for twelve backsides at once; all soft and shimmering it was, like a throne. But then I caught the sight of myseln in the mirrors: fat and old and dirty, with Bill shuffling next to me a walking skeleton with demons caught in his hair. So I said to Bill that we should find the showers and have a scrub like. 'Certainly,' he said, still with that damned fixed expression on his face, and the puppet on its strings shuffled through the far doors and didn't return, calling out instead, 'This way, two rooms, two bathrooms! Hot bloody water!'

I found the lad in the bedroom scoffing posh little chocolates from the pillows. He said he wanted to wait a bit to shower cause he was enjoying hisseln, so as I was just as desperate to wash as Bill, I told him to take a cola from the minibar and entertain hisseln a minute. I reminded him that dogs can't have chocolate, but that he could give Jip the stick of salami in there, and he set his little face to the instruction and kicked his legs.

Sometimes when I'm kind to a child it frightens me how easy it is to turn their minds.

I put on the great flat telly for him an' all, and amongst the fuzzing channels, cartoons ran on the automatic, so I handed him the doofer and went to wash.

I hadn't had a real shower eleven year. It was a weir sort of shower, with a huge aggressive nozzle like rain stinging my skin, polished steel knobs all along the wall would be more at home in a railway yard. And the soap smelled of my mam:

LILY OF THE VALLEY it said on the label, a bit old-fashioned
I'd of thought, but Mark had said that old vintage stuff was
back in fashion, so maybe it was the nostalgia for my mam
started my brain turning.

Mam had seen a lot of death herseln. That's why she chris-
tened me Hope. What with two of Mam's sisters going young,
and her parents in the ground only months apart, she'd taken
to her ideas. Once you've been that close to what death is,
she'd say, you see it all, what's waiting on the other side. What
is it? I'd ask, and she'd say, hope.

I tried to explain it to Bill when us bairn died. I knew in my
bones she had not disappeared. She went *somewhere*, I told him.

I've seen it myseln. Like, when they die, for a moment
they're in both places, here and there, and I've felt it burn
through me when they've let go and emptied themseln of
here. *They go somewhere.*

But course, Bill was calling me Glory by then, not Hope,
and he couldn't feel a thing.

The beach down by hotel is a fishy sort of place in town, int it,
Ms Elgar, with that great flat silver bay. Like a giant's footprint,
and the tide hardly floods. Fine brown sand full of worms from
the rich soil behind it, the fields almost touching, and yon
mucked with the briny ribbons of seaweed and the hollowed
bodies of anemones crunching under stones.

The coast here battles with the bog, see. The coaled outlines of dinosaurs and the skulls of dire wolves are preserved in
the maw. Used to be all sea round here, Jurassic period, they
say. You can dip down your fingers in the gaps of rock and drag

up fossils in flats of grey stone, perfectly formed skeletons of tiny things from thousands of years ago pinked with the stains of heather and brine, but still pretty for a child to find.

Up the cliff instead of wolves naw, there's them strange Gothic buildings with rusty tiled faces and iron spires, towers spiking the cloud-filled sky. The majestic front of the Victoria Grand Hotel gazes lazily on – a pale ald eye it has, velvet curtains flapping at the edges in dark red like veins. And the monstrosity of The Diana curdles the cliff with its ugly long windows, gorgeous on the inside, but from the beach it has the black eyes of a polished insect, watching.

Bill had not wanted to come with us down front. He was paranoid there could be cops or army come and catch us, but me and the lad saw no one.

Jip raced up and down the waterline, his underside all wet and muddy, barking, jip, jip. How he got his name, that funny yap.

The arcades to the back of us were silent as tombs. They would of been shuttered on the night of the sound, seeing the shop signs with the opening hours written on, closing time midnight. So then, for the most part, they'd all been home tucked up in their beds, with only one pewr homeless bastard in a bus shelter on the promenade, quietly rotting inside his winter coat and hat on his newspaper cot. A scattering of gulls and terns lay spread around him, winding the path back to the cliff, twig legs caught in clumps of bitter dark wrack: a wreath sent up from the sea for the mourning of the land.

We skimmed stones a while, and the lad was bursting with joy, laughing with red sweaty cheeks, them moles come up excited in black, flapping his hair from his young eyes every naw and again. He'd rolled up them school trousers he still had on, sand up his back from Jip jumping with sticks and bits of old trash. I noted to myseln we'd to find the lad sommat else to wear than that bloody school uniform and fleece.

As the sea started to gold with the afternoon, I was somehow alert to Bill at us spines, my mouth full of the metal of fear the whole while, mingled with a faint taste of blood in my gums I'd noticed as we strolled along. I kept glancing up at that towering hotel, its deep windows for eyes, thinking I'd catch sight of Bill leaning at the glass, surveying the gifts of his new kingdom.

And the lad.

My view come down to sommat orange washing gently in the tide farther up. I first took it as seaweed, old rags, a body's limbs. But there was a familiarity in it. I went up kicked it with my boot. Yellow pockets, blue toggles. All torn up. Gurgling bloody in the foam of the sea's filth. It was one of the ugly orange anoraks from them two ramblers we'd sent village way couple days back.

Aye, I thought. Sommat's gan on we don't want no part of.

Just then between the buildings I caught a flutter, a sense of watching: the shimmer of metal non-animal height. Jip come to heel, gave off a low growl. Then all was still just as sudden. I watched Jip for a clue, touching my knife in my breast pocket, but he wandered back to sniff the sand. Being so near land, I ken danger. But there was no sense o' it, and Jip had lost interest.

'We should get back,' I said sharp to the lad, peering about creeped, and pushed him off spying the anorak in the water. He wanted sore to go search out a candy floss; said he'd never had it in his whole life, his voice raised high to be cute like lads do when they want owt. 'That's a long shot, fella,' I told him, eyeing the shuttered arcades, but the lad was determined, and in any case, the pup had to shit before we settled all the way in the top of that blessed hotel.

We walked that lonely front a while, an eye up my back, and for the first three or four beaches, the scattered sand on the promenade told a story of bloody feet running, tens of people fighting and pushing, then rubber soles of boots printed in the sand. And blood, so much blood, blackening the ground. We kept quiet. The lad here-there kicked a print with his own foot as we went, comparing the sizes. Jip found the print of a dog, caught in the chaos somehow.

And there were other prints, bigger than dogs, sliding.

But the footprints all cut off sudden, a stink of sommat acrid, wet and heavy. Strings of flesh and skin trailed down to where the sea hissed, swelling in its craw. 'Look away,' I said to the lad, but honest, it was more for the horrendous image of it feeding my own fear.

You can still make out these lines of neon pink paint, sprayed on the ground massive at the head of the pier. Just like my flock's smit, they are. A circle with a cross. Dozens of discarded plastic glo-sticks popped and faded, as if teenage witches bereft of candles drew up their circle with what come to hand. A spill of fuel. And in the walls behind, a smatter of holes encrusted with blood. A mural of bullets.

The lad asked, 'What's it?'

And I says, 'Helicopter pad,' not really knowing, walking quick past the wall. 'Make-do one.'

'Ya wha'?' said the lad, rubbing his eyes all tired from it.

'Fer taking off survivors, suppose.'

The lad scraped his foot on the pink for a bit. 'Not us, though.'

I noticed as we walked how the beach was dug over in a great circle, almost invisible where we'd come from. At the edge, the stinking carcases of gulls and crabs had been arranged in geometric lines. I stared at it a minute, trying to make out the code. And the sour flavour come up off the sand. Jip scampered over, digging, pulling at sommat sticking out.

It was a child's hand.

Mass graves, then, these circles we've been seeing. Did you know, Ms Elgar? The way you just paled tells me you did. What's that you say?

(Inaudible)

Oh aye. I agree, woman. No military would of marked them with bitten brids. How impossible that anyone would dig such perfect circles, make such mass burials decorated this way, abandon the place for dead.

You know, there was a ritual for the old gods I ken somehow as a child, sommat the elders may of spoke of to the barrows of Vikings, the carvings of animals. But the memory of these stories was too dim in the fear as I stood there, gazing at it all. This ritual had always been here, had it? In the dark of us?

My mind went wandering over the land like a kite, to the ancient sites decorated with them stone beasts, to the shallow graves me and Bill had scattered and forgot. I stood in that circle, and a wail in the distance threaded them together, all canny beaks pointed to me.

And I thought: has the land come to mimic us vile deeds, or did we only mimic the land's?

The sky dimmed then as if it answered, though there was no cloud overhead.

Jip come away from it quick, shaking his head like it both-ered him, and the lad took the pup in his arms, crouching to hide his face in his fur. 'They're gan, lad, whoever did it,' I said.

The lad looked up at me, eyes red and sore like a prayer. Questioning, his little lips moved, but nowt come out. I yanked his arm near out the socket past it all, up pier, till we were free of that scene.

I'm loath to say it's quite pleasant farther this way, no louts to shout and leer on the promenade – even with the few left ripening, lining the edges. We were taking the dead for granted already, the devils we'd become, though naw and again the lad would take up a fistful of sand from the planks of the walkway and sprinkle it over the bloated bodies, a custom he must of seen somewhere, and Jip would go up nosing an armpit or mouth in reverence. 'Not too close, biys,' I'd say.

The lowering sun started getting in us eyes, and the stroll was tedious with all the places shuttered up and not a soul about, but we at last come to a kiosk, a small man in a striped apron on the tarmac in front, fingers stuck in his ears, all cloyed black. See, all the dead, bleeding from the ears straight off. All ground level, sky in sight; or else very near to that blessed mast at Morton like that Rob. The rest out there, put down, murdered, like stock that's no longer viable.

Polythene bags of pink frothy sugar hung all about his kiosk like mouths foaming blood, popcorn like cracked teeth, red shiny sugar dummies on ribbons that reminded me of choking. I blinked these images away and tried to think only of the lad.

I noticed the machines were on inside the arcade on the pier, all lights flicking and flashing with electric, and outside by the kiosk, an air hockey table. 'Come on,' I said to him. 'Let's have a game.'

'Smart!' said the lad, over the moon with it all, and I filched the coins from the stall's till, and we played for a bit, him stuffing sweets in his gob between smashes, and he laughed and screamed, and Jip ran around us like the hand of a clock barking, till I let the lad win massively, thirty-three to four, and he was so giddy when the line of pink tickets popped out at the end that he sang along with the music coming off the machine and puffed out his chest, beating it, skidding about on the planks.

Then the lad sped off down the pier past the dodgems and the roulettes, and for a moment I could only see his shadow, flitting between machines and rides and the colourful sidings. And then he was giggling past the slap of the waves, talking soft, raising questions in surprise, and Jip growled low, so I cried out, 'Bill?' thinking he was there, come down to join us, but then the lad come running back, pleased with hisseln, and alone, and when I asked him what's to do, he went blushing, like I'd caught him in a lie.

'Just, the machines are funny down thar,' he said finally, a thin attempt to appease me.

'Nay, nay, lad!' I felt the temper come up in my voice at him, catching the edge of his lie. Jip was making feet at my heel like he does when strangers are close. 'Who's thar?' I cried out, almost a question to him, but more to the end of pier. 'Show yerseln!'

'Jeez, Glore,' the lad muttered with a derisory snort. The nipper was only focking mimicking Bill. Two minutes with my husband and he was turning rotten already.

Well. That riled me proper. I grabbed his shoulders, shook him hard spiteful. 'Don't you tell me fibs!' I says to his twisted little mouth. I swear if I'd had a pin I could of hooked the lie on a seam of spit easy as a wrong stitch of wool. Jip was creating, so I yells to him, 'Gawn, pup!' and he went galloping up pier hunting all tail and eye.

'You's pinching me, Glory!' the lad whined, chocolate moles all sore on his cheek, and he sobbed for good measure, blinking his pretty wet lashes, expecting a beating to next Thursday. If I'm honest, I was on the edge, when I heard some wooden thing sliding, far up the pier, but Jip trotted back like nowt had gan on, a half-eaten toffee apple in his proud jaw, and I reckoned it must of been the wind after all. I let the lad go and stood very still like my da had once shown me for locating a lost beast. I wet my finger for the ley of that wind. The air was still as broth.

'Stay 'ere,' I said, and though the lad begged me not to leave, he was enough entertained with Jip's making short work of his apple, grasping it in his paws, and it struck me in that moment the lad had no fear.

I wondered where Jip got that apple an' all, Ms Elgar. So I did.

I went quite aggressive up that pier, swinging my boots; their stomping made me brave. But when I reached the end with the world all three sides, it was sommat quite frightening to behold. The sky went too low, all greasy and yellowed like unskirted fleece, and the water was still, and very blue. A distant squall settled ragged like blood in milk. And the air wore that newly breathed skin of sommat just gan, the decking all sodded with sand. Someone had been there recent.

In the arcade, I made out the settling of a flung coin on a table, but given the games' light bulbs only flashed weak, with so many nooks in the dim of the place, it would of been stupid to enter alone. I'd no choice but to give it up.

I walked back, a shiver in my step, but glad to have eyes on Jip once more. 'Could of sworn you was talking to someone,' I muttered, and the lad heard, but said nowt, a new and wary stillness in his eye, and we left the pier then, a strained silence betwixt us for a little while.

Taking some of the bounty on us arms by their ribbons, we carried us haul back along the shore. Cheered by the good- ies, I suppose, the lad was soon chatting merrily about the stones, the sea, how he'd thrashed my arse at air hockey, how he was so proud of them tickets, and he was going to tell them about it.

'Who's them?' I said. Aye.

'Oh,' he said, worried like. 'Bill? Bill, is his name?' Like he'd forgot. He was almost hysterical. Like what my mam would say of the bairn: overtired, fussing like that. But I wondered, did he just lie to me? Was that a lie?

I ken children's heads, and how they yatter on and on when they're frait. But the lad, I could almost hear the cogs moving as he pondered. Then he asked me with great concern, 'D'ya reckon tha' Bill is okay?'

What do you say to a child? Well, lad. Let's see. Bill Gleason is the most dangerous serial killer in England. Bill Gleason, who stole a little biy just like you, and wouldn't tell his mammy what he did with him after, even when she begged. Bill Gleason, The Devil O' Th' Moor. And you, my young friend, are exactly Bill Gleason's type.

I reached deep. 'Bill might'n stay wi' us much more. Or we might'n.'

He breathed out slow and hard, and I wasn't sure if it was the comfort of the red sugar dummy he'd started on, or relief at my reply.

We're animals, all of us. We sniff it when sommat's not right, when a person's not all there up top. And the lad had a life of it with his own pikey of a mam already. Imagine the types a woman like her brings in of a night.

'Can I go t' pool when we get in?' the lad asked, desperate to change the subject.

'I'm not yer mam. You do what ya want, lad.'

'Yessss!' he said, as little lads do when they've scored a goal.

Anything but the death, we spoke of then. Anything but what he'd seen them last days, or how he felt about it all.

I need to think it over, how I'm telling this. The truth is, just like all stories, the trope plays out: monsters are lonely. They destroy everything on account of needing love. They grab hold of any slight chance too tight, and squeeze it to death.

For a long while, I reckoned that's what'd happened with Bill. That he wanted so much to chase a feeling that turned him on, that made him feel so alive, that the rest of how he come by it didn't matter to him. And when I break it down to such simple elements of greed and want and vanity, I see that's my sin too. The less love Bill showed me, the more I longed to please him, and for that, he filled me with what he wanted, and in the end, my sole satisfaction was in his. And to tell on Bill would of been to lose him.

Like in one of my romantic novels by a girl same age I was then, we become monsters, cut off from the world, yet closer through all us deeds.

The sky was turning a wash of grey as it skimmed the sand, draining the day of colour so the gold-reds of evening could flood in. So quiet on the beach you could hear a celestial energy racing in with the night, and I was reminded by that colour of the big orange tod in the grass, and the lad poking him with a stick, curious like.

Then other ground surged in me, red earth dug open, wet. A thin memory of small hands grasping, my heart like a brid's, pulsing. Legs tumbling heavy, white skin bloody, scratched in brambles. A soft empty blanket folded simple on the back seat of a car, having served its purpose. How I'd stared at the blanket's form in the reflection of the wing mirror all the drive home, its perfect pinkness, like a child's cheek full of life.

'Glory!' the lad was shouting at me, amazed, proudly showing me a great dead crab he'd hauled on a stick by its claw.

'Sorry lad, miles off.' I sniffed away the horror and looked far cross the water where the hollow shapes of gulls were calling. That's when I spied the low black line, scuffed at the offing. 'Lad?' I said. He looked too. 'You see that?'

'Aye.' We stared, trying to make it out. 'What's it, d'ya reckon?'

The line sharpened for a beat, but then it faded into the mirror of water. It could of been a vessel, bloody big if it were, or maybe just a trick of the light. 'We'll see clearer when it's dark. If it has lights on.'

Jip was snorting at the rotted crab, tail wagging with small pleasure. I squinted up at The Diana's long windows, into that creepy gleaming glass where Bill was waiting for us to come back.

'Funny, y'know,' Bill had said at the door of the penthouse, just as we were leaving for beach. 'I've felt more alive, since the sound.' And he'd smiled as thin and pink as that line of blood in his nail.

The satin edge of that pink blanket. Cheryl Ann gripping it, sleeping and warm.

The sky rolled over, and a breeze caught death on its edge. A stench fell up in us faces. Bill had said he'd never got that injection he was due. That he'd felt more alive since the sound. Since them pills were thrown down Crag, more like.

The lad had to be taken straight. 'Listen, pet, let's go to yer nan's naw,' I said quick, a ghost run up my back.

'Wha?' He was mighty confused. Jip was eating sommat from the shingle. I called him come bye, for we didn't know sure if it was safe to be eating things that had perished from the sound. I noticed my throat getting quite sore as I spoke, and I wanted to put it down to thirst, and I gave a cough to clear it. To clear the dread.

Jip come by chewing, the dead thing hanging from his jaw, and I saw it was only an old cheese sarnie covered in sand. 'Good biy,' I said. But I was thinking on that Rob, back in the farmhouse with the nice ceramic tiles, hacking blood in the doorway.

'Funny ya coughed,' said the lad, all matter-of-fact. 'I got a frog in me throat an' all.'

'Don't you fret on it,' I said, heart sinking. 'Probably just sea air cleaning us pipes.'

'Aye,' said the lad, dragging his stick in the crook of his arm like a shepherd; he wasn't convinced.

But I reckon we're unaffected, except for this damned cough. You were underground when the sound come, away from the sky. Bill had thick prison concrete. The lad was in cop shop, anti-mobile walls. Me, in wood. And dear Mark, far out, and the land had protected him.

I moved us first to the next breaker, all slimy and black with seaweed, over to next beach. Out of the eyeline of them windows, we went quick up the cliff, close to the wall, past the back of The Diana and to the car park. Jip was just about still happy to walk, but I could tell he was worn down, and he kept making tippy-toe circles heading back to the hotel.

I took a quick look about and jumped in the motor, shut the door as quiet as I could. The lad copied me careful, getting in the front with me, feeling that cold panic looming like a thread tugging, watchful, and Jip crawled under the seat. What if Bill was spying on us? What if he was storming down in that farcy glass lift, legs all kneeless, to stop us from leaving? What in hellfire's name would Bill Gleason, The Devil O' Th' Moor, do, if he thought I'd betrayed him?

But was I betraying him? When I went over the scenario where Bill comes charging at us in that car park, me explaining I was only taking the lad to his nan's and coming straight back, that felt like a damned lie an' all.

I kept swinging my head about, peeling my eyes, blood beating painful through my chest. I'd parked on a slope, so I let the handbrake go without the engine, and silently we flew downward, thankfully on a cement path and not gravel, out the gates and onto the road, where I swivelled us to head west.

When we slowed, I started the engine, but it was so loud and sudden in the quiet I knew Bill would of heard us, watching or not. 'No goin' back naw,' I said to the lad, or rather to myseln. The lad murmured in reply, sucking on his sweets, looking out the window at the blue falling dusk, not bothered what I was going on about. 'We'll head off to Pettingrew, and you tell me if ya see owt ya recognise ont road.'

'Landmarks,' he said firm, like he'd been waiting his whole life to have a situation to use the very word. He stuck his head out the window like Jip might as we drove fast away down coast, and I could see in the mirror how his silky young hair caught on his damp lips.

The wheels I kept tight to the cliff edge, an old brant path in the trees I ken off the main road that used to be the trail, snagging nocturnal beasts that had been out hunting when it happened. A smatter of stale blood would fly up with mud to the windscreen every so often as we climbed the narrowing flanks of slender pines, rustling through ferns as big as wolves. I put on the wipers, squirted some stuff. I let in the night air on the dash filters, and it was good and clean. 'Smells green 'ere, don't it?' said the lad, leaning his sweet face in the breeze.

As I said previous like, you can taste the colours of this place, once you've a mind.

After some rummaging, the lad was pleased to find an unopened bag of crisps in the glove compartment. 'Pickled onion!' he said, holding them up like a trophy, a lot of noise opening the packet. Jip had a sniff, but I told the lad dogs can't have onions, and he said, 'OhHHH!' like little lads do when they miss out on a treat, shoulders slumped.

'Don't mean ya can't give me a couple,' I said, and he pushed them in my mouth like medicine with his little sweaty candied fingers, grinning at the game of it.

We turned west hard to the farms, and I grew more nervous naw we were out in the barrens for miles till the dales. The light was fading fast, and I knew we'd have to use the head-lamps soon, become a pair of moving beacons seen all the county if anyone come looking for life.

'Eyes peeled,' I said to the lad, and he stared out not blink-ing, stuffing his gob. Jip licked his ears, and he didn't mind one bit. It hit me he'd not once questioned why I didn't want to meet anyone on us way, for help. I realised he was thinking we were watching for lunatics roaming, not help. He was sure frait to meet their sort again.

The sky had taken on that funny skein once more, some strange flicker of a lens put wrong on another. The stars blurred and doubled as they appeared for their shift in the fabric above, and the earth gave up a low hum. 'Like pylons again, the swooshing,' said the lad.

'Queer, eh?' I coughed, this time unable to stop, and in the end I had to hold my breath to still it. I put my foot down to get out of the creep, and soon enough we slipped over a roundabout into a few welcome amber street lamps, first past a car up the siding crashed, then the village sign for Pettingrew glinted its reflective white surface in the row.

'I know it! I know it!' said the lad then, jumping in his seat. 'It's up 'ere, the bend where the round things are, fer wheat!'

'Silos?'

'Yes! Yes! And a big black barn, a landmark!'

'Very well done, lad,' I said, smiling to myseln. I hoped to Christ his nan was alive.

We whipped the tight country bends hemmed in by brush, the road diminishing to nowt but a hacking path, and I caught the wet long grass on my cheeks through the open window, the moon coming through like a damp stain over fields.

More crop round thar than I'd imagined. An idea climbed in me that I could come back, take perhaps a couple of sacks of wheat for bread. And beets could be frozen, their tops for greens. Maybe there were seedlings in the stock rooms, for potatoes. I could stay here, I drifted, with the lad and his nan; help with the stead, if she was willing. I could leave Bill behind, start again...

We next come upon the black barn just as the lad had said, and then two great silos like alien temples in this dark rising at us over a corner.

'It's the pink one up 'ere!'

We turned into village proper, and the first cottage after the last farm was the only pink, a thatched roof over several long buildings behind the stoop. The lad was out running before I'd a chance to park, but I knew it was useless to call out. I put on the handbrake and rushed over to stop him going in, Jip already pissing up the flowers by the wall.

'Nana?' The lad was on tiptoes, hammering with the brass knocker shaped like a rabbit. 'Nana!'

I could see the desperation in him, so I peered through the bottle-end windows, but so dim it was, both inside and out. 'Tell ya what, I'll go in,' I said, told him to keep an eye on Jip, stay put.

The door was unlocked, like most places round thar, so in I went. Out of habit, I wiped my feet on the mat.

The place was proper cosy. A typical sort of set-up. An Aga in deep blue, a huge farmhouse table covered with a plastic Laura Ashley cloth like my mam favoured. The teapot was one of them pigs in waiscot and breeches, and the cups all made out as chickens and cats. On the stove, a green china plate of fresh gingerbread had been cut into fingers, with a tea cloth covering it where flies gathered.

I first found a calico cat, curled up nice on the armchair. If you didn't know better what had happened, it looked alive and all well, just snoozing. I prodded it with my pinkie, making sure, and if the stink that come off wasn't enough, there was a thin streak of blood from its ear on the cushion. I thought of Jip, running nervy in the flowers out front, and it made me retch a little. Whatever slip of love I felt for that pewr dead cat caught in my throat.

And next to it, a great ticking grandfather clock, a painted moon and sun on the face. A pretty clock, sommat I'd like in a house of my own, and the cat I'd of liked too, and in that moment I wondered on it, whether we could stay there anyways, make a life, just me and the lad and Jip. For sure naw, given the cat and the flies, they were all the rest of them dead.

I walked slow to the back of the sitting room, all floral print and wood with leaded windows out onto a yard with stables. A chestnut horse lay dead with his great feet to me in the rising moon, glimmering horseshoes recently shod. Least seventeen hands, a heavyweight, and I was sad for that, seeing a handsome big animal dead in the open.

I was reminded of sommat I'd not thought on for year. As a girl, maybe eight or nine, one Sunday morning I'd been sent to my room from goings-on in the yard. This happened when they took the sheep to slaughter, but I knew it wasn't that.

I sneaked to my window anyhow, despite best advice, and spied careful, as big Pattinson, only a lad then, tried to shoot a big bay horse to death, over and over. Three hands I didn't ken were keeping a tight circle away from the scene in disgust, for it seemed from the scraps of conversation I could make out that this neighbour, their boss, would rather see his beast put down by Pattinson than pay for the vet to come. They were muttering about it being a hunter. Gone lame jumping a ditch on a fox hunt on us land. Smoking into the steam of their breath in flat caps and body warmers, rocking on their heels like they were at a funeral already, the great black saddle between them as the altar.

Course, Pattinson couldn't kill a horse for trying, and the blessed beast kept getting up like a seven-headed demon, with more and more of its dear face blown away hanging in red chunks, throwing itseln back distressed crying like a person begging, grotesque.

With my fingers stuck in my ears, I carried on watching, stubborn little bugger I was, just like that horse, and in the end it took the three men to come hold it down whilst Pattinson slit its great heaving white throat with a knife. All thrashing in pain on the ground it was, still fighting, fighting to live, battling slick in its own blood, Pattinson's great shining forearms wet through with it as he held its beautiful head back to make it go quicker, eyes churning in its skull to the reds. That is how death is, I thought. Gasping, gasping.

When it was over, they took Pattinson to the hospital in Eversdale. The horse had bit into his shoulder, leaving deep red squares in a massive arc. Quite beautiful, really, Pattinson would say later about that scar. Like a progression of stars.

What an arsehole, my da said to me, shaking his head as they hurled the precious carcase onto a tipper, driven away for dog food. No reason he couldn't of studded it out instead. What a waste! He ran the stiff broom all quick and angry cross the yard as I held the hose over the sea of crimson that seemed to go on forever. Furious, Da was. He told me the git who owned the horse was a rich American in a big stately home up

Cresswell way. Probably ruined that, an' all! he said. Turned
out the Yank had paid Pattinson fifty quid for his dirty work,
and this disgusted my da even further. 'We might kill creatures
fer a living,' Da said to me then, 'but the way a man treats his
stock is the way a man is.'

My da must of thought he'd done his honourable best to
keep me safe, and that he failed. I heard folk saying on the
wireless he'd campaigned for me to hand myseln in, saying
they loved me with the pretty hanky to the eye, and while
I never heard it myseln, I found that reet confusing, cause he
damned well never said owt like it to my face. Or maybe he
just hated me after a while, and moved on these eleven year.

Past the sorry ald horse I slipped into the nan's barn at the
side, its cracked wooden doors tilting in the breeze. A storm
lantern hung on a hook, its bulb still burning dim.

I found them straight. The nan was in her housecoat and
wellies, a green cardigan over, like my mam would of done.
Hippy-looking, tiny silver things knotted in her hair. An older
man, flat cap, perhaps the hand. Another, younger, big and
blonde as a Mack, stethoscope at his neck, elbow gloves: the
vet they'd called in the night, his new gold wedding ring bal-
anced clean on the handle of his Gladstone bag.

And there in the straw, a beautiful grey mare, eyes gone
with flies, coat dappled white and perfect except for the black
line of blood from her ear. Her belly was swollen still, one
spindly bloodied leg of her pure white unborn foal between
her own.

This was the story of what happened here.

But then? Well. Ms Elgar, what I'm about to impart next will sound like old wives' tales, all green eggs and hogswash. But I'm telling thee, cause you've been living through this an' all, and by naw we both ken the shape o' it somewhat, do we? I keep telling myseln it's just nature evolving, cycling. But this, whatever it is, it's not any of what we can explain proper.

So, I was sat down hard on the dirt floor outside the stall to let out a sob. The scent of the stable was a comfort to me, the sweetness of manure and hay coated the death somehow.

Then I heard it. A weir sound like chewing. Like them maggots on the dead, but so loud. Slobbering, licking.

Coming from the next stall.

A pile of tack hung on a line between. Bridles, reins, girths. A pair of stirrups swayed, almost imperceptibly, on their black leather straps. A saddle on the post, I watched its pommel jump, just a little bit, over and over. The D-ring flapping, catching the wood. A tiny quiet tap, tap, tap-tap.

I slid my back up the wall, silent as I could. Praying the lad would stay off. I could hear Jip in the bushes. I made a single click of the tongue, ever so slight. Heard him still where he was.

I got to the edge of that stall. It sounded like an animal feeding, maybe a pig? But such a stench, and that strange glub-bing in my ears once more.

The air turned thick and electric.

Careful, woman, I thought. A quick glance. I pulled out my knife, slow and sure. Held my arm cross my breast. Lining my head with the stall post, I readied to turn, look. Make myseln known.

Over the way, just opposite, a great mirror was leant against the wall, I suppose abandoned from the house. Cracked cross its corners, foxed to all hell.

There, in the reflection, stood a black shape guzzling, suckling prey. On two legs, kneading the death, long earthen claws, teats dribbling. Tongue and teeth soil, snarling. Gorging on the rot of this land.

A bright iron eye in the mirror come open, finding mine.

And I know this is going to sound mad, but. Well.

It had my face.

It had my focking face.

Sudden, the chewing stopped.

Listening.

The lad appeared in the corner of my vision, an expectant figure with Jip on the threshold, holding the tray of biscuits. Maybe I was screaming.

I scrambled from the ground, grabbed him by the arm running, dragged him to the motor. Jip started up barking. I fumbled the keys, got the door open, knife in hand. But a knife was useless against what I'd just seen. 'In!' I screamed, terrifying the lad. Christ, I thought we'd die!

He glanced back to the stable, his little face drained. 'What's —' he said.

The motor went first time. Foot to the floor, down the winding road to the coast. 'Don't bloody look back,' I said, wet through with panic.

And he buried his face in Jip's fur and gave out a single cry.

We flew down that road away from the land, a new darkening around us, a damp fog fallen sudden, filled with whispers and animal screams. I rolled up the windows, and we kept going, kept going. For sure there was nowt left for us in the barrens.

After a while, the fog cleared and we gradually saw the stars, and my heart slowed, and I left off glancing in the mirror, longing for the sea and the safety of buildings. And there was sudden a change in the land, as if we'd crossed some unseen boundary to us own world once more.

The lad's voice strained in the quiet of the motor and the land. 'What d'ya reckon?'

I thought about what to say, what he was asking after. The horror of the stable stuck to us in fragments, a glimpse of us ends. I sniffed. 'I reckon yer nan got rescued and is waiting fer ya somewhere safe.'

'Reckon?' he said, letting me take his mind off with that thin shred of hope. He was able to let hisseln be protected.

'I do, aye,' I said. My hands felt tight on the steering wheel, full of nerves. Jip was huddled on the floor sticking his wet nose on the back of my ankles. Sommat in me gave way with it, and I swerved off and stopped the motor. We sat for a minute in the gloom on that road, the only sound the ticking of the cooling engine and Jip's little whimpers. I felt so weak.

'What?' said the lad, quite forceful.

'I don't know what to do!' I said, gripping the wheel to steady myseln. The panic was sharpening my voice. I didn't understand my own emotions. 'I don't know where to bloody take us! To be free of it all!' Was I shouting?

I looked to the lad for answers, and found him calm, considering. He put his hand on the wheel next to mine, rocking it a little in a game. 'Let's go back to Bill, fore he misses us, yeah, Glory?' he said, quite normal like, with a shrug of a lad who knew to move on once there was nowt left for him in a place. Course, that's how I read it then. A clever lad.

You can say why not just keep on going and going the other way, but us only real option was to get to the hotel in the growing night, with all the food and locked doors, a roof over us heads with the only man standing to keep watch, than to flee into the wilds with nowt but the remainder of a seaside kiosk to rely on and whatever that was come gorging at us backs.

That weir circle of brids with the wings all bit.

'You can have a go in that pool when we get back,' I said, turning the ignition again, and the lad nodded, somewhat wan. Cold comfort, I suppose, after what he'd been hoping, but he must of understood it was suicide to go poking about empty houses in the dark with no plan.

So, there I was, driving back to Bill once again, chancing playing focking happy families with The Devil O' Th' Moor. That homing set in me deep. The same that had taken me first light after to Bellemere.

'Tomorrow, we'll find a better place,' I said, more to myseln than the lad. One night, only one night, I told myseln, to get through the horror, as we headed into that faded light between wolf and dog.

'I like the beach anyways. And the pier,' said the lad, and we chomped on handfuls of the biscuits with the worst of the land behind us, quelling us terror. The stars come up clean in front over the sea, and nowt seemed so nightmarish as it had back thar. 'She must of known we was coming, me nan,' said the lad finally, through sugary biscuit.

'Why ya say that?'

'Allays makes the Grasmere biscuits special when,' he said.

'Oh,' I said, trying to be casual about it, head filled with the beast in the mirror. The night spread falcon quick, and once we got out from the roundabout, it was too dim to drive without headlamps. I couldn't decide what to do. It was as if the lad was attuned to me by then, and he answered my thoughts. 'This is a military vehicle, int it?'

'Aye, it is.'

'It'll have them special orange military lights, fer driving, so nobody can see us. They call 'em blackout lights.'

'Where did ya learn that?'

'Off telly.' He sighed, maybe remembering another time he'd been stuck in front of the box as a distraction or protection, some incident with his mam that couldn't of been great. 'I like the army stuff, see, and motors.' He studied the steering wheel carefully, moving his tongue about in his cheeks with concentration. 'Look fer a thing wi' a little cross symbol o'er it.'

I looked down and it was so obvious. Right there, a black switch by the wheel with a sticker over it, BLACKOUT LIGHTS.

I tried a laugh. 'Reckon that's it?'

'I reckon, aye,' he said sarcastic with a grin – smart kid – and we laughed too hard as the two tiny glowing streams of orange come out in front, just enough to drive with through the trees, and in that way, my mind went over and over that calico cat and the clock with the moon and the stars. A flash of the horror, the suckling. How it had stopped dead, and listened.

Dog, like the verb, not the noun.

And so, I pushed on quick away, all the while mithering what to say to Bill. 'Pretend we went looking fer grub, yeah?' I said as we parked up at The Diana once more. The sky peered through the windscreen from over the sea. The lad went quiet for a time, screwing up his fists, and we both sat waiting for his permission.

In the end, he said, 'No worries,' like an adult might, and we got out of the motor.

There was a hush in the car park as we trod quick to the glass lift indoors. The clouds were ash with a cobalt of the insides of flames, stars scratched with the strangeness of speeding colours. And that sky reminded me of what Bill had said that first morning about beauty and dying.

I mean, he hadn't quite said it; that was Bill's way, like with his notebooks. But the sentiment sudden hit me anew. For Bill, death and beauty were entwined. And naw we were surrounded, by all of it, all, all, all!

I looked down at my charge; pinks and greens skimmed reflections in the pools of his young eyes. And I scried all what Bill had done and would do, naw the world was his alone.

The lad stared up at me with his red sugar mouth, careful studying my face. 'I'll look after ya, Glory,' he said, strident and calm. And it struck me he'd probably said that often to his mam in times of desperation.

A tear seeped his lashes as we rose to Penthouse 2, little sticky fingers wrapped ginger round mine, alone and tired. I suppose he was fed up with it an' all.

Despite all feelings brimming, all prospects, all possible coming hells, we languished together in that rising box with the dying sky, and the fleeting peace of his child's oath.

All that beauty, makes you want to die.

'THE DIANA'

Gelatin silver print, mounted on board

160 cm × 250 cm

Bill had a proper surprise waiting for us when we arrived back at the suite. Thoroughly bored, and sensing his crown slipping, he'd got off his imaginary throne and raided the hotel kitchen. Steak and chips three times, all laid out on the posh table with high-backed chairs and smelly candles in them holders, lit and guttering like magic, the feast naw quite cold. I felt a bit guilty for doubting him, but my hackles were up just like Jip's. The air was blue. 'You've been busy!' I managed, still full from the Grasmere biscuits, chilly with fright.

'It were better an hour back!' he said, acid like, sitting down heavy with a cigarette sideways to the table, skinny legs crossed, tapping. I couldn't read him. I suppose being locked in a glass case for years on end must destroy the last fibre of body language in a person. But I never could read Bill. Not really.

He'd hauled up great catering tubs of coleslaw and sachets of ketchup, and even cooked a steak for Jip, garnished with fried eggs on a silver banqueting platter like you'd get at a wedding. Jip took to shivering with excitement when Bill put his nose to it, and the lad just kept on saying, 'Wowsers, wowsers!'

We sent the lad off to wash his face and hands, as if we were a real little family having a normal tea on holiday, and me and Bill sat either end of this great posh table like Lord and Lady Muck, watching Jip gobbling the steak for want of a conversation.

There was, course, a hole where the story of the thing in the stable should of gone. But that story felt like mine alone. It could of set Bill off sommat chronic.

I drank hard and deep, trying to forget. We were safe for the night, away from the land. It was all I could hold onto.

But there was naw an awkward, dangerous sense to Bill, since he'd combed flat his hair and got on some farcy gold embroidered silk pyjamas. Cause he looked so very much more like his old self. Handsome, sharp. Dark. Alive, just like he'd said.

Bill smiled to hisseln as he surveyed what he'd laid on. It was a vain, smug look I'd forgotten till then, as if he was plotting, choosing his next move, but three moves along. He was annoyed, sure, but he'd clearly decided to take the game in a different direction. I mean, with Bill, there's always a bloody game.

He held up a scrap of paper, a finale of some kind, torn from the hotel stationery, and he read aloud what was on it, written in a swirly hand, '*Dear Room Service, gone for a late-night swim in the bay. Please leave champagne on table, tip forthcoming. Ta!*' He cackled. 'Tip forthcoming!' He was very tickled with the last occupants' note, laying it down next to his plate like a precious keepsake. He started nipping at a chip with his blackened fangs, still grinning. I watched him, careful like. 'Good job they went out fer that swim, else you'd hafta do some reet cleanin' up!'

Cut your finger, pull a tooth, it bleeds so much you think it'll never stop. So you have to understand, Ms Elgar, just how much blood there'd been, with Bill. We were stained with it, by the end. It got so I cared more about the mess than anything else. Soaps by the sink fingered a pale foamed red. Car handles rusted, and sticky. Flies in the corners of rooms. Pillowcases smeared with nosebleeds, bites, thrown over heads, parts removed and fondled. Spoons and strings and old towels stuffed down the backs of chairs till maggots ate their way through the covers. Tins and cups hid with relics in the sideboard, plastic carrier bags burst under the sink.

Aye, I'd hafta do some reet cleanin' up a'ight, I was thinking to myseln. Whilst he played King of the Castle.

Bill stared back heavy at me awhile, the smile fading when I never joined the mirth, and he lit another cigarette. 'Took up smoking while we was off?' I tried.

He ignored me. Smoking, wasn't he. Why should he waste his breath answering? 'Where d'ya go, Glore, after beach? I were watching yous walk up, then ya took motor off.' His eyes said the rest about deceit and betrayal.

I swallowed my drink, felt the truth go down. 'We went looking fer scran. The lad'd this idea we'd go up big new supermarket he knew, fore the freezers might go off.' I tried to say it as easy as that. Wriggling I was, in my chair.

'I see,' said Bill, face still as a sphinx. 'And yet, no fockin' food.' He made a big show of peering about us for shopping, lifting the tablecloth an' all.

'We only went and got lost!' I was too loud, and laughed it off gay as I could, brushing the Grasmere crumbs off my trousers. 'Hafta try again tomorrow.'

'I see,' said Bill again, this time with an edge, narrowing them animal eyes. 'But look at all this, you stupid fockin' bitch,' he spat, leaning in. 'I already provided fer us.' The room was instantly heavy with his rage, and I waited for it to sink.

That's what you do, Glore, when he does this, I heard myseln advise. Wait, then change the subject. Always a game. 'Oi, let's open that pop then,' I finally managed, a ringing in my ears, nodding to the champagne left by the ill-fated room service.

Look, I bloody well needed a drink, right? All this talk had given me flashbacks to this one mite of a lass, Maggie I think her name was, her little mind going over and over in them clear blue eyes, a doll blinking, trying to make sense of it all.

When I lie in bed of a night, things like that come to me as ghosts. The feeling of rubbing my nervous thumb down them sharp-edged buckles of her cherry-red shoes as I chucked them full of stones in the lake up Cresswell, where the mud washes the rusted diamond dust between your toes. The same cherry red of the lipstick on the lad's slag of a mam.

Bill swooped up from his chair, all suave and casual in them dumb pyjamas, and he got the bottle open flat and poured without any cheers, and we both threw it back like a remedy, twice, three times, staring at the ceiling, where the shadows had come crawling from nowhere. And my thoughts turned to the legend of the Black Dog, and the thing in the mirror at the farm.

But then, in the warm of the room with no sky or land staring back hissing, I got to thinking that all I'd seen in Pettingrew was my own reflection somehow distorted in the dim with a beast, some animal left dying in the stable. I settled myseln to this explanation.

I had to.

Teeth marks. Not animal.

By the time the lad come back all cleaned and combed in a huge pink towelling robe, Bill and me were loose enough to be sipping the wine nicely, having exchanged a few pleasantries about the room and the facilities, much like you might with a depressed ald uncle in the hallway before leaving a family do.

Could it work out with Bill if I kept calm, if he kept calm? A lot of years had gone by since, and I'd changed, had I? So why couldn't Bill of? *Stupid fockin' bitch*, he'd said, but wasn't that always his way with harsh talk? Almost affectionate, was it? Though I was racking my brains to remember if it was before. He must of been given lots of therapy and that. Wasn't it part of the conditions to be admitted to Bellemere?

But then my stomach was sour with them little cherry-red shoes.

The lad grinned. 'Look at dog!' he said, pointing, bringing me out of my stupor. Jip was on the sofa, legs splayed, tongue hanging, totally wasted from the last terrible days.

'Like a pup that's just had steak and eggs!' said Bill with a wink to the lad, and they giggled together in their robes. A sigh left my body, that maybe it wasn't so bad as all that, things considered, to be left at the end of the world with my husband and a nice little lad.

We tucked in heartily then, for however I'm holding my
guard I can always eat. Seemed the lad was the same, and soon
we were picking us teeth with the little wood sticks Bill had
brung up from the restaurant – orange sticks, he called them,
which tickled the lad – and Bill pulled out a few chocolate
biscuits in little plastic packs from his pockets, a bit melted
but perfectly good, and he said little comments in the lad's ear
while we ate them, not about much, just whether he'd enjoyed
the seaside, and did he like his dinner, and the lad kicked his
little legs on the chair with pleasure of all the attention he was
getting. 'I'm absolutely stuffed!' he said finally, sticking out his
belly, and I could see he'd fallen for Bill cause he was showing
off, almost flirting like children do. So relaxed he was, so open
and happy, like he'd been given a new path in life and could
leave his slag of a mam behind with the dead village and the
sound, and naw we could go on, living here in this palace with
all the food we could eat, forever and ever.

Bill leaned into his sweet face and stared vicious. My heart
lurched. 'Enjoy it while it lasts,' he muttered, sitting back to
light a cigarette.

The lad giggled a bit, and looked to me, unsure of Bill's
joke.

'He's not wrong, lad; best we eat as much as possible
tonight. Tomorrow, we'll set out again!' I said, sunny as you
like, and I found him a can of pop from the minibar.

'And go where exactly, Glory?' Bill said, flat and dull and
hard like a done knife, the spiteful edge in his voice grating,
and the lad, he kicked his legs a little quicker, and them moles
in his skin had come up black in the guttering candlelight as

his pewr brain searched for sommat social to say to stop it all being anything but damned nice and good and happy between us, sucking in the pop like a cure for it, just as me and Bill had done with the bubbly, and the air seemed to tingle with fright.

I found the doofer for the telly and got on one of them automatic radio channels that just plays music with no talking on a loop. There was a silly one full of musical show numbers, and Bill's cloud passed with the tiniest smile under his smoke, and he said, 'Thar, leave that on!' He hadn't heard music for ages, I suppose.

The lad got up on his chair and started larking about all elbows to the tune. It was sommat brassy and jolly, and soon enough we were all dancing about on the furniture, making faces in the mirrors, Jip barking and barking, tail wagging, in a stupor of glee, though throwing a quick growl over one shoulder whenever Bill come too close spinning the lad around and around, the robe naw forgotten, the lad in his trunks, bare-chested and giddy, and I caught Bill's long hands running the pebbled little spine of his dear back as he threw him about.

I went to draw the velvet curtains, make it cosy for us. And far out where the grey met the black of the sky, a row of amber lights naw glared.

So, that line we'd caught on the sea, me and the lad, it was a ship after all.

I said nowt on it, pulling the curtains tight so out there wouldn't spy the lights from the window. But it felt too late. They'd of seen the only light go on for miles.

Well, I said to myseln. If me and Bill's going down, if they come in the night, let's get fockin' bladdered. There were six or seven bottles of expensive-looking red wine on the side, so me and Bill, we took to one each, him shoving the corks in with a knife, us guzzling from the necks, while the lad kept shovelling in handfuls of coleslaw and chocolates one after the next, smeared face and shining eyes. He raced off, saying, 'Come on, come on!' and he showed us the people who'd been staying there had all these posh clothes and feathered scarves, as if they were in a musical too, and we laughed a lot then, big belly laughs, trying on all the clothes, Bill in a red kimono, me in a bow tie, the lad in a great hat and feathers, me drunk as a fiddler's bitch, all jumping about on the massive bed as hard as we could, laughing, laughing, and the lad, he said to me at some point, 'I've never 'ad such a good time in all me life!'

When we run out of puff, we sat there on the bed, the three of us legs out in front like rag dolls under the piles of feathers and sparkles, huffing with excitement, and I thought on the rich Yank with the shot horse and the big stately home. I mean, we had to go somewhere. Staying in the hotel could be a danger to us freedom, with the ship coming in, and I suppose in the warmth of that magical moment, I didn't feel like giving up Bill.

'I wanna tell yous sommat,' I started, trying to quell the panic in my voice. 'The pair o' yous.' I looked round like I was going to do a conjuring trick, and they were enthralled. It was the glittering lights and colours, and the candles, or maybe the way Jip was lying all content and fat on the pillows. But for that moment we were together, and I was relieved the lad was on that side of it. For Bill used to say there were us two, then everyone else. How nobody else was real.

'The three o' us,' said Bill. He smiled and touched my hand. It scared me, what he meant. I wanted to ask, but I couldn't, could I? With the lad there.

I let it go. Blurted my idea out loud. What a daft caw. 'There's this big stately home. In the middle of nowhere. Used to be a nunnery.'

'Where at?' Bill said, picking at his teeth.

'Far off, Cresswell way,' I said. 'Ya need to know to head there, else you'd drive past.'

'What's a nonerish?' said the lad.

'Cresswell?' Bill said, incredulous. 'That's a long ways off, int it? How'd we get thar then?'

'Driving. Got a full tank in the back.' I looked to the lad. 'It's a faraway place on the coast t'other side, where nuns live, to be alone.' Bill was just staring, thinking. 'Maybe we could gather up any stock still alive ont land, make a start of it? There's a walled pasture, some gardens.'

'No bloody way,' Bill said finally, scoffing into his chest.

'Why?' said the lad. 'Sounds good.'

'Fockin' stupid idea,' said Bill. 'What if they see us? I mean, first thing army's gonna do is commandeer all them big places round abouts, setting up bases, making them field hospitals and that. Like they did in the wars. Nay. Dumb, dumb, dumb!'

'It's true, tha',' the lad said. 'I seen it on telly. They do tha', Glore.'

'Dumb ald Glory!' said Bill, laughing, nudging the lad with a sharp elbow.

The lad suddenly started up laughing too, open-mouthed, tittering like he was acting it all out to please Bill. 'Yeah, dumb ald fat Glory! Stupid bitch!' the lad yelled, smiling. But then he caught my eye, knew he'd gone too far. Bill took a moment to enjoy my pain, and the three of us sat there a minute in the misery.

It hurt me, no doubt. The lad saw it in my face, some shadow passed over, and he flinched, expecting me to thump him one I suppose, eyelashes fluttering. But I just buttoned my lip and looked on him. Was this the way it was naw? The laddie and Bill turning on me, while I tried to save us all? I couldn't stomach it.

When he was satisfied the insult had taken hold, Bill took up his fags like an instrument. 'No need fer that talk, laddie.'

The lad murmured, studying his hands. He'd meant to impress him. 'Sorry, Glore.'

I didn't have the energy. 'They probably took it over by naw when ya see it like that.'

'None of that, see, Glore? Stay put. Fer the best.' Bill raised his arms to present the room as his case. 'Even if they did come, take 'em ages to find us, and that scran downstairs, enough for a year!'

All the luxury? I had to agree, it wasn't half bad. Bill threw me a leaflet about the hotel he'd got from the desk. 'And read that. Solar power. Ont roof. Even if the power goes down, we'd be grand. No way we're leaving. We hit the bloody jackpot!'

I looked over the leaflet, all the smiling folk in their posh rooms. A smile must of crept onto my lips an' all, cause the air changed like after rain as they both settled to it.

Bill wasn't thinking long-term. He didn't understand how it was inland, did he? Then there was them pills he'd been on eleven year, no longer going in his system. I wondered vaguely if I could get me and the lad out for a while, let them in the ship find Bill. I'd do that in the morning, I remember thinking. We'll get away till they've been. But it was such a faint notion I could hardly keep it in my head, what with all the booze and emotion I was suffering with.

We were in Bill's house naw. To hell with it all, in that moment I loved the thought of Bill. And so, I convinced myseln all was well.

'Can we dance, like?' said the lad then, rubbing his noggin. 'All getting a bit serious like fer me in 'ere!'

Bill let out a ha, such an old soul was the lad. Just his type.

I turned up the music and got off the bed, dancing about. Silly mare. Cause if I'd said nowt about it, me and the lad could of fled easy to Cresswell early doors if we needed to, and Bill wouldn't of known a thing.

Despite my smiles, at some point last night I mithered on what punishment would await, if them on that ship would come in the night to find us while we slept. Would they put us down on the spot, judging by what we'd seen at pier?

At some point last night, I stopped thinking.

And we danced.

At some point last night, I must of put the lad in the little bed in the back, cause I know I said nighty-night and tucked the covers round, and Jip went on the bed with him, all sleepy and content.

I know some juncture I was naked on the floor, and Bill was on me looking like old Bill reborn, his body hot on mine, and there was that feeling of desire and wanting, rolling that tide of Bill Gleason deep as hell and perfect; perfect you are, he said, and I loved him and his rotten open mouth and the black of it, and his face the way it had aged and browned like leather, a book of secrets I used to read, over and over again.

I must of said I loved him, and he said, *Oh Glore*, like I was sorrowful mistaken. And the last thing I can tell you is I was gazing in his feral eye looking for answers, and I was lying in the bed, and thinking we were happy. Aye, we were happy, and it was going to be beautiful, somehow in that light, like a dream I never let myseln have. 'Just you and me at the end of the world,' he whispered, and that worried me, and I've the memory I made him promise to leave the lad out of it, begging I was, just leave him be and have me instead, have me. And he took my wrists hard in his fingers and kissed my hands, but he never promised.

I was wasted and tired, and I hadn't been intimate with a man in all that while away. I just wanted to believe in some good after all the bad we'd endured to be together in that place. That poor judgement, or my strange moral code, I'm not sure what you'd call it, but it has sommat to do with the beginning of him and me, how he'd formed me, how he'd brung me into his fold.

It's funny. I only recall it naw talking to you, the dream I had last night, so vivid in the senses. The particular way the red earth turned with the spade, how together we tucked her in the dark of the shallow, black as Bill's eyes as he tore the soft white throats of the lambs.

Hold on, Glore! Bill said.

And I gripped the folded pink blanket tight in my arms.

I'd held that same blanket the morning we buried Cheryl Ann in that broken church with the weeds in Bill's town I despised so very much. See, in my dream, it was us daughter we were burying, and not in that place, but in the low field at Clark Farm with my nan and the brids and the big orange fox, and all the flowers that come up in the fallow.

So, I was quite content when I woke this morning in the hotel, till I got my eyes open and the hangover come in like a dump. The sun had already reached the windows of the bedroom cross the sea, pale and glaring. I found myseln wrapped in the soft hotel sheets, a feather scarf in that unnatural neon pink arranged cross my head on the pillow. There was an empty bottle of vodka rolling about in the covers like a ship in a storm, and I didn't remember having any of it.

It disturbed me I recalled a whimpering sound some time off, scratching, being half aware of it hours ago. I looked around for Jip, but not seeing him, I gave a soft whistle to come bye.

He darted from nowhere onto the bed; a gripper he is, but dipped quick under the covers and there rested, quivering against my bare legs, heavy as lead.

'Bill?' I said, thinking we must of slept together in the same bed, but I called softly as to not wake the lad. I reasoned Jip must of been frait of us antics last night. He probably didn't remember me and Bill in the bed together before naw, and it must of looked violent and abusive to him. Like many other times. I went to pat his head to calm him under the sheets, but he growled.

250 · CATE BAUM

The room turned dim and grey. My body reacting to an alarm my mind had forgotten all about. That singular breed of quiet. Aye, a memory kicked in me hard. I flung back the covers and threw on a shirt. 'Bill?' I shouted, checking the bathrooms. Jip stayed put, trembling. 'No, please no,' I whispered, stumbling about the rooms, all decadence deformed, faces in the marble snarling, the gold surfaces distorted mirrors, watching. The silence was too loud. I thought of that silence from before. I couldn't hear myseln think.

I dashed to the lad's room, but all that was there was a bundle of sheets made up like a small body. A smear of chocolate on the pillow. 'Where ya at, lad?' I hollered jagged, skidding from room to room, shuddering with the fragments of joy from last night naw splintering my insides.

I forced myseln to stand still for a moment, listening, thinking, reasoning with myseln, blood beating wild in my ears. They'd probably gone for breakfast, maybe a surprise for me still sleeping, chatting merrily in the hotel kitchen, the lad swinging his legs on the counter eating crackers or sommat while Bill fried the eggs. Or maybe they'd gone for a swim in that pool the lad so wanted to try out.

Head banging, that's when I noticed the float of the white curtain at the mirror, calling to me, a sea breeze carrying it in, a ghost at the door. Course, they were on the balcony! I laughed, fancy being that daft, I told myseln, to forget about the great balcony this penthouse has out to sea! They couldn't hear me from out there, was all!

Too cheerful, I strode over, hoping to be pleased to discover their hiding place, expecting the pair of newly acquainted friends to be languishing on the posh bamboo deckchairs looking out to the water through the glass balustrades, as if they were born to it. I pulled back the thin curtain. On the gauze, a small handprint in red. My fingers come away wet.

The lad had done well. Must of struck hard and up, the left side in the soft. Just how I taught him. I was almost proud when I saw it.

Bill was slung on the floor of the balcony. The blood was pooled in the crook of his arm, between his fingers thick as wine, robe soaked gristle pink. My knife's handle shone with the sea's reflection, halfway stuck, jolting with each beat of his heart like a sail. A stab wound will do that. Leaves you weak as a lamb. He squinted at me through the weir light. Muttered. 'About fockin' time.'

Sommat keen and beast-like kept me poised, alert, while the whole world belted infinities about us. I kept to the threshold. 'Where's us lad?'

'Gan.' Bill grasped at thinning hair, grinding teeth. 'Run down beach.' Wheezing. 'Spied him wi' some long'un in a black coat.' He coughed with the effort of speaking, a fist at the blade in his flank.

'Some long'un? Thar's nobody left, Bill.' Jip was nosing the curtain, whining.

Bill shrugged best he could. 'S'pose thar's some still rattling abouts.'

'This fella, he could be…' What? I thought, worse than us? But see, I'd had conversations with Bill over the years where he's come in early doors and bare lied to me about his evening's event. I reckoned he was doing it naw, even in this rotten state.

My whole body slunk away from me. The lad would only of wet Bill if he was shit-scared and sure to die.

That's that then, I thought. The lad is dead.

I was choked with the grief of it. 'What d'ya do to 'im, eh?'

And I felt the words echoing, echoing back at me, from past times.

Like when I slipped out with Bill's keys in my fist that night from the bathroom, freezing in slippers. Peered through the dim truck window. Saw for myseln what Bill Gleason was. Like when I got in to find half the towels from the airing cupboard dumped in the washing machine, soaked in black blood. Like when he smacked me in the mouth when I was expecting. Like when that little lass was shivering, pissed herseln, bit him like a fox. And when I come in after, seeing them bed sheets, all he had to say for hisseln was, *Get truck round*.

'Wha'?' was all Bill said naw, eyes moving rheumy in the back of his head. In dying, the arrogance prospered in him.

It all come rushing then, infestations I'd harboured years, scratching at the walls of me. The death, the loneliness, endless possibilities I'd recklessly abandoned, all to play demons with this incubus! And naw he'd destroyed the one chance I might of had for salvation. 'Don't tell me nowt, Bill, fer I ken the lad!' I shrieked.

He smiled a little, mocking. Course, in his dim view, I'd turned into a nag by raising my voice. But I saw some confession in that smile. His tongue shook in streaked cheeks. '*Ken* 'im? Nay, nay.' He reached out a hand to me, beckoning, pacifying. I saw the knife was a part of him naw, and I reckon we both knew if I touched it, he'd die right off. A tide of love swelled in me. Only, it wasn't for Bill.

'Glore,' he whispered. I gazed on the sorrowful sight. It would be a long death. Exhausted, I got down next to him, lay in the hot blood. I suppose I wanted to watch. And he wanted me to.

Close up, Bill's eyes were glossy with pain, like a rabbit when you find them in the wire nare don-fer. We lay there for a while, facing each other, with the sound of Bill's laboured breath and the rumbling sea below. Oh, and the stink of adrenalin, and iron, like the killing floor of an Easter. 'Are you frait to die, Bill Gleason?' I whispered, searching his face for humanity.

Haggard skin, wet leather, distorted in a smirk. He rested a hand, cold and wet, on my cheek. He said it so low. 'You and me, at the end of the world.'

Slid his fingers round my neck. Squeezed.

First, I took it as sommat sexual, seductive. And so I let him, for a bit. But when Bill took to grinding his jaw like a loose trap, all broken and rotted, the horror bled in fast. I tried to tear his hand from my neck, but even in that state, Bill was exceptionally strong when it come to killing.

He meant for us to die together.

You and me, at the end of the world.

As the realisation flooded me, I kept playing out how he must of raped and killed the lad in one of the hotel rooms, or down beach in the late moon, leaving the tide to take the mite's broken body off. And I'd gone and slept through the lot. I deserved to die, I was after thinking. I should let him. And I closed my eyes to the three scars of sun.

But survival kicks in hard with me, cause next thing I'm clawing at my throat, blood in my eyes, dragging nails cross Bill's face. He just watched me, calm and tender as I struggled, his tongue flicking, tasting it all. 'Remember, Glore, before?' he gasped, pressing my neck, studying me, eyes glittering with the taste he'd had of the lad, the violence between them, or me, or all of it, and 'before' wasn't the just gone night.

Was I really such a victim? I'd never loved this monster. I'd only ever joined him enthusiastically in not loving me.

He must of seen sommat pass in my eyes, cause then Bill Gleason pressed harder.

Time sighed, and my mind wandered back to Bellemere, to that big pink bastard Clive. And so, I bent my knee between us, and I pushed on that knife handle just as Bill had then, and the blade slid easy deep, scraping bone and vein to the bolster, and his darkness poured out.

Bill let go his grip of me, squirming in his own mess. He was only focking grinning. Reet high on agony, awed by the sheer gall on me.

He was almost turned on.

Well, aye. The word swam from the depth of me as a curse, that word Bill had used at Bellemere, and out my lips in a growl. 'Nonce.'

I studied him after, for quite some time, sat back on my knees; the curious shank of him fleshy pale at the blade as if the blood refused to stay in this devil of a man, spilling off the edge of the balcony to the rocks far below. I'd a panicked notion he'd pushed the lad over, but when I peered down, there was only a tiny smatter of Bill's blood on the lime, and dead gulls smudged like pencil marks.

I lifted my face to the sky, took in the whiteness of the sun, and the roar of clean water hissing at the land. At its dirt, and savage secrets, and burned-away lives. And us.

And still, the line of the ship, blackened and frayed through the thickening fret.

When I looked back to Bill, he was curled to one side like a child, eyes naw shut, a thin trail of brown blood trickling from one ear. I remembered one of the kiddies' mams saying that Bill should be put to death, so he'd die understanding his actions.

But Bill never understood shit.

I stepped in from that balcony, away from Bill, and I locked the door with the key, three times quick, a final clickclick-click, and I flipped up the bolts on the frames hard, rage pushing into my thumbs, and I rammed the electric shutters down with the button on the wall.

My thoughts were only with the lad naw, his dear face smiling up all bright and knowing. His little head, worried and hot, asleep all wrapped round Jip. The sugar on his lips, his brave tears, and the way he'd make the best of it all the way round. See, it was the first time I'd let myseln get close to a child, and I'd grown to care for him. Jesus, I thought. He could of been my salvation!

'What have ya done?' I murmured over and over, shivering with the pain of it, not sure who I was talking to, myseln or to Bill. The land.

Jip come low from the bed, sniffing at the bloody door, took to whining, scratching about. A rattle started up with the breeze on the shutter. A phantom in chains come haunting, it took the shape of Bill, fifteen floors and the height of the cliff to the ground. 'Come naw, Glore, love,' I was after hearing him murmur ghostly through the gale, imagining his face pressed to the metal, beady raptor eyes peering through slits to find me.

I drew cross the curtains, remembering all the times I'd shut out Bill's acts previous: locked a door, wrapped a blanket, bleached a floor, burned a suit, told a lie. And like that, in the lonely murk of that hotel suite, I turned the music to some classical thing so I couldn't hear the calling no more. So I couldn't hear as I reasoned with myseln on his behalf.

I loved him, see.

Me and Jip went back to bed for a while. Bloody, exhausted. To empty of the grief; to make out it was Wednesday last, before the sound from Morton Hill, the little lad, and Bill. As if it was how it used to be, after. Before.

We must of slept hard, Jip and me, cause when I woke again, the day was half done, and I'd dreamt that we were on the beach again with the lad, just in images, all still, and the sky in my dream was so very blue. But the images had threaded into days with other little lads, and I woke up coughing in the light, and for the first time I realised I dream in colour.

By then, the room was silent.

'HELFOLD STONE'

Gelatin silver print, mounted on board

160 cm × 250 cm

All and country called it Clark Farm, by way of us family name, but the stead's title on the deed is Helfold, built on sacred ground settled by invaders from the North, named for the carving of the goddess Hel, hewn on a standing stone in the far pasture.

Aye, well, Erskine Elgar, The American Artist. You understand the nature of story and its calumny. That this ancient carving should be on my farm.

We're all told the tale coming up: that Hel means 'to run to the dead'. In Valhalla, the Norse hall of the slain, she spirits children to the underworld for Odin, the god of wisdom, death and frenzy. On the carving, she dances naked with a black wolf, chasing the sun.

When I was a girl, I'd sit a long time at the helstone, dawn a shining liquid poured into the budding trees, the gentle sounds of the heft brung in to graze the new warmth. The quiet ''ow-do's on the flat air of my da's shepherds, pink-faced lads much younger than you'd probably expect, a low slape or two winding their legs. A thousand-year procession, a part of the ever.

Here, the soil runs quick through us veins, and heads us out to the sunrise whither we want it or not, driven by some godly force bigger than any of us can imagine – sommat to do with us heritage, or what's ours by rite. And so, we go out, deeper and nare lost as the flocks of a snowy night, cause we're happy there in the cold and the mud just staring at the rolling sky, watching the storms come over, wrinkling the stars. Like that, we're hefted to the land, and there's nowt to be said more about it.

And so, the world goes on.

There was one time as I watched the flock come in, when from the sparse knot of trees to the north appeared a huge red fox sniffing, sensing difference in the day. Got close, he did, great golden eyes flashing, nose flicking, fur in light like fire; twitching, burning, a beauty in his wildness.

And for a moment in the still, we reached a brave understanding. I opened my hand flat, a greeting. But he smelled the civilisation on me, instinct kicked curiosity, growled a warning, and bolted back to wood.

To this day, it makes me sad. Why did I open my hand?

Trust me when I say I wept a good while in the shower after washing Jip with some farcy shampoo, an idea in my head to wash off the stink of what had occurred. It was my doing with the lad, was it? Scolding myseln, Jip whining in the water. And there in that hotel shower, I convinced myseln I'd wanted it to happen, that I'd used the lad to find Bill's truth, to see if I could stand it and yet be with him again.

My bones heaved with the familiar weight of after. Between, in the sinews, was sharp and tight, lungs stiff and fat, cheeks all thin with sorrow. I was to carry this again.

Jip was clear depressed with the lad gone, giving a shudder naw and then as I towelled him. I wondered if he'd seen the whole damned thing and was suffering from it, or else sick like the other animals that had died. I reckon he remembers the kids he'd played with before, and the lad was yet another I'd taken from him.

When I went to the room to find clothes, I saw the lad had left me some shells and a feather on the bedside table, like a lover might leave an extravagant gift. *All that beauty.* The sand from the shells glittered in the light that crept through the gaps in the blinds, a pure white like church that catches and reflects everything in colours and strange shapes through glass and mirrors as one great fake ocean of shadow on the walls. It tormented me, calling in brightness like that, and so I opened the drawer and scooped the whole mess inside, too much reminded of when the lad had asked me about the little kiddies on that damned newspaper clipping sticking out my drawer, and he was naw one of them, and it was all my doing. He'd asked me was I a witch, the lad. Was I the Black Dog? I never did give a straight answer.

My hands trembled as I called Jip to heel. I'd started coughing regular, like that Rob from Morton Hill. Didn't bode. I had to get some grub in me, think about what to do next. It seemed at first useless to search for the lad, knowing how well Bill could hide his prey. But naw, just maybe at the end of the world, he hadn't been so careful.

For some time, we went round trying the doors of the other rooms, up and down the empty corridors with that terrible jazz playing gently in the corridors like everything was lovely. But all the doors were locked, a stink rising with what was behind.

With heaving dread, I remembered the pool in the basement.

Down in the lift, I peered out every floor, looking for any sign Bill had been there, but found none. A woman lay rotting in diamante earrings. Another, in her dressing gown, curled in the hall, in one hand a phone, ears dried with blood. Perhaps she'd lived longer.

We slid out the lift and followed the signs to the health suite, as it was called. Through the great window to the side, you could see the pool was empty, nowt but a clean smell of chlorine, the door to its changing rooms locked tight with nowhere to enter. It had been night, after all, when it happened. Such a relief the lad wasn't there!

Me and Jip found the hotel kitchens in the basement too, where Bill had left another sort of massacre on every surface and sink: eggshells, rinds, bread crusts and empty tins. Well, he'd never cooked in all the time I'd known him, except last night just gone. There were plenty of clean pans for us, it being a bloody great hotel, so I cooked up some bacon and eggs from the massive fridges, with a bowl of milk and a sausage for Jip.

While the pup was distracted, I went looking in the great walk-in freezers, convinced the lad would be inside. Pickles and fish and sides of lamb and beef, stacks of bread rolls and massive tins of beans and tomatoes. But no lad.

Bill was spot on about the hotel. There's enough food for months in that kitchen, and nobody about. And if that changed and someone come, it's easier to hide in a massive hotel than a two-bedroom farmhouse.

The last one we'd taken together, Wren, his family name. It was his mam who said the thing about Bill deserving to die. When I'd gone up to him at the school gate, he'd on a little dark blazer with the name sewn on the pocket. I reckon they don't do that with kids' jackets no more, on account that a complete stranger can use it to convince them they're known to their mothers, and it's an easy way to get a child to trust what you're saying to them, that their mammy said they was to get in and have a ride up top while she run some errand or other: *Mrs Wren sent me, is that yer mam?* Then: *Don't ya recognise me? I met ya when you were a bairn at th' house, when me dog were a pup.*

You like dogs, do ya?

I use to burn inside, guts on fire, thinking on all what I'd done for Bill.

But I'd done it the same this time an' all, had I? An invisible thread pulling on my mind, puppeting me, soon as the little lad was with me. 'Nay,' I said to Jip in the kitchen, wiping my face where it was stressed puffy and red. 'Not me intention, pup! Not this time.'

Jip looked at me, head cocked, waiting for bacon scraps.

I threw him the rest of my sarnie and washed in the big square porcelain sink, same as the sinks we'd had at farm to scrub up after mucking out, and where I'd wash my newborns of their cauls a springtime when I was a girl.

I scrubbed my neck with the hot salty water, but I still had the stink of Bill on me, so I got in a frenzy scraping with my nails – weeping in the water, I was, coughing slightly, and my throat ever so sore, and then I noticed the water itseln. It wasn't the stink of Bill after all, but the smell from washing. There was a slight blue tinge in that water, a taste of metal and sommat bitter I'd taken for my own adrenalin.

Jip shook his head like he'd bashed it and gave a whoop, a funny noise like sneezing. 'You got it an' all?' I said to him, and my heart gave. He trotted about my ankles, cautiously wagging his tail, but he was only trying to comfort me, bless his little heart.

I wondered if they put sommat into the supply, chlorine or owt, trying to save us what remain from dying. They. Think that white stuff melted into the soil, its unnatural spores over stones and then under, into the roots of the land?

When I was a girl, there was this farmer, Griffiths, up top aside, dead some year back naw, but it would of been the year I turned fifteen that he took to being an idiot and dumped a load of soil that was infected with anthrax spores in the beck on his land. All cause a caravan of crusty travellers from the south had camped up for one of them free festivals they used to do round some bits of old stones on his stead to try and save the world from ending, and he wanted rid. At Clark Farm, we hadn't minded them really, these southern hippies. They'd bought eggs off us a few mornings, and one of the lads, all dreadlocks and rags, he'd done a bit of drystone for my da cheaper than any of us lot, so they weren't all bad.

But time went on, and they danced naked round the helstone at night, harping on it was sacred. Their painted collarless dogs were worrying the flocks, their litter blew cross with the stink of human sewage they poured on the bog. I worried for the fox.

The local coppers turned up and told Griffiths he'd only gone and poisoned the whole water table cross five steads, and of all things he was given a bloody police caution.

I heard they all went down with the hands sunrise to the stones and saw off the stinking hippies with other bigger dogs.

The authorities had come up after put chlorine in the water, to kill off the poison Griffiths had dumped, and we got a paper notice stuck to all us taps and doors saying we weren't to drink it for seventy-two hours, nor to have a wash or a cup of tea, nor give it to the stock for at least a day on, which was an issue seeing as a flock like ours could drink upwards of three thousand gallons a day, and we had to order a great shining tanker of water like they have for well-filling in the hills.

My mam was well pissed off at the lack of water, cause my mam, she loved her brews. But I do remember what it looked like if you ran the tap, much like it did naw, a slight tinge of blue to it, and to drink, it come off a bitter edge in the gums, like when us kiddies went to daring each other to touch us tongues on a salt cake in the snow.

We've drunk a load of tap water since the sound, eh? Who knows how sommat like this pedals its machinations? We'll not know the truth of it. Not here, naw.

Anyroad. We had to get out, sniff the air. It's an itch in me and Jip. Not used to being inside, see, not having had much of one these last eleven year. I couldn't of watched Jip sniffing and whining at that blessed balcony door no more, and it was so quiet in that kitchen, and so still, that things from before come up in me like bile.

Those nights with Bill, the vast moor sky held the pulse of a wound, the print of a scream, the cold. I would name its stars out loud, like counting. With pup Jip, I caught up flat stones, weeds with pretty flowers, animal eyes glinting in us head-lights, waiting. And there too, Bill's neck, scratched with tiny fingers, mouth smeared wrong in the dim of the truck. There were so many stars I didn't yet ken.

I hate to think on all this again, but it means I *did* see, that I *did* watch, *not* turning my eye to the dark. Instead, I took it all into my head. Else I'd not have the memory of it to view, to feel naw.

I used to believe that how I behaved those times with Bill was like a slave, and what Bill had done was his business; that I simply assisted him as his wife, helping with a terrible deep need that he couldn't shake. That I did it so he'd be happy with me, so he'd show me love and gratitude. The same moti-vation as when a wife scores drugs for her addict husband was how I'd made it out in my memory all of back then, all before my eleven year in village.

But this was only me lying to myseln. One of them London shrinks might of said it was a survival mechanism, a story I could paste together with the edges of the pieces. Some scabby shapes of truth I made out to be able to live with myseln and what I'd done.

In these last few year, I've had to come to terms with the fact that if these memories are so strong in me, it means I *did not* sit away in the car, waiting for it to be over. I *did not* leave the room quick and go and cover my ears, as I'd convinced myseln was the case. See, I'd had it down solely that it was a fetish in Bill, and nowt to do with me. That was my line for a long time. Though, sure, I'll admit the line does change.

Till I started reading about evil Hope Gleason in them books what they wrote about us after, I'd certain carried this other story in me, about who I was. Till I heard extracts from this one book on the wireless, read out by a famous Northern actress who sounded a lot like me.

They printed some of that book in the paper, too. And it was all there, the story laid out in plain word, us pair of faces side by side and equal in the deed, with the evidence from the murders all quoted and labelled and photographed so as there was no escape from my part in it. I would pore over this inventory, checking, checking,

- *Chair arm bound with trap wire, pastoral tapestry, of a set Mrs Clark gave the couple for 'Sunday dining'*
- *Dried blood, unidentified, on nursery carpet, ruler for scale*
- *Lock of hair, blonde with scalp remnant, in red Vestas matchbox*
- *Child's pants embroidered with rabbits, shredded by animals*
- *Blue paper kite, ripped into grave*
- *Girl's red shoe with buckles, washed up Cresswell lake*
- *Lamb crate, pink smit, scrape marks inside, dug from abbey fallow*
- *Green velvet button in bedside table drawer by Clark's childhood bed, 2p coin for scale*

What shocked me the most is that they said, in this book all read out by that actress, that I used to hold the kiddies down. They reckoned Bill said in his police interview that I was the one to tell the kids to shut up mewing for their mammy, that I'd slap them and grip their tiny wrists hard tight.

And when I read this, at first, I was extremely cross that they believed these things of me, that they'd written that Bill had said them like it was true – indignant, I suppose I was, cause I had no memory whatsoever of being there with Bill when it went on. I was convinced these so-called experts and journalists had made it all up to sell papers. Vicious-like about us, after all.

But recently, with strength to set myseln to exploring this further, I'd get a creeping sensation of the squeezing of fine bones like the necks of tiny brids, or the feel of a pinch of shiny pale skin catching between my nails. The memory of a blue shiver in delicate veins under young new flesh, beating.

I come to after that, like I'd finally woken up: I must of done it, must I? How else would I of ever known that sensation so strong, so real, so dug deep in the whorls of my fingers, unless I'd actually experienced the feeling of it some time or another?

As I stood there thinking on the little lad, I stretched out my roughened moor hands and studied them, expecting revelation, perhaps a map to the past in them creases and scars. See, my recollections of that time with Bill, before, there's parts entirely missing, and no matter how much I think on it, how to account for the hours, the things I read in the papers and heard on the wireless about what had happened, all them strangers talking about it, seems to have naw mixed with my memories and dreams, so that all the things appear as one truth. A thick skin has formed from the trauma of it, like cross new milk, not coming away.

And what had gan on with the lad in the night? I was telling myseln I'd been blind drunk knocked out and nowt to do with it, but I'd set it up, eh? The closed space I'd afforded Bill. The night with the lad, all made accessible, Bill's cravings with no meds to keep him down. The way we'd both built the lad up for confidence in us, with all that dancing and scran, and laughter.

If I screw my eyes tight and go back to the last thing I remember, it's being pished out my face on posh wine, jumping up and down on the beds with the lad laughing to music dressed in feathers and sequins, and Bill banging on the table like a drum and Jip barking, barking. Oh, the lad was laughing so much his face was all red, a big wide-open mouth with that excited little pink tongue a darting minnow inside. I could see Bill in the mirror, clocking this lad, his mouth, and staring back at me with this heavy communication all woven through with needs and desires.

I prefer to think that I imagined it, that look, that I'd pushed Bill away from the idea. That I made a concerted effort to get Bill to bed and did what I could, and I know for sure it went on a good long while, cause it's sommat quite particular to me and Bill, that kind of drawn-out ritual of being together in the bed, heavy and slow and hurting.

And it did feel like I was protecting the lad, sacrificing myseln for him, all Bill's desires dampened with me. Or maybe

I thought us being farm folk so used to patterns of hours and the tides of night and morning, that having achieved a fair lot we'd put a pin in it and go asleep. But I'd only gone and sharpened Bill's memories with that damned pin on what it's like to be with Hope Gleason.

I can't know sure how it ended with Bill stabbed on that balcony with the red on the gauze. Maybe it happened in the morning, I thought, for it mattered little naw the world was dead if the sun was in the sky when Bill snapped shut his jaw.

For the lad in The Diana, more than any of the others, believe me, I was so very truly sorry. I didn't even know his name.

I suppose when the world ends all that's left is devils and monsters come out to see what havoc to wreak.

'GALLERY'

Gelatin silver print, mounted on board

160 cm × 250 cm

Then I says to myseln, maybe you're wrong, woman. Seeing as it's so very normal for it to be death around Bill, I'd jumped to bloody conclusions. And the notion grew in the still that I'd been far too quick on the balcony. Had I filled in too much of what Bill was saying? He interfered with the lad in some way, that's not up for debate. But in my panic, I took his story of the lad taking off as Bill's way of saying he'd disposed of the mite. I mean, it was from experience, that assumption. But then, I thought to myseln, the lad did wet Bill proper. Maybe he did get away.

'Come naw, Jip. Ya get to workin',' I said to the pup, lacing my boots real tight like a punishment, and we set out for beach.

A diluted sun's cracked through the clouds this afternoon; it's been raining at sea today, drifted over. Did you see it come fast in, cross the water, that weir light? It was the sort you get ont moor of a winter with the bite of a one-dog night, weaving in the gilt of clouds. Mist addling the waves in a hush, like metal flung with salt and tipped, and the water is all so blue, did you see? Same as the water from the tap I said about.

Jip had started with these odd little attacks by the time we set off down front. Coughing. And the blood had come up sour in my own gums an' all by then, swelling and tearing as we walked along the edge. That swooping in my ears. This time, it's not faded off.

Jip rushed to the water as we left the hotel's path, case the lad was there after all and he'd made a mistake, hunting frantic with wide doggy nostrils flapping round the shoreline where him and the lad only a few hours back'd been having a laugh together, dear fellas, Jip jumping for sticks and skimmed stones with an almost human joy spread on his face.

Then I saw the pup was on a trail; sommat kicking off.

There's a strange twist of fate here, let me tell you. As we went walking past the Victoria Grand, I hear this screaming. A lass, going mad she was. Then, fellas, hollering loud. Jip went growling, but I told him wisht, and we crawled into a nearby bus shelter and made usseln small.

The voices got louder. Immigrants. Loads about coast town these days. They passed the bus shelter, her whimpering on, the men putting up with it. I peered through the window, went to touch my knife. But it wasn't there, was it? Damn and blast, I thought to myseln. But they were just three scruffy gippos, left over like us, pulling along a trolley of food, so I waited till all I could hear was the faint scuff of wheels as they turned down the narrows where the shops have their bins. Well, they do say that all that's left is cockroaches when the world ends.

Giddy I was, worrying on who else I'd meet on my way, and why they might let me live. Oh, how I missed my shed in that moment! But look. I know better than to doubt my historical self.

Jip was sniffing, sniffing in the corner of this shelter, giving little trots backwards with a hum. I looked at what it was. Thrown down and abandoned was the thick brown fleece I'd borrowed the lad, all crusted with blood! 'What th' devil?' I reached over, Jip nosing the smells of his little pal, a corner of paper coming out the deep pocket. I yanked at it, and crouching there, I smoothed it on my knee. A permission slip from his school. Course, his slag of a mam had not signed it. A trip to see an exhibition on the coast. And there in black and white, a picture of the gallery,

SHIPMAN GALLERY PRESENTS

LAND OF HOPE

The Artist's Residency of Erskine Elgar

That weir witch name, Erskine Elgar. The American Artist, who'd come round asking after me the last summer in village, taking nebby pictures like a peeping Tom with her map. Your posh 'residency' in the coast town, on a grant paid up by the council. *This* coast town.

And I thought on them flashes of movement between buildings in town yesterday, what it reminded me of. Last season, when you come up wood, with the clickclickclick and them big gold eyes. And on the pier, when the lad said there was nobody there, he'd sure been laughing, and talking to someone.

And then it come to me. Hadn't the lad's dead mam from the cop shop cleaned that gallery of a night? Oh aye, everything made sense then. You'd given a talk at his school, in village. Bridget, she'd said, 'especially the little lad', and nodded to me, cause she meant the lad who fed Jip the biscuit.

My little lad.

Sure they'd done all about Erskine Elgar in his class. He *knew* about you. At least well enough to trust what you said. Hiding in other people's stories, that's your place, int it? One of them folk trails the shadows of heinousness, catching vicarious on the threads.

Jip caught the scent, past a small row of fishing boats tied on the jetty by the rocks to the clean white stone shaped like the howes for some nod to heritage.

To the gallery.

The glass doors were whispering, open and shut, open and shut, a delicate, broken machine breathing, and we waltzed right in, simple like that, us feet no louder than feathers fell from a wing.

The Romans once ruined this coast town. Invaded. Did you know if you dig up the gardens round here you can still find these perfect little Roman coins and coloured glass dice? Not worth owt, cause there's so many of them dug up so often, and course, things in this world are only valuable when they are very rare, no matter how beautiful or ugly they are.

I thought that, about rare things, when we met at the Pyre. The magic in the lens.

See, this gallery was Roman-built, originally. Carved into the cliff, made three floors down. Council's added this great thick glass window looking out cross the sea, with the sky, for the natural light. I come here on a school trip once an' all. This mosaic flooring is from when Claudius's soldiers used the place as baths. I loved the swirls of the blue tile when I was a lass. Like waves crashing on iron-lined roads. This sweet portrait of the traitor queen, Cartismandua. Red hair, like me, tiled in shell and clay, ends caught blue in woad. Night after night, the South was being decimated by a Roman invasion crawling northward. Against her husband's wishes, she made an alliance to save her tribe. Course, the bastard never forgave her.

Us weir women, witches and hags, we're never forgiven, while the men, even rotten bastards, are heroes and stars. Just look at Bill. A national legend with a mythical name, while I'm just the dirty wife.

Down the stairs, me and Jip, following the lad's trail, down these clean white gallery steps, the sky watching through that window over the rocks. Towards the space that used to house the Roman hypocausts, these red brick hives for underground heating. Into your exhibition, where nobody was when the sound come but you. Still alive, you, no doubt, due to the thick Roman stone that lines these walls double; solid ancient slabs hewn by rapists and polished by slaves.

As we reached the last run of steps, we were greeted by a cacophony of voices, telling stories of this land. Words formed in mouths in mine own way. The land's way.

> ... the Vikings were not the first to rape, pillage and slaughter here...

> ... tribes of witches roamed the land thousands of year
> before, taking sacrifice and ritual with sky spirits hid in
> stone and soil, and in the brids... watching, calling, wait-
> ing fer empty souls to commune...
> ... thar's been a decline of interest in the night sky...
> ... the flocks are in us blood...
> ... the stories passed generation to generation, in us skin...
> ... the stars hold the mysteries of the universe, but naw folk
> are scared to ken what's to become of us...
> ... sudden, it feels too close. The end...
> ... well, aye. Perhaps we already know what's to become...
> ... we are all connected by the land...
> ... a living heritage...

Your recordings, triggered by us passing into your exhibition. Moor folk, naw dead, their testimonies lost on account of there being nobody left but me to hear them.

It is a powerful thing what you did, Ms Elgar. And why I agreed to this taping.

As we passed through the exhibition hall, the voices faded to whispers, almost imperceptible, but constant, fragile. And if you listen, you can still hear them, even naw, come out the gallery doors, hushing cross the silent land.

I peered desperate round the gallery. Eyes on me from some-where. Them stories all whispering down the stairs. So many corners, pictures hanging, such a big place, all white and cool. And that massive great window, with its fierce vista of the sea and rocks. It made me reet nervy when I first seen that view; nature coming at us all raw. But Jip was relaxed; the trail was done.

I told you when there's death in a place, you feel it in the silence. But when someone's alive? The air tingles and brights. Even through them voices, I felt you down here before I saw you.

Erskine Elgar, there, not a bit surprised to see me. Sitting on a pile of rucksacks in the middle of your exhibition, cameras and devices going in as you packed. Another few bags about, woollies thrown on top. Head freshly shaved, ready for the off. You stopped buckling, smiled a little as I come in. Jip wagged his tail, nosed your stuff, perhaps remembering you. But no lad.

'Hope.' That gravelled voice, a kindness in it. You smiled.

'Where ya off?' I threw. Places, not names, with us.

You took a moment, a tremor in the throat. 'See that ship out there?' Your steady gold gaze pierced the window to the line on the horizon. 'There's a Seahawk going back and forth over the north end of that cliff.' Lifted a camera to your eye, zoomed the lens. 'Helicopter. I photographed one of those at RAF Morton.' Put it down, eyes glinting. 'That's a US vessel. Has to be crew, at least one pilot.' You looked at me hard, fear tight in your teeth. 'I plan to take him there on a boat from the bay at high tide.'

Them, the lad had said.

So, *them* was you; with him on the pier, laughing, flashes of movement between. Enchanted, he must of been, when The American Artist had stepped from the shadows. Must of told the lad to come here to the gallery if it didn't work out with his nan. With me. 'Let's go back to Bill, fore he misses us,' the lad had said all docile in the motor, in the dark of the land.

I leaned against the wall, weak with it. Heart swelled. 'He's here, then?' I managed, voice cracking.

You took me on square. 'He's sleeping downstairs.'

'Bill's dead,' I said straight.

You nodded. Not quite certain the lie I'd told. Sure the lad couldn't of wet Bill to death, you ken that. But you come over calm, observing, and stood up, bags between us. Hands out like calming a beast cornered. 'Hope. I've no weapons. No way of stopping what it is you came to do.' Your breath was ragged. 'But I'm begging you; appealing to your finer nature.'

I laughed sardonic, Bill's blood up my side.

You tried again, all earnest, big eyes turning. 'It's not what you did before that counts any more. It's the choice you make now. Clearly, you made choices in the last days that kept that young boy alive. So, please. Make the good choice.' You sighed a bit then, tattooed hand chopping thin air. 'Look. If I ever get to tell anyone what happened here? I'll tell them how you saved him. People remember the end of a story more than anything else. This ending could be your redemption.' You glanced up the stairs, the frait washing in. No words to describe what was coming. 'You know we need to get him out before…'

And that I do know, woman. Get him away. *You and me at the end of the world*, Bill had said, like it was a beautiful thing. And it was, for one night. But only the one.

'Hide tide's about sundown,' I growled.

You collapsed on the bags, a muffled sob. How long you must of sat before I arrived, practising what you might say to evil Hope Gleason. Not knowing when I would hunt you, if

I would bring Bill. Not knowing if today you would die. Aye, suppose my reputation doesn't inspire much confidence.

But it wasn't just the thought of me had you in this state. A few days old, that bruise up your cheek, spread yellow and blue. You caught me looking, turned your face, closed your eyes for a second. I thought on them trucks we'd seen, driving cack-handed. The wall outside, the bullets, the circles with the brids. Teeth marks on the wings. *Not animal.* Sommat had gan on.

'You mustn't go out when you hear it,' you whispered, by way of an explanation. Shuffled a little. Touched your face. I understood enough.

We must of arrived in town soon after. That big motor tearing through the silence? Nare died, did you, when you saw it was me and Bill, and the little lad!

Seems us fates are tangled in some other rotter's tale.

I started up coughing then. You tossed me this posh bottle of water. Legs weak, I pulled the low white bench they have for viewing the art, plonked down opposite you, lifted the bottle, ta. Jip had made hisseln at home by the bags; a wheeze in his snout punctuated the air. I poured half the bottle on the floor for him, and he took to lapping. 'Lad's reet, though, yeah?' I ventured. *Please, please.*

'He will be.' You shifted in your make-do seat when I sighed. 'You know, his mom told me his father's in the fighter wing at Morton. Some one-night stand.' You crossed your long legs all neat, found a baccy tin in a coat pocket, made a fag. Liquorice papers, course. 'When she cleaned here the two nights a week, we'd talk.'

'She told him his da's in Thailand.'

'Oh, right. Kick-boxing.' You tried to laugh, sarky like, nodded, lit your cigarette with a shaky hand. Exhaled. Considered me through the cloud. 'Strange, smoking in here.' Scraped the bits of tobacco off your lap. 'Doesn't matter now though, does it.'

I can just imagine you in here, after folk had gone off from peering at your pictures of an evening. Come up from your jammy little flat. A bayard parading high-hoofed, the invader drunk on power, admiring maps of ill-gotten territories. Gabbing to that slag of a mam while she scrubbed your floor about the meaning in light, reflections in lenses. About your fragile creatures.

'Everything's strange,' I said, and together we gazed around at your pictures, eyes lingering in lieu of words.

You smiled a bit. Old fear disguised with new relief. Looked at your watch. 'We've hours yet,' you said. 'Let's talk awhile.' Rummaging. 'You could tell me your story.'

You love your stories, don't you, woman? Anyone ever told you that?

You drew hard on your rollie, the entitlement coming off you in its crackle. Pulled out a little fluffy microphone, no wires. And the little metal stick I seen previous at Black Dog Pyre. 'Surely more than anyone else, I deserve to hear what really happened,' you said.

Despite your crust, I reckoned it might do us both good. Like a confession, int it? And so I said, 'A'ight.'

You come over to me all flat feet, clipped the microphone to my collar, slow thumbs, fag between your lips. You know, you smell like some place far off; clean. Plastic, black ink and spice. Older, close up. I can see the loss in your skin. 'There,' you said, all pleased, put the stick near the mic till a beep went up. 'When the blue light is flashing, they're paired.'

'Paired?'

'Connected. Like, wires in the ether. So I press this button, and it will record until they can't find each other any more.'

I nodded. Wires in the ether. 'Ask us sommat then. Get started.'

You stepped back, clicked the stick and the hollow voice said, '*Ask us sommat then. Get started.*'

'Huh,' I said. 'That were me?'

You stared above my head for a moment. 'I've noticed moor people talk round a subject until they find a way in. I usually start with, "Tell me about the land. What it means to you."' You closed your eyes. 'And I'd like to know why.'

'Big subject.' I felt a bit violated, you asking that, but we both needed sommat to hold on to, waiting in that empty place for the tide. And so, I rambled on about the land and its customs, the old gods. How everyone thinks they know my story.

Then I told you it all.

No single explanation would feel like I've told you the why. The same as them 'experts' down London, who dedicated entire lives to poring over us deeds in this way and that. See, those who don't work the land miscomprehend the grandest thing: In nature, more than one thing can be true, contrary to each other, and yet coexist. Sun can shine warm through snow. To live, we must kill. I reckon there must be infinite sides to a person's soul by design, cause there has to be, to survive. Like in one of my old romantic books, perhaps terror made me cruel.

Or perhaps it's what my da used to say. The quiet dog's the one that bites. It's in us nature, that quiet line, roaming blackened through the calling; and sometimes, when dreadful things break us, some of us, the broken? We follow.

That's all I can tell you of who we are. Me and Bill.

And the land.

I suppose by the time you left me here, with all what went on in them last infernal minutes, you forgot about your little farcy mic clipped on my collar. That blue light, it's still flashing, so like you said, we must still be connected 'in the ether', and recording.

And as you told me, folk remember the end of a story more than anything else, so I'll keep on with us story to its conclusion. It might be the last the land ever tells.

We'd sat in the silence pooled around us in the gallery for quite a while after I finished talking, staring on your black-and-white photos, massive on the walls around us, seeming so much more with the skin of my words naw hanging on them. Pictures blown so big as to make them appear as wide windows looking to the deep vistas of moor, miles off northwest of here, swathing me in my past.

I asked you why black and white. What did you say?

'Colours are nature's way of distracting from the horror. Poisonous plants and flowers have the most beautiful colours. A burning pyre. Ruins verdant with moss. A storm at sea, as blue and pale as, well, your dog's eye.' You smiled close as Jip got up from where he'd been sleeping, lazy wagging his tail, nosing your hand.

'Just like wi' them lights,' I said. 'Colours.'

You frowned at that, and we glanced out the window together, fearful, but it wasn't dark enough yet. 'I work with lines,' you said, returning to the safety of black and white. 'Shape. Print on paper. It shows the subject in its truest form.'

No matter, I thought. I ken the colours by heart. Brids with tapestried wings flying high cross an early moon, a fox in wood with his tail sparked in evening light. The trees, the clouds. The red earth. The white low sun. You sure captured the way the land moves fast cross the eye. Like a hawk come scraping the edge of its pitch. Folk forget that England's on an island, and that we're prone to the swift flow of weather as it meets water, drawn by the moon and the fish, and the chill of it.

And there. Framed and glazed as its own historical artefact, that great torn paper map I scrawled on atop the cairn for you that foggy day at Black Dog Pyre. It's muddied naw, well used, my rain-soaked hand in scrubby pen.

I told you then I was sorry that it'd entertained me so that day in a spiteful fashion, to send this nebby posh artist from America to take photos of 'local beauty spots' when unbeknownst she'd be documenting me and Bill's work in perpetuity! Kiln Narrow. Helfold. Village. Abbey. Bellemere Crag. Wood. All the places you'd been for these pictures. You must of caught on who I was when I marked the graves for you that morning on the map.

'I knew for sure-sure yesterday. When I saw you with Bill.' A twinkle. 'Maybe I should make a citizen's arrest.'

'Oh aye,' I said flat.

'It's strange. I had this idea you would come see the show, and I would know by your reaction, call the cops. But, if we're doing truth?' A shadow moved over your face. 'Having you arrested, it would have compromised the work.'

Damned rich to be tasked with taking back the land from The Devil O' Th' Moor only to crown me guest of honour.

You shrugged, shook the lighter. 'But the world ended, so…'

We looked together at the graves on the walls, smoke in us eyes. I told you Bill said five when they got him, how they found two more elsewhere. They were 'happy' with that number; enough to send him down sure. I'd laughed out loud with the incredulity when I heard that on the wireless. Seven! Lucky for some, I suppose. But it's so very fascinating to me that all them kiddies could drop off the face of the Earth with not one feckless bugger looking for them! Makes the world seem satanic, don't it, that so much evil runs free under us toes without as much as a whisper to catch it.

But you, Ms Elgar, I reckon you set out to catch that evil. In each photo, you chase the deeds of Bill and Hope Gleason, and hold them in your frame. If folk bothered to look close, they would see you laid the clues. Did you think in return that those who visited your exhibition, slid in sniffing your art like foxes at a bin, they'd leave sommat behind for you to taste, a native grease in the air, a word in breath hanging that you might fathom?

When most go over the story of me and Bill, they imagine a sense t' it, like a child making out faces in the clouds. But you don't take things as church. The explanation everyone else swallowed so willing as to why a madman and his wife went out murdering, you rolled it in your own mouth: 'They were born evil.' And you spat that reasoning out. Erskine Elgar, The American Artist. Here's who I am, and the sum of me. And it might just be that those two things are entirely different.

I says to you, as we looked at it all in the gallery, LAND OF HOPE, the title of the exhibition, it wasn't only my name, was it? It's your play on words, I ventured, ever so clever. 'In the mix', as they say. 'Meta'.

It was your hope for this place, you told me, as we studied the views. Convinced you might resolve sommat bigger, sommat to do with the world and the way it was broken, you took on the residency. Maybe healing the land would be healing yourseln.

As we stared at your view of Clark Farm, it come to me how you'd fancied the future in the emptiness of landscapes wiped clean with your lens, in the eyes of them fighter jet girls. To me, they represent death. Did you believe the world builds on itseln forever, higher and higher, and better, simply with the passing of time, I asked you, as we moved to a view of Bellemere. The world does not move upward, but in cycles and seasons, bursting and fading, day turned to night. As we traced with us eyes the serpentine patterns of the howes at the Crag, I told you the Viking tale of the world as a snake god so greedy it eats its own tail.

'Bill once wrote sommat in them damned notebooks of his,' I said. *All is a circle, a line without end / The future comes at us, always with death.*

'The sun is also a circle,' you said, tearful, 'and it rises from the dark.'

We hard looked at each other, hearts beating loud and slow, pulse pushing my three suns ghost-like in red through the stare. 'Wipe your face, Ms Elgar,' I said cold. 'Death is fascinating.'

I'm an arrant mare, but you ken I was right. Roaming the land like a wraith in your black coat, stealing pretty pictures of where other women's bairns are buried, picking at carcases? We'd be witches in another time, Ms Elgar, you and me. They'd of burned us kind for acts like these.

'Who's that great bure?' I says, turning to the picture of me, and you brightened a bit, getting back to the work. You went to speak, but your eyes trailed off, soft and tired. Had you imagined me seeing it here a thousand times, practised what you would say? I suppose platitudes naw rung wretched hollow.

Dead luck, my da would of called it, what you had last summer when Providence sent you Hope Gleason herseln. You'd gan sniffing the shapes of witches in fog, and sudden, there she was, delivered by the Fates atop Black Dog Pyre, hair flame red and a great fat behind on her. Not much of a disguise.

That photo's what you took of me that evening in wood, when you come by shed. Took my breath away, if I'm honest. Didn't even ask if I minded, clickclickclick you went through trees, and I raised my hand with the axe like a tribal hag, and you got me coiling away from the flash, all screwed up and angry. Peculiar to see how I've weathered. Ugly and twisted, that wyrd sliver of face showing behind my fist, like an ancient tree uprooted in storms. I mean, sure, I'm dirty most the time and I've put on years. My hair's no Boudica, is it, definite more Medusa. Cursed to a head of poisonous snakes for loving the wrong man. Nobody could look her in the eye neither.

As we looked on it I asked if you'd hoped to expose me in the grandest of ways. A scandalous front page? A discovery of witches? Nobody'd said owt to me up village about that picture, see. But then most never ventured far as coast town. Ones that did see the picture would of said, oh look, it's Glory from us village. And that's that. Eleven year I've been cunny enough, I told you. I ken how to hide.

A smug laugh rose, acid like. Folding a jumper in the quiet. 'The council asked me to make The Devil O' Th' Moor disappear. The *dirty wife*? Nobody cared about her! This work, hung for all to see, and not one person asked about her.' You smiled nasty a moment. 'Did you know they called off the dogs the day you ran, after only three hours? It wasn't even dark! In the books —'

That's not true!' I cried. A memory of panic in the night, dogs barking close, lights going over, searching. It could be a scene from another tale I read, a dream, a film. I can't honest say what's true when it comes to Hope Gleason.

You spoke over me. '*In the books*, it says that "an unsaid consensus went round the men that day". It was agreed that "the land would do its worst and swallow her up".' You looked on me sidewards. 'I think it did. The whole moor a pyre! Hope Gleason, the cautionary tale. Crawled into the land, turned to ash!'

You don't ken this place, I thought, rather bitter. 'Folk round 'ere —'

'*Folk round 'ere?*' You smirked. 'During this project, I learned a fundamental truth about your "folk round here". Given a choice between beauty and monsters, they choose beauty every time.'

And your cocky artist hand pointed to the card on the wall by my picture.

Burning inside, I stepped in to see what's written. Words in gold ink, just like your eyes,

'GLORY'

Gelatin silver print, mounted on board
160 cm × 250 cm

An artist working with wood at her shed in remote moorland. Nobody knows who she is.

Well, *you knew* straight off. Black Dog Pyre, you told me you were hunting monsters, and I warned you, did I not, Ms Elgar, they'd end up hunting you back. Look at how you took your pictures; the proof is damning enough. It's as if in each image, the two of us that acted, and the one of you who later watched, we've called another to come out in front of your lens. 'There's a sentience to this land,' I said. 'It's…'

'Something akin to magic.'

Oh, oh, you sudden looked grey at the gills, Ms Elgar. Cause you saw it clear in your photos soon as I was in the gallery to see it with you. In the old days, they thought when someone died you could look in their eyes and see the last thing they saw, just like a picture painted on the orb. I reckon your camera is like that. Scrying into the eyes of a place, seeing what it last saw.

In the Bible, it says the eye is the lamp of the body. *Take care lest the light in you be darkness. If then you are full of light, the world will be wholly bright.* What you let in, that's what comes out of you an' all.

It's not folk who choose beauty in this world.

It's the monsters, devouring it whole.

And so, Erskine Elgar, The American Artist. Stood there all arrogant fists, hoisted in the circle of your own lens. You had to ask, somewhat hysterical: 'Did we *summon* it?'

Folk have been summoning the land thousands of year. This land, made of blood and bones, and cinders. Only naw did it return the call.

But it's always been here.

I went over to one of the prints, and I says to you stern and pointing, I said, 'Bloody take this view, fer one.' Your studied lens catching the flats at dusk. The way the picture shudders. Where me and Bill buried the boy with the blue kite, in the cold hard ground just there, shallow. Only five inches deep on rock beds, that earth, settled over slabs patterned like the backs of lizards. I'd squeezed his little hands together in the warm brown peat like praying. He looked as if he'd always been there when we finished, a buried angel discovered after thousands of years. Not a carcase covered hasty with dirt so's we'd make it back to town for last orders.

'Look wi' me!' I banged my fist on another with its sweep of earth – grey in the picture, but you can taste it, can you, all blood red. And you did look. I recognised it clear, cause that's where we put that wee lass Maggie, beautiful bare, inside the howe on Saxon Lane. In a storm, it was. Oh, how the clouds had come at us like bruised ogres as we took her up from the truck! A precious offering to an older god than Death, Bill had said of that sacred place underground, where other children had been laid out sacrificed to the land centuries ago. I put two flat stones on her wide blue eyes like sommat holy, and my wet hair dripped rain like tears on her cheeks but I wasn't crying.

You captured perfect how the weather turns up thar. At the east, a gale can turn the pink cloud mackerel-like in spits, whereas to the north the cloud gathers in thick pelts of white, given the way the gusts go round that glen. Then gold in the late afternoon, running threads through the eye of the narrow, where the maen coves and the sky never really seems blue.

Not like her eyes in the howes. They were as blue as my mam's Dutch china.

'And this.' I kicked one with my boot, that view cross Houlsdale; oh, Houlsdale, right on us land! My mam and da's grazing! With the deep welkin digging in them pits by the ridge, and the bare trees almost white in sun. Their long blue shadows claw scraping towards us, do they, as we stare, looking in as if it's all alive, dancing and talking with itseln, a great symphony of winds and whispers.

Course, it is. Alive, I mean. Anything wild is greater than the sum of its parts.

It's just how it is vanna, your picture, if you take a minute to be still. A lonely spot where quite often, when I was coming up, I'd sulk or weep if a lamb I'd been weaning had been sold, or if a lad had lied to me, or if I'd played up with my jobs and been sent out far on foot to call in the stragglers before night. That's probably why this one makes you sad. See, the stories don't leave a place, but instead wait till someone's listening.

'And this hollow.' I stabbed a finger and you come in with your wet owl eye close to the smudge of ink deep printed in brant trees. And you felt it an' all. Me and Bill, we laid another there, all curled up in his football shirt. They'd volunteers searching with sticks in the bog weeks, a notion he'd fallen down a forgotten well or a sinkhole kicking his ball about. The ball was in us back yard some month, torn up proper by little pup Jip. When I passed that hollow some week on, I found it fascinating a great mound of frilled mushrooms had flourished through the fern the exact same red colour as his shirt. His picture on telly look nowt like him.

Maybe death makes us strange in the face.

As for your believing choices as different to deeds, I've had them demons an' all. Feverish thoughts. Like, if I'd just gone on that writing course, written a book, I'd be in some far-off city where folk sip iced drinks and wear my hair long. If I'd never got in Bill's truck, instead married a Mack, merged the flocks: a farmer's wife with a broken bed. If I'd not run, a prisoner reformed, playing 'Kumbaya' on the recorder. If the bairn had lived, would I of been happy? If I'd turned Bill in, would I be good? Would I even of met my Copper Mark? If all these graves were empty, never turned? Erskine Elgar, The American Artist, would we of been friends? Give over, woman! Wherever I go, there I am. Just look at my portrait!

With your lens, you held a mirror to my soul, reflected what I really am. You want to know? There! The Medusa at shed! Ugly, stained with horror, lifting the axe. *Clickclickclick*!

I am the suckling beast in the stable. The Black Dog.

I am Hel.

I am Hope Gleason, the most dangerous female child serial killer in English history.

'HOPE'

Undeveloped film

The last known photo of Hope Gleason, standing ashore by the Shipman Gallery

While I was holding fort in the gallery, the lad had slipped out from behind the studio door. All thin and dry-looking, a piece of stale loaf in his hand. Bill's blood crusted down his shirt. You went pale as oats. Did he hear all we said, do you reckon, Ms Elgar?

'Been lookin' all over fer ya!' I said cheery as I could to clear the atmosphere. The lad wouldn't look at me no more, would he, took to petting Jip instead, feeding him the bread. They were relieved to see each other a'ight. Jip made feet, licked his ears, singing a little. The lad managed a giggle in all the darkness, but I was dizzy with it. The water. The sound. My head heavy, throbbing, damp at the back.

You strode over, folded arms, nudged me too familiar with your black coat shoulder. 'Go easy on the child,' you said at the end of the world to Hope Gleason.

The lad blinked slow from one to the other of us, moles on his cheek all sore-looking. Searching my face for mercy, a slump, a whine. 'You said, Glore. If ya couldn't protect us no more!' He wiped his face on his soaked sleeve, one hand on Jip for comfort. Bill's blood on his cheek.

I crouched, knees clicking, and squeezed his little shoulders kindly this time. Jip went down beside us. I felt behind me your gait shift, a horse with a cat, but you ken this had to happen. I looked on him. My little lad. 'Take the knife, I said. Use it like I showed ya, aye.' I scuffed his head. 'Don't fret.'

Trembling, the lad was. I forgot I was soaked in blood. 'Did I kill 'im?' he said in a final release, casual like. Wringing his hands white, heart still full, despite it all. 'Were prob'ly playin' wi' me, when I think on it.' His eyes fell to the floor, ashamed. Giving Bill an out? Such a good lad. Tears thick as glue.

'Nay, nay, lad. Just a scratch! He'll be reet.' I tried to laugh it off, and you made some noise towards it an' all.

I tried to catch your eye, give a sign, but you wouldn't let me in. The trust had shifted, sommat sweaty. I wasn't your charity case no more. My throat was closing, a trickle in the back. The gallery heaped with the stink of Bill. We stood all three together and Jip in that tall white space surrounded by the land, all trying to catch us breath, and the atmosphere seemed to change about then, folding in. That first scream, high-pitched and desperate, went up in the quiet. Jip's tired grey ears stiffened. Could of been a fox, but sounded human, did it?

'Time to go,' you whispered frait, slinging bags to your back. The lad picked up a folded pink blanket from the pile, to help, I suppose. I took the duffel you were struggling with. 'Thanks,' you said, wary like. I nodded. It made me wish again things could of been different between us.

Through the great gallery window, the tide was lifting the boats, clanking and drifting, the late sun dipped red. 'Leave now, we'll make the ship before dark.' You took a final look round at your project. Me. Not wanting no more truths from Hope Gleason.

Then, up, up the white steps, through the hush of stories, silent past the howes. Along the beach we slid, you peering through that camera, zooming the lens like binoculars, searching for movement. Clinging to the lad. Not a soul around. Just that strange glow of blue in the air, clouds like craft in spits, an electric swoop caught in us ears. The sea was feverish at the edges, the cliff turned black in the shadow. A close stink of salt and rot, an earthy thrum of bodies, flies. It'd been a warm day.

We hung back a moment, looking together out. The ship was purple and blurry like a bruise on the offing, pins of light hovered on rigging lost in the haze. You lifted your camera, took a few shots. 'All this, and you still taking pictures?' I said, cynical like, a bit annoyed.

You turned sad to me then, a kindred smile. 'I'll do a book about you. About the land. When all of this is over.' You brung up a hand, the name in lights. 'A *Retrospective of the End of the World*.'

'It's just the end of theirs,' I said. And you chuckled dry, despite the panic that hung on us harsh damp like bed sheets forgotten on a line, the air all charged like a storm.

My dear American Artist, part of the 'theirs', charged to the cluster of fishing boats clanking on the low concrete jetty, quick boots on the deck of a fourteen-footer: a filthy white, no rig. Shook a green petrol can, fiddled with controls. I flung on your bags; heavy, they were. 'I'll write up your story as soon as we're settled on the ship,' you vowed, struggling with ropes and valour. 'In case there's no power later.'

I wanted to say, Ms Elgar, there's nobody much left to read it. But you found that important, I reckon, to offer restitution. Perhaps it's a comfort to you, like whittling is to me: the idea of sommat to work on whilst all else falls down. It gives you that distance, does it, your pictures, other people's sad stories? So as you never have to think on your own. Aye, well. That's what it is.

Jip was pulling seaweed from stones, muddying his belly. He'll eat greens when he's sick. The dear lad was lingering on jetty, was he, while we had them few words, pointing to the side of the boat with his little finger, almost smiling, eyes lit up, *wowsers*, he said, sommat-sommat-grin against the wind I couldn't hear, wet-faced and quiet.

A wilder scream pierced the beach. *Not animal.* I watched Jip shiver.

A woman alone in all that nature knows. That deadening in the belly, a shift behind your shoulder. And I closed my eyes to the three scars of sun. *Dog, the verb, not the noun.*

The land was finally flooding in.

'Best get to goin', Ms Elgar,' I called to you as that first electric whine come crackling over beach at speed, but I'm not sure you caught me. From the deck of the boat, I watched you dare lift your eye to the camera, zooming in on the cliff. Mouth dropped in terror, rushing to the rope's knot. The motor hardly flinched before humming into motion.

I didn't turn to look. It would be closer, later.

Jip whimpered, making feet for the lad as you helped him aboard gripping the rail, tiny, longing. 'Wisht,' I said quiet, and Jip come to heel. My dog, see, and nobody else's.

A strange sense of beating started up in that crackle, a murmuration of bones far inland drove fast cross water in hollow thuds. We looked to the oily sky, almost to check it wasn't caving in. That's when the air turned all thin and hot.

'No!' you yelled, primal almost, and I see the boat listing. You, holding that camera like a weapon, cause the lad had only gan an' jumped off the boat, throwing hisseln headlong into Jip's fur, who was naw licking his own face, all nervy and stiff.

I pulled at the lad's wrist. Jip's too old for all this naw, and not well.

That's when that front rolled in sudden, and the sun seemed to dim, and the cliff was bathed in a glimmering blue. That white seed stuff started to fall again, just like snow, blowing cross us faces, stinging us eyes. Not too far off, gunfire, a man's shout.

'Glore!' the lad implored tearful, time against us, flinging hisseln at me through the deluge. 'Why yous not getting ont boat?' I let myseln enjoy his hot child bones all pressed in, his faith in me, the regret for what he'd done. His heart. 'Come on-ah!' he whispered, cheek all feverish like a secret.

He was mine, was the issue. And what happens to kiddies that are mine, we all know that story. 'Daft 'ap'orth,' I whispered in his soft ear, inhaling his hair all sweet with tears and Bill and everything I wanted. Instead, I put him at arm's length for a memory, rubbed his fine-boned shoulders. 'Go wi' the artist lady 'ere.' I looked over at you, your face all urgent and darkened with worry. 'She's a nice woman, int she?'

He was all lip out, clinging to my coat like a damp cloud. 'Let's run,' he mouthed. He was clutching that little wood fox I'd whittled, and oh, my heart gave.

'What about yer da?' I said loud, no conspiracy. I took the fox, tucked it in his pocket. 'Thailand, ya say? He'll be wantin' to see ya!'

'Don't tell me stories!' he wailed, burying his head in my shoulder, breath all snot.

That golded American eye of yours traced my every word, begging me, please, please, do the right thing. And I caught my reflection in your eyes in that moment: a spectral form in stereo, two fragments of mirror, windows in sun, a couple of tears, a lens. Aye, woman, I thought. Recalling that time in yon farmhouse when the lad had played up just like this. He was going, 'I wanna be wiv' you!'

'Tha' so?' I said, spiteful naw, setting his face close to mine. Then I whispered it right into his little mouth so he tasted the words on his tongue, grinding them dirty into his nice pure cheeks with my thumbs, muttering slow, careful, to soil his insides, bleed out his heart: 'I'd only take you back to Bill.'

I pushed him away sharp, brung up my hand, snapped it like a jaw.

The Devil O' Th' Moor'll come cut off yer tail in the night!

His young gaze stormed o'er me in terror, and he stumbled backwards up the jetty gasping, hands instinctively at his ears. You got him back by the scruff, dug his sweet face into your black wing of a coat. And this low bestial noise come off him,

like when they're made sudden aware of their own impending.
This surprised me as much as a needle in my eye.

Ms Elgar, you ken it was the only way. Trust me when I say
nobody much wants these ideas in their brain for the interest
of it. Just look at the scrap in your arms for the proof. Well,
aye. Look at *me*.

And you did, as always, look at me, with that big gold stare,
lifting your camera halfway considering, then, clickclickclick.

For the book, you mouthed.

So you took off, motor raucous through metal waves,
gloved hand on the wheel.

'Glory!' The lad was sudden yelling to me over the engine,
breaking away, and he was pointing down the side of the boat,
to the word painted there. 'It's me name! It's me name!'

I did squint to read what it said, but I'd the white stuff in
my eyes. The sea was kicking up a strange thick foam over the
curly blue lettering, remnants of seaweed spooled dirty at the
crest. I couldn't read it. 'What's it?' I shouted over the noise
to him. 'What's yer name?' But he couldn't hear me neither,
just kept waving till the boat faded into the shadow of water.

A tear did fall heavy to the sand. A grey star. I scrubbed it
with my boot.

I love him, see.

And naw, me and Jip will follow the land's brambled path
up the wild cliff past The Diana.

I tell you, Ms Elgar, if I had your camera, I'd take a last
photo of here. Of the smudges of ship and boat on the mirror
of luminescent blue, the evening sky doubled in it soaring low
with a great burning pyre of celestial sparks, the fall of white.

For a time, I could make out the lad sprawled on deck with his blanket, a tiny bright dot, lights in the sky like fireworks in his eyes. So many more colours naw, all pinks and greens and orange, racing with the cosmos. Towards the dark line of elsewhere.

I dig in my heels, and my roots reach up to meet me. I feel there's an ordering under way, a shifting of sentience through renewal and death. It's a familiar calling, as ancient as the moor, a nature to this place we must shepherd. As with all invaders the breadth of time, soon, us deeds will be buried as if they never happened, and the land will carry these stories forever.

In this last sunset, the whole world could die, burning into the night. But oh, how beautiful the dying is!

As if in this glorious ending, there is still hope.

ACKNOWLEDGEMENTS

First, to Henry, my mirror, my love, for endless hours given to the last word. To Jonathan Myerson, Clare Allan, and my agent Sabhbh Curran for tireless championing and patience. And to Claire Fuller, for brilliant advice (and diagrams, and tea); Maxine Peake, Danny Robins, Viktor Wynd, and Yo Diablo (my soundtrack) for otherly inspiration; Brian Kelly and Steve Carter for reading. My own black dogs, Harbour and Nuno, for Jip. And to my parents, who walked me to the ends of the English earth when I was a child, to where I found the magic.

Transforming a manuscript into the book you
hold in your hands is a group project.

Cate would like to thank everyone
who helped to publish *Land of Hope*.

THE INDIGO PRESS TEAM
Susie Nicklin
Phoebe Barker
Michelle O'Neill
Will Atkinson

JACKET DESIGN
Luke Bird

PUBLICITY
Sophie Portas

FOREIGN RIGHTS
The Marsh Agency

EDITORIAL PRODUCTION
Tetragon

COPY-EDITOR
Sarah Terry

PROOFREADER
Maddie Rogers

THE

INDIGO

PRESS

The Indigo Press is an independent publisher of contemporary fiction and non-fiction, based in London. Guided by a spirit of internationalism, feminism and social justice, we publish books to make readers see the world afresh, question their behaviour and beliefs, and imagine a better future.

Browse our books and sign up to our newsletter for special offers and discounts:

theindigopress.com

Follow *The Indigo Press* on social media for the latest news, events and more:

ⓧ @PressIndigoThe

ⓞ @TheIndigoPress

ⓕ @TheIndigoPress

ⓘ The Indigo Press

ⓙ @theindigopress